EROTIC TALES

Also by Alberto Moravia

FICTION

The Woman of Rome
The Conformist
Two Adolescents (Agostino and Disobedience)
The Fancy Dress Party
The Time of Indifference
Conjugal Love
Roman Tales
A Ghost at Noon
Bitter Honeymoon
Two Women
The Wayward Wife
The Empty Canvas
More Roman Tales
The Fetish
The Lie
Command and I Will Obey You
Paradise
The Two of Us
Lady Godiva
The Voice of the Sea
Time of Desecration
1934

GENERAL

Man as an End
The Red Book and the Great Wall
Which Tribe Do You Belong To?

PLAY

Beatrice Cenci

EROTIC TALES

Alberto Moravia

TRANSLATED FROM THE ITALIAN
BY TIM PARKS

FARRAR STRAUS GIROUX
NEW YORK

Filmset in Great Britain in 10/12 pt Monophoto Photina
by Northumberland Press Ltd,
Gateshead, Tyne and Wear
Printed and bound in Great Britain by
Richard Clay (The Chaucer Press) Ltd, Bungay, Suffolk

Contents

To Carmen

The Thing

Dearest Nora,

Know who I met recently? Diana. Remember her? Diana who was at the French convent school with us. Diana the only daughter of that big brawny country character who had some land in Maremma. Diana who had never known her mother because she'd died in childbirth. Diana who was so cold, white, clean and healthy, with her blonde hair, blue eyes and statuesque body, that we used to say she'd become one of those insensitive, frigid women who maybe have dozens of children but never experience love.

The memory of Diana is oddly bound up with the early days of our own relationship; and this, in turn, with a famous poem by Baudelaire that we discovered together in our years at school, a poem whose meaning we still disagree about now, just as we did then. The poem is "Women Damned". Remember? Instead of getting excited about the humanitarian poetry of Victor Hugo which the good nuns used to recommend, we would read "Les Fleurs du Mal" on the quiet, with that burning curiosity of early adolescence (we were both thirteen), a curiosity that's always on the lookout for something it can't yet define, but which all the same it feels predestined to experience. We were friends, close friends, perhaps even then something more than just friends; but we certainly weren't lovers. And so, almost fatally (because there's a fatality in what one reads, too), of all the hundreds of Baudelaire's poems, the one we lingered over was the one called "Women Damned". Remember?

To tell the truth, it was me who discovered this poem, me who read it out loud to you and explained what the lines meant, pausing, one by one, over its fundamental points. There were two that really mattered. The first comes in the verse: "My kisses are gentle as day flies/At eventide, embracing lakes serene,/And those of men their ruts will multiply/Like chariots or ploughshares harrowing"; the second in the verse: "Cursed be the dreamer ineffectual/Who first desired, in his stupidity/Loving a problem void, insoluble,/To mingle thoughts of love with honesty."

As you see, the first verse champions lesbian love, so delicate and affectionate compared with the brutality and coarseness of heterosexual love; while the second verse clears the air of moral scruples, which don't have anything to do with the things of love.

Of course even I, for all my explaining, understood these verses only very vaguely; but I understood them well enough to choose them out of all the others as the ones which would favour my passion for you. This passion, now so exclusive and self-aware, had a confused beginning. In fact, my very first advances I made to Diana.

As you may remember, occasionally, when there were exams early in the morning, the non-boarders at the school used to sleep in with the boarders. Diana usually slept at home, but one of those nights she stayed over at school and, as luck would have it, her bed was next to mine. I hardly hesitated at all, even though, I swear it, it was my first time: my senses demanded and I obeyed.

After a long, anxious wait, I climbed out of my bed, reached Diana's in a single bound, lifted the covers and sneaked in, hugging myself to her in a slow, irresistible embrace, just the way a snake will coil itself unhurriedly around the branches of a beautiful tree. Diana certainly woke up, but partly because of her dull, passive character and partly, perhaps, out of curiosity, she pretended to go on sleeping and let me do what I wanted. As soon as I realized that Diana seemed to accept the situation, I felt that same voracious impulse you feel when you're starving and you see some food: I wanted to devour her with kisses and caresses. But after a moment

2

The Thing

I imposed a kind of order on myself and began to creep along her motionless, supine body from top to bottom; from her mouth, which I brushed with my lips (my desire, why deny it, was directed to the other mouth); to her breasts, which I uncovered and carefully kissed; from her breasts to her stomach, where my tongue, like a love-sick snail, left a slow, damp trail; then from the stomach down, down as far as the sex, final and supreme goal of my little excursion. To have it at my mercy I took her knees in my hands and opened her legs wide. Diana went on pretending to be asleep and I eagerly tucked into my love food. I didn't leave off until her thighs closed convulsively on my cheeks like the teeth of a trap of fresh, muscular young flesh.

My boldness, however, was limited by inexperience. Today, after bringing a lover to orgasm, I would repeat my journey in reverse, from the sex to the stomach, the stomach to the breasts, the breasts to the mouth, and, after all that passion, I would abandon myself to the sweetness of a tender embrace. But I was still inexperienced; I didn't know how to love, and I was afraid of being surprised, by a suspicious nun perhaps, or a sleepless student. So I came out from under Diana's bedclothes at the bottom of the bed and, still in the · dark of course, got back into my own. I was breathing hard, I had my mouth full of sweet sex juice, I was happy.

The following day a surprise awaited me, one I might have expected in the end, given the stubbornness with which my very first lover had shammed sleep: when she saw me Diana acted as if nothing had happened between us; all day, cold and serene as usual, she kept up a front that was neither hostile nor apprehensive, but just completely and utterly indifferent. Night came; we went to bed next to each other again; when it got late I got out of my bed and started to get into Diana's. But the big, strong, athletic girl was awake. As I slipped under the covers a violent shove forced me out and sent me tumbling to the floor. At which point I had a sort of flash of inspiration. Your bed was next to Diana's too, on the other side. Suddenly I realized that you couldn't not have heard the commotion I'd made with my noisy love-making the night before; and that now you were waiting for me. So it was with the confidence of someone going to a promised date that I crept to your bedside. As I had foreseen, you didn't refuse me. And that was how our love began.

3

Now let's go back to Baudelaire. We became lovers, then, but we observed certain, let's say, ritual precautions which you insisted on – you always were a little hesitant and frightened. You asked, and to please you I accepted, that we make love only in two well-defined sets of circumstances: at school on the rare occasions we slept there; or at my house when your mother, an attractive, worldly widow, left Rome at the weekend with her lover and let you come and sleep at my place. Except for these two situations our relationship was to be chaste. Although I accepted, I couldn't make sense of this curious way of planning things. Now, with time, I have come to understand: you were obsessed with the morality Baudelaire speaks about, and to lull your sense of guilt you wanted everything to happen between us as though in a dream, between sleeping and waking, in my house or at school. All the same, you never got used to our relationship entirely; you never accepted it completely as a lasting, stable way of life. And here I want to quote another verse of Baudelaire where he gives a perfect description of your attitude to me: "The lazy tears that fell from her dulled eyes,/The broken air, the stupor, the delight,/Her vanquished arms, cast down in armistice,/All served, adorned her beauty delicate. /Reclining at her feet, calm, full of joy,/Delphine devoured her with her ardent eyes/As a strong animal observes its prey/When with its teeth it has marked out the prize." ‚

The way you saw it, I was Delphine, the tyrant, "calm, full of joy", and you Hippolyta, the poor creature devastated by my desire, the prey "marked out" by my teeth. This bizarre idea of yours led to your suffering from an uncontrollable fear that once again Baudelaire describes perfectly: "I feel some heavy terror fall on me,/And black battalions of spectres thin,/Who want to lead me along moving ways/On every side by ruthless skies shut in." Obviously, this is all written in the romantic style of the time; but it catches well enough that aspiration to so-called normality which was to obsess you after we had been lovers for two years. Oddly enough, with you this aspiration took the form of a violent impatience with your virginity. I was a virgin too - still am, thank God – and didn't feel at all impatient with a natural condition which in no way prevented me from being a complete person, or rather a complete woman. You, though – remember? – seemed more and more convinced that something was preventing you from living freely and to the full; and this something you identified as your virginity and you said that if our relationship went on, you'd never be able to get rid of it. Speaking of which, I remember a phrase of yours which hurt me: "I'll grow old with you, I'll become that sad figure of the maiden aunt who gets it on with women."

We stayed friends with Diana even after we left school and around that time she invited us to spend a weekend with her in her villa in Maremma. We took the train as far as Grossetto. Diana and her father were waiting for us at the station. Tall, thickly built and bearded, Diana's father was dressed like a Tuscan cowman with a red woollen overcoat, corduroy pants and untreated calfskin boots. Diana was less countrified in a white sweater and green jodphurs tucked into black boots.

We drove for about an hour up and down bare hills in brilliant sunshine that gave no warmth: it was winter, with a northerly wind blowing. At the top of a hill, along a muddy road, we arrived at a kind of farmstead, very rustic and not at all the wealthy villa we'd been expecting. There was no garden round the house; just a muddy, trampled patch of ground like the earth round a stable. When we arrived, the horses whose hooves had done the trampling were grazing in the meadows below the farmhouse. I counted six of them. As soon as Diana and her father appeared, they climbed the slope to meet us, more like dogs than horses. Diana and her father stroked the horses a bit, then suggested that you and I go into the house and wait for them there: they had to go on horseback to visit some tenants. They climbed into the saddle and rode off; we went to sit in the living room in front of a blazing fire in the big fireplace. Remember? After a long silence you said: "Did you see Diana? Fresh, white and red, clean – the very picture of physical and moral health." All at once I was hurt by the implicit reproach in what you'd said: "What do you mean? That I'm stopping you from being like Diana, physically and morally healthy?" "No, that's not what I mean. I just mean that I'd like to be like her and in some ways I envy her."

Enough. Diana and her father came back; we ate T-bone steaks grilled right there over the fire in the hearth; then, after coffee, the father went out again and we three went upstairs to a bedroom on the second floor to rest. But we didn't rest; we started to talk, all three of us stretched out on a huge double bed. I don't want to go over all the chat that led up to it: all I remember is that at a certain moment you began to talk about the problem that was obsessing you then – your virginity. At which point something extraordinary happened: with her clear, calm voice, Diana informed us that she had already sorted out the problem and, in fact, had lost her virginity some months back. With ill-concealed envy, you asked her how she had managed it; who was the man who'd offered his services, done her the favour. "Who?" she answered candidly. "A horse." Amazed, you exclaimed: "But hang on, isn't a horse too big?" Diana laughed; then she explained that the horse was only the indirect cause of her losing her virginity. What had happened was that, with all the riding she did, one day she had felt something like a sharp, painful tear in her groin. When she got home she'd found bloodstains on her pants. In short, she had lost her virginity without noticing, as a result of being constantly in the saddle with her legs apart.

After that trip to Maremma, things between us two changed very fast. A kind of awkwardness had got between us: you began to go out with a man, a lawyer from the south, a handsome type, fortyish; and I didn't see you anymore except for a few brief moments, partly because school was over and partly because your mother had broken off with her lover and spent the weekends at home with you. A year went by and you announced that you were going to marry the lawyer. Three years later, at just twenty, you left your husband, claiming "incompatibility of character", or at least that's what your mother told me over the phone. You went back to your mother. I came back into your life and we began to make love again, although always in secret and with plenty of precautions. Finally, after two years of secret love, we threw off the mask and came to live together, happily and freely, in the house we still live in today.

Now you probably want to know why I have mixed up our story with Baudelaire and Diana. I'll tell you: because deep down you continue to identify with Hippolyta and persist in seeing me as Delphine; you the downtrodden victim and me the cruel tyrant. You continue to see us, perhaps not without a certain masochistic gratification, as two "damned women". And yet, no, it isn't like that. We are not two damned women, not in the slightest; we are two brave women who have saved themselves from damnation.

The Thing

You will ask: what damnation? And I shall reply: that of slavery to the male member. Saved ourselves from an illusion of normality that now, after your miserable matrimonial experience, you know full well to be a figment of the imagination.

Which brings us to Diana. Seeing her after two years gave me the chance to meet precisely the pair of women who do fit Baudelaire's epithet, "damned". Because Diana hasn't been alone for some time now; she has got together with a certain Margherita in a relationship not unlike our own, apparently. I had never met this Margherita, but you have I think, because once – I can't remember when exactly – you told me about her and described her as "horrendous". You'll say: okay, she is a horrendous woman; but you've said yourself that she and Diana have a relationship like ours; so how come the damnation? I answer: take it easy; I said "apparently" like ours. In reality, I discovered that Diana and her friend have remained more than ever worshippers of the member, and what's more, in a sort of inflated fashion. But I don't want to run ahead of my story. All you need know for the moment is that their enslavement has gone far beyond the human sphere, to a dark zone that has nothing to do with humanity, not even the blind, brutal humanity of male aggression.

It happened like this. After you had left for the States, a letter arrived one morning with the postmark of a village not far from Rome. I looked at the bottom and saw Diana's signature. The letter was short and it went like this: "Dear, dearest Ludovica, you've always been so good to me, you're so serious and intelligent that now, finding myself in a difficult situation, I immediately thought of you. Yes, you're the only person who can understand me, the only one who can save me. Please, I'm begging you, help me; I feel I'll never get through without you, I'll be damned for ever. I'm living in the country, not far from Rome. Use any excuse – the fact that we were schoolfriends for example – and come and see me. But come *now*. Until we meet, then – soon! Your Diana, who has never forgotten you, not in all these years."

I must say that the letter made a strange impression on me. That poem by Baudelaire which prompted so much discussion on damnation has never been far from my mind, and here was Diana in her letter using that word "damned" and even reinforcing it with a desperate "for ever". The word was strong, much stronger than in Baudelaire's poem, which after all was written in a different age; then not only was it strong, but exaggerated too for a love relationship, however unhappy. Of course, there was always the possibility that Diana wrote "damned" because she couldn't manage to break off with the horrendous Margherita. But there was something in that word that went beyond the desperate desire to free oneself from an unbearable sentimental slavery; something dark and impenetrable.

So I phoned Diana right away, in the country, at the number she'd put in the letter. I pretended, as she had suggested, that I wanted one of those so-called school reunions, and was immediately invited to lunch the following day. Next morning I got in the car and headed in the direction of Diana's villa.

I arrived shortly before lunch. I drove through a wide open gate and on up a laurel-bordered drive which opened out into a well-groomed Italian-style garden with green flowerbeds and gravelled paths in front of an attractive two-storey villa. I drew up in front of the door, but I didn't have time to get out of the car and go to ring the bell: the door opened and Diana appeared, exactly as if she had been lurking in the hall, waiting for me to come. She was in her bathing costume, topless, because of the summer heat, but with this peculiarity: instead of sandals she was wearing red boots, the same colour as her costume. On taking a second glance at her, though, I could barely control my amazement at seeing how much and how strangely she had changed. In that instant, looking at her, I made a sort of lightning list of all the physical features she had once had and now lost. She had lost her hard, pronounced shapeliness: in place of the arrogant bust were two small, scarcely outlined breasts; in place of her curved, well-fed belly, a flat depression stretched between the two protruding bones of the pelvis; instead of her fine muscular legs were two ungainly sticks. But the biggest change was in her face: it was white and emaciated, dominated by blue eyes that her thinness had made enormous, and beneath them were two etched furrows of sexual fatigue. Her mouth, once a natural and never made-up pink, was now crudely enlarged with a smudged scarlet lipstick. Her whole body gave off a strange impression of liquefaction, like a candle consumed by its flame. You'd have said she hadn't so much slimmed as melted.

In a delighted voice she exclaimed: "Ludovica, at last! I've been waiting for you since dawn!" I didn't even recognize her voice. I remembered it as clear, silvery; now it was hoarse and deep. She coughed and I saw that between two long, skeletal fingers she gripped a lighted cigarette.

We hugged. Then in a casual kind of way which seemed in contrast with the desperate, urgent tone of her letter, she said: "Margherita has gone into the village, she'll be back soon. In the meantime, come on and I'll show you the house. We'll start with the stable. There are some really fabulous horses. You did like horses, didn't you?"

So saying, without waiting for an answer, she led me across the garden from one path to another, in the direction of a long, low building I hadn't noticed at first. The line of slit-like windows told me it was a stable. Diana walked slowly, head down, occasionally lifting the cigarette to her mouth, as if concentrating on something important. In the end, the result of her concentration was pretty feeble. "There are six horses and a pony," she announced. "The horses are thoroughbreds, worlds apart from my father's. The pony is simply a marvel."

We arrived at the stable door and went in. I saw a long, narrow rectangular space with five stalls on each side. The horses Diana had been enthusing about took up six of the stalls, and although I don't know much about horses, I quickly realized they were very handsome beasts; two white, one roan and three chestnut. Sleek and lightly built, in their clean stalls with scrubbed majolica tiles, they gave an impression of luxury. Diana stopped in front of each of them, telling me their names one by one, pointing out their best features, stroking them; but all this fairly distractedly.

Then she went to the pony which, because it was so small, I hadn't yet noticed, and in a light, detached voice she said: "This is my favourite, though. Come and look at him." And so saying, she went into the stall. My curiosity aroused, I followed her. The pony was a light chestnut colour, like a young deer, with a blond tail and blond mane. It stood still, as if meditating, under the torrent of long hairs that formed its mane. Diana began to praise the animal's beauty and while she was speaking, proceeded to stroke its flank. I had the strange impression then that Diana was talking aimlessly, just to talk, and that rather than listening I ought to be watching her, because what she was doing was more important than what she was saying. Very naturally, my eyes came to rest on the long, lean, white hand with its thin fingers and scarlet, pointed nails, that she was passing back and forth along the animal's trembling flank. And I noticed that at every caress her hand would go down a little further in the direction of the pony's belly. At the same time, she continued to speak with a strange, almost hysterical urgency; but apart from not listening, I wasn't even hearing her now. Instead, as if isolated by a sudden deafness, I was watching her hand – slow and hesitant, yet all the same animated by I couldn't tell what intention – which had now got down very near to where the pony's sex lay all closed in its sheath of chestnut hair. Two or three more strokes, and the hand made an almost mechanical jerk and blatantly moved to lie over the member. After a moment's hesitation, the fingers closed around it.

As if suddenly freed from my transitory deafness, I heard Diana saying: "He's my favourite, I won't deny it, but I ought to tell you something else, except that I don't know how to say it. Let's say he's my favourite because with him 'the thing' happens. It's this 'thing' that keeps me here, that made me write to you." She was standing right up close to the pony now and you couldn't tell what she was doing. Then I distinctly saw that her arm, stretched under the animal's belly, was moving back and forth, back and forth, and, logically, though not without a certain incredulity, I came to the conclusion that Diana was masturbating the pony.

While she did it she talked and talked as if accompanying the rhythm of her strokes with her voice. "What I call 'the thing', then, isn't so much him as what Margherita and I do with him. So I ought to call him my boyfriend, my man, the way women do. Because as Margherita's always telling me, there's not the slightest difference between him and a man, absolutely none. Of course his head, body and legs are different from a man's; but *there* he is exactly like a man, except that he's thicker; still, according to Margherita, that's not a defect, on the contrary, at certain moments it's a plus. Don't be ashamed, go ahead and look at him, and tell me if he isn't a real beauty. Go on, isn't he beautiful?"

Suddenly the pony reared up, lifting itself upright on its two back hooves and letting out a long, resounding neigh. Diana was quick to soothe and calm him with her voice and caresses. I left the stall. My expression must have been eloquent because Diana broke off her rhythmic monologue and murmured softly, as if speaking to the pony: "Stop it, don't get excited, you pig you." And with a different, suddenly imploring voice, she called after me: "Ludovica!" I was going away, but struck by the tone of her voice I stopped. "Ludovica, I wrote to you because I've got myself caught in a trap, in a real trap, a loathsome trap, and only you can get me out of it." Moved, I stuttered: "I'll do what I can." "No, Ludovica, not what you can, but one definite thing: take me away from here, today." "If you want, you can leave with me." "But you have to insist, Ludovica, because I'm a coward, a terrible coward, and at the last moment I might back down." A bit annoyed now, I said: "All right, I'll insist." She went on, as if speaking to herself: "We'll have lunch and then I'll say goodbye to Margherita and you take me away." Without a word, I hurried ahead of her out of the stable.

In the garden Diana caught me up, grabbed my arm hard and started to speak again. But I didn't listen. I was remembering that incredible, yet logical declaration she had made, that the pony was her "man"; and I couldn't help telling myself that the slavery of so many women to the male member had found a caricature confirmation in the example of Diana, transforming that so-called normality, to which you once aspired, into something parodic and monstrous. Yes, Diana and her girlfriend had got together not to love each other like we do, no, but to adore in the pony the eternal phallus, symbol of degradation and slavery. I remembered our arguments about Baudelaire's poem, and I told myself that it was Diana and Margherita who were really the "damned women" the poet speaks of, and not you and me, as you, in your moments of doubt and depression, sometimes still insist in believing. I recalled the end of the poem: "Go down, go down, oh victims pitiful", and I felt certain that this didn't refer to us, because we are not victims at all, but to the miserable Diana and her Margherita. In reality they were the victims of their own perversity, partly because they couldn't help prostrating themselves before the male image, but most of all because they pretended to love each other the better to hide their perversion, and with that disgusting farce profaned the pure and affectionate love that could have made them happy.

Diana, meanwhile, was saying: "I'll come and stay with you, for the moment. That way Margherita will think we're lovers and she'll leave us alone." Near furious, I answered: "No, not with me. Out of the question. And get your hand off my arm."

"Why is everybody so cruel to me?" she complained. "Now you've started as well."

"I can't forget that a few moments ago this same hand was squeezing that 'thing'. How could you?"

"It was Margherita. She persuaded me bit by bit. Then one day she blackmailed me."

"How, what blackmail?"

"Either you do it, or we separate."

"So? That was the right moment to get out."

"I didn't feel I could leave her. I loved her, I thought it would be just one time, nothing else: a whim."

"But where is Margherita?"

"There she is, over there."

I raised my eyes and, in doing so, saw Margherita. I thought of that adjective you had used so decisively – "horrendous" – and I looked at her hard as if to find a confirmation of your judgement. Yes, Margherita really was horrendous. She was standing under the portico of the villa with her legs apart, her hands on her hips. Tall and thickly built with a chequered shirt, big-buckled belt, white polo pants and black boots; I don't know why – perhaps it was her arrogant pose – but she reminded me of Diana's father that time we saw him in the country on his farm. I looked her in the face. Under the round mass of dark, kinky hair, her unusually low forehead came down like a helmet on two small, sunken and penetrating eyes. The tiny snub nose and pouting but thin-lipped mouth made me think of the snout of certain large apes. In short, she was a giantess, a female freestyle wrestler, the kind you see on television grabbing each other's hair, kicking each other in the mouth, bouncing with both feet on the stomach of their opponents.

She let us come near; then with a cordiality that I felt was false and calculated, she cried: "You're Ludovica, aren't you? Welcome to our abode. I have a feeling we're going to be friends; I sensed it the moment I saw you. Welcome, welcome." Her voice was like her body, seemingly jovial, but deep down cold and commanding. The voice of a school Headmistress, a Mother Superior, a ward Sister.

Naturally, we embraced. Then, to my amazement, I realized that

Margherita was trying to turn this welcoming embrace into a love kiss. Her pouting lips slid, moist and clinging, from my cheek to my mouth. I turned my face away as much as I could but she was holding me firmly in her powerful arms so that I couldn't prevent the tip of her tongue from penetrating the corner of my mouth for a moment. Brazen and pleased, she drew back and asked: "But where were you both? In the stable, of course! Diana has been showing you her passion, that blond pony? Pretty, isn't he? But come in, everything's ready, lunch is served."

We went into the house and found ourselves in a traditionally rustic sitting room with black beams across the ceiling, white-washed walls, a sandstone fireplace and heavy, dark furniture – not antique. One of those long, narrow, refectory tables was laid at one end with places and food for three.

I'm not going to go over what was said during lunch; it was Margherita who did all the talking and the only person she talked to was me, as if excluding Diana from the conversation. What did Margherita talk about? About this and that, as they say, about nothing of importance; but while she talked she never for a moment stopped hinting at the fact that she had taken a liking to me over the last few minutes, a liking quite bewildering for its suddenness and unexpectedness. She stared at me with those little, sunken eyes which shone, burned almost, with I didn't know what animal lust. Under the table, her two enormous calves squeezed my leg in a vice-like grip; she even went so far as to stretch out a podgy hand and, with the excuse of looking at the amulet I wore round my neck, she stroked it across my breasts, exclaiming: "My! Isn't our Ludovica beautiful, Diana?" Diana didn't reply: she was twisting her large mouth into a grimace of painful perplexity; she turned away from me and looked into the hearth. At which Margherita said brutally: "Hey you, I'm speaking to you. Why don't you answer?" "I've got nothing to say." "You whore, say that Ludovica is beautiful." Diana looked at me and repeated mechanically: "Yes, Ludovica is beautiful." Throughout this embarrassing scene, I was trying to free my leg from Margherita's calves, but without success. It was exactly as if I'd put my foot in a trap; that same loathsome trap Diana had spoken of in the stable.

We ate some excellent ham with melon, barbecued steak and a dessert. After this, Margherita did what speakers do at the end of a banquet: she banged her fork three times on the table. We looked at her in amazement. Then she said: "I have something very important to announce. I've chosen this moment to announce it because Ludovica is here and she will be able to testify that I mean what I say. Well then, as from today, I have put this house up for sale."

Instead of watching Margherita I turned to Diana, since the announcement had obviously been meant for her. She was twisting her mouth more than ever. She asked: "What do you mean, you're selling the house?"

"I've given the job to an agency. From tomorrow on there'll be an ad in a Rome newspaper. I'll sell the whole property, including the land round the house. But I won't sell the horses. No, not them."

A shade mechanically Diana asked: "You'll take them to another house?"

Margherita paused for a moment as if to underline the importance of what she was about to say; then she explained: "My new home will be a flat in Milan: however big it may be I can't see how I'll be able to find room for seven horses. On the other hand, I love them too much and couldn't bear thinking of them being handled by other people. I might be able to let them go free and live wild, but unfortunately that isn't possible. So, I'll kill them. After all, they are mine, I can do what I want with them."

"How would you kill them?"

"In the most humane way possible: with a gun."

There was a long, a very long silence. And I'll take advantage of this silence, my dear Nora, to tell you what I thought of Margherita's declarations immediately upon hearing them. I thought they were false and groundless, in the sense that they were really a kind of game between Margherita and Diana. Margherita had no intention at all of selling the house and even less of killing the horses; for her part, Diana didn't believe her friend really meant what she said. But for some private reason Margherita needed to threaten Diana, and for the same reason Diana needed to show that she took these threats seriously. So I wasn't too surprised when Margherita went on: "Yesterday morning, Diana told me she was planning to go back to her father's. That's why I decided to sell the house and kill the horses. But if she changes her mind, quite probably I won't do anything after all."

The Thing

It was an explicit invitation to Diana to decide. I watched her, I must confess, with some anxiety. Although it was clear, as I've said, that this was all a sparring match, I couldn't help but hope that Diana would find the strength to free herself from Margherita. Sadly, this hope was dashed. I saw Diana lower her eyes. Then she announced: "But I don't want the horses to die."

"You don't want that, eh?" Margherita seemed to be enjoying herself now. "You don't want it but the truth is that by deciding to leave you do want it."

I don't know why, perhaps out of stupidity, but I decided to intervene in this game: "Excuse me, Margherita, but that's not quite right: everything depends on you, not on Diana. At least as far as the horses are concerned."

Oddly, Margherita didn't take offence. She took what I said as an indication of my willingness to play another game, the one that she had been trying to set up between herself and me. "Well then, Ludovica dear," she said ambiguously, "let's say that everything depends on you."

"On me?"

"If you are ready, even on a temporary basis, to take Diana's place, I won't sell the house and I won't kill the horses. But you would have to say so immediately. If you accept, you could go back to Rome to get your things today and Diana could take advantage of the lift to leave."

A look of near fright must have crossed my face, because almost at once she corrected herself: "Of course, I'm only joking. All the same the invitation stands. I like you. I'd be happy for you to come and stay here, with or without Diana. So, Diana, you still haven't told me your decision . . ."

At this point I should explain that while Diana didn't appear to have taken the threat of killing the horses too seriously, this new threat of being replaced by me seemed to have a definite effect on her. She looked at me with those huge blue eyes of hers, wide with sudden suspicion. Then she said decisively: "I'm ready to do anything to stop those horses being killed."

"Not anything. 'The thing'."

Now, Nora dear, at this point I ought to have made a determined attempt to snatch Diana from the clutches of the horrendous Margherita. But despite my promise, I didn't do so. And this for two reasons: first, because after Margherita's far-from-jokey invitation, I was afraid that if I intervened I would only be able to save Diana at a price that was really too high, by agreeing to be a substitute for her myself; and in the second place because at that moment I hated Diana even more than Margherita. True, Margherita was an utter and incurable monster, but Diana was worse precisely because she was better: a treacherous, weak, sneaky coward. You will say that my judgement was prejudiced, perhaps unconsciously, by the memory of my unfortunate experience with her at school. Maybe. But hate is a complicated feeling, made up of different elements: you never hate for one reason alone.

So I kept my mouth shut. I saw Diana looking at Margherita with a shy, beaten expression. Then she whispered: "Okay."

"Okay what?"

"I'll do what you want."

"Today?"

"Yes."

"Right away?"

Diana protested with conspiratorial sour grapes: "At least let me digest my lunch."

"Okay, let's all go and take a rest. Diana, you go to the bedroom. I'll be there in a moment. I'll just take Ludovica to her room."

"I can take her myself. After all, it was me who invited her."

"It's my house. I'll take her."

"But I want to talk to Ludovica."

"You can talk to her later."

This squabble finished as expected: dejected and uncertain, Diana left the sitting room in the direction of a door that probably led to another part of the ground floor of the house; Margherita and I climbed up to the second floor. Margherita led me along a corridor, opened a door and we went into a little attic room with a sloping ceiling and a window. Margherita's insistence on wanting to show me up to the room had already made me uneasy, but this uneasiness grew when I saw her turn the key in the door. I immediately protested: "Why are you doing that?"

Margherita remained quite unruffled: "Because that whore is perfectly capable of coming and bothering us without any warning."

I said nothing. Margherita came close and with a light, careless gesture, slipped her arm round my waist. So there we were, standing, almost embracing, under the low attic ceiling. Margherita went on: "She's jealous, but with good reason for once. She's spoken a great deal about you. She's told me everything: the school, you going to her bed at night, her pretending to be asleep. I had built up a certain idea of you, a good one naturally. But you're a hundred times better than I imagined. And what counts most of all, a hundred times better than that whore Diana."

To interrupt this weighty declaration of love, I objected: "But why do you call her a whore? You called her the same thing at table, just a few minutes ago."

"Because she is one. She throws tantrums and turns up her nose, but in the end she always says yes. And don't be fooled by her sentimentality: she only thinks of one thing – you know what – and nothing else matters for her. The horses for example. Do you really think that if I killed them tomorrow, she'd feel as terrible as she claims? Never. But since you were there she wanted to show you that she has a sensitive spirit. A whore, that's what she is. But I'm fed up with her. So, what have you decided?"

I was genuinely amazed: "What are you talking about?"

"Do you agree to come and live with me here, for a couple of months maybe, just to start with?"

To gain time I objected: "But there's Diana."

"We can do something to get rid of Diana. You'll have to take her place." She was silent a moment, then added: "I spoke of killing the horses a few moments ago. All I'd have to do to make her go is kill the pony."

I exclaimed: "A few moments ago you were threatening to kill the pony to stop Diana leaving you. Now you threaten to kill it to make her go away!"

"A few moments ago I didn't want Diana to leave and I knew that the threat was sufficient to make her stay. But to make her go away I'll have to carry out the threat. If I kill the pony, she'll go."

She was pressing up against me and she bent and kissed me on the neck and then the shoulder. I tried to free myself, but couldn't manage. In spite of myself, I said: "What do you want from me?"

"What Diana can't give me, will never give me: real love."

I tell you, at that moment Margherita nearly had me frightened. It's one thing hearing certain things from you, but quite another to get them from a giantess with piggy eyes and the muzzle of an ape. I protested, weakly: "I already love somebody else."

"Who cares? I know everything about you. She's called Nora, right? Bring her here; you can both come and stay with me."

While she was speaking she pushed me towards the bed and a hand clumsily pulled up the front of my skirt. Now you know that often, especially in summer, I don't wear anything underneath. Up came her hand between my legs; she grabbed at my pubic hair with all five fingers and pulled hard, just like a brutal, lecherous man. I let out a cry of pain and freed myself with a shove. At the same moment someone knocked at the door. Her eyes shining with excitement, Margherita made me a fierce sign with her hand, as if to order me not to open the door. My answer was to go and open it. Diana was there. Before saying anything she looked at us both in silence. "I'm ready, Margherita," she said.

For a moment Margherita didn't know what to say: she was still breathing hard; she seemed flustered. Finally, with an effort, she got out: "Haven't you slept?"

Diana shook her head: "I was here all the time."

Surprised, I asked: "Where here?"

She replied in a whisper without looking at me: "Here in the corridor, sitting on the floor, waiting for you to be finished."

I felt again that I hated her; she was so cowardly and weak-willed. When I arrived she had begged me to take her away; now instead she curled up like a dog outside the door waiting for us "to be finished". Margherita said impetuously: "Okay, let's go." And then, turning to me: "Agreed then! See you soon."

They went out and I threw myself on the bed to get some rest after all the tension. A few minutes later I jumped up and went to the window: I was sure there was something I ought to look at, though I didn't know what exactly. I waited a long time. From the window there was a view of a meadow which stretched away behind the villa. At the bottom of the meadow was a large swimming pool with blue water surrounded by a high hedge of trimmed boxwood. The boxwood hedge was divided in the middle and through the gap beyond the pool you could see, in perspective, a long, low construction, doubtless containing changing cubicles and a bar for drinking an aperitif after taking a dip. I looked at the pool and told myself that it was nothing less than a backdrop, like in a theatre; soon something was going to happen. And in fact, a few moments later, a little procession emerged from the direction of the stable and crossed the meadow.

First came Diana, topless, with her red bikini bottoms and boots; she was leading the pony with a halter. The animal followed her quietly and slowly: covered by the long hairs of his mane, his muzzle bowed down as if in thought. He had a garland of red flowers round his neck; they looked like roses, the simple kind with just one ring of petals. Behind the pony, holding the animal's long blond tail in both hands, with the same solemnity that one might use to hold the train of a sovereign, came Margherita.

I saw them head straight for the gap between the two, high boxwood hedges, disappear, then reappear behind the hedge to the right, though now I could only see their heads. The pony was too small and I couldn't see him at all.

At this point it was as if they took it in turns to act and watch. First of all Diana made the gesture of bending down to where the pony was; her head disappeared; Margherita's head, on the other hand, remained visible: she seemed to be watching something going on just beneath her eyes. Maybe a minute went by; then, unexpectedly, the pony reared up as it had done in the stall, its head and front hooves suddenly appearing above the hedge. It dropped back down almost immediately and disappeared again. More interminable minutes went by; then Diana's head reappeared above the hedge and it was Margherita's turn to disappear while Diana watched something going on beneath her eyes; the pony didn't rear up again. Then Margherita came up again as Diana had done; both women's heads were visible now, facing each other. Perhaps Margherita spoke, gave some command; I distinctly saw Diana shake her head in refusal. Margherita stretched out an arm and pressed her hand on Diana's head, the way you do in the sea sometimes to push someone underwater for a joke. But Diana didn't give way. For a moment they were still; then, with just one hand, Margherita slapped Diana twice, once on each cheek. And I saw Diana's head begin to sink down slowly till it disappeared again. At this point I drew back from the window.

Without hurrying, because i knew the two women were busy with 'the thing', I left the room, went down to the ground floor and out into the garden. With a feeling of joy I found my car parked in front of the door. I got in and just a minute later was already driving fast back to Rome.

You'll want to know why on earth I have told you this whole, rather sinister story. My answer is: out of repentance. I confess that when Margherita was pressing against me up in the attic room I was almost tempted to give in to her. I would have done so precisely because she was repugnant, because I did find her, as you put it, horrendous, because she did want me to take Diana's place. But fortunately my memory of you didn't desert me. When Diana knocked, everything was already over; I had already overcome the temptation and was thinking only of you and of all the good and beautiful things you mean to me.

Write soon.

Your Ludovica

To the Unknown God

I saw Marta fairly often that winter. She was a nurse I'd met some months before at the hospital I was sent to: I was getting these mysterious bouts of fever, something I'd picked up in Africa probably, on one of my trips to the tropics as a special correspondent.

Small, minute, with a big head of bushy, tightly curled, fine reddish-brown hair, parted down the middle, Marta had a round, baby face. But a baby who had been worn and drained of colour by a precocious maturity. In the absorbed, worried expression of her big, dark eyes; in the quiver that would often flicker around the corners of her mouth, the idea of infancy was strangely mixed up with that of suffering, or even martyrdom. A last detail: her voice was rather hoarse and she spoke with a rough, local accent.

But Marta would not have aroused in me what was, in some ways, a sentimental curiosity, had she not, during my illness, behaved towards me in a way that was, to say the least, unusual from a professional point of view. To put it bluntly, Marta caressed me every time she remade my bed or tidied my bedclothes or helped me to perform my natural functions. They were fugitive and extremely brief caresses, always round the crotch and as if stolen from the very secret that made them furtive and hurried. But they were also in some ways impersonal caresses. I felt that they weren't addressed to me, but to that part of my body and no other. I never got so much as a kiss from Marta, and I knew all along that she would have given the same caress to any other patient, if she got the chance.

This was all rather mysterious. So it was curiosity, more than any desire to resume this relationship, that led me, once out of hospital, to telephone Marta and ask her to meet me. She fixed a date but with this peculiar reservation: "Okay, I'll see you, but only because you seem different from the others. I feel I can trust you." These words seemed like the pathetic clichés people trundle out to save their dignity; instead, as I realized later, they were the truth.

We had arranged to meet in a café that had one of those backrooms, near where Marta lived. She had suggested it herself, using a phrase whose true meaning I hadn't grasped: "The back room is always empty, that way we'll be alone." I must confess, I had the impression that in the half-light of the empty back room, Marta might *perhaps* make another of those strange raids on my body that she'd made at the hospital. But as soon as I sat down opposite her in a darkish corner, I immediately changed my mind. She had her head held back against the wall and she watched me doubtfully while I explained how pleased I was to see her and how her being at the hospital had helped me get over a difficult moment in my life. Finally she shook her head and said firmly: "If you've come here to get what you got at the hospital, tell me now so I can leave without wasting any more time."

I couldn't help but exclaim almost ingenuously: "But why at the hospital, yes, and here, no?"

She watched me for quite a while, then answered in a disdainful voice: "You're acting just like all the others, unfortunately. Still, there is something about you that makes me feel I can trust you. Why here, no, and at the hospital, yes? Because here I don't have the hospital atmosphere round me. Here I'd feel I was doing something dirty."

"But what does this 'hospital atmosphere' consist of?"

"The hospital atmosphere," she replied somewhat impatiently, "how can I put it? The doctors, the nuns, the smell of disinfectants, the metal furniture, the silence, the idea of sickness, of healing, of death. But, without going further than is necessary, the fact that the patient is in bed covered with his bedclothes – which means you can't do certain things except through the sheet – creates what I call the 'hospital atmosphere'."

"The sheet? I don't understand."

"But you must remember that those caresses which made such a big impression on you were never made directly on your naked body, but always through the sheet."

She seemed relaxed now and spoke completely openly about our relationship. I don't know why, but I said: "Sheets are also commonly used as shrouds for corpses."

"Not for me. For me the sheet means the hospital."

"What do you mean?"

"It's what reminds me that I'm a nurse, that I am there for the patient's good and that I mustn't go beyond certain limits, namely those of the sheet. Instead, here, in the backroom of this café . . ."

"But it was you who suggested it."

"Yes, because it's near my house. Here in the café you'd probably like me to stroke you through your trouser fly and the slit in your underpants. How gross!"

Spurred on by I didn't know what experimental curiosity, I said: "You'll have to excuse me. The fact is that I've rather taken a fancy to you. Let's think: would you like to come to my place one of these days; I'll get into bed and pretend to be ill; I'll be covered in a sheet."

"It'll be your house, not the hospital."

To see how she would react I insisted: "If you like, I'll say I need some tests done and get myself sent back to hospital again. On the condition, though, that every now and then, even if only for a moment, you come to see me in my room."

"Are you crazy? It matters that much to you then?"

"I told you, I've taken a bit of a fancy to you. Or rather, to your vice."

She hit back immediately and forcefully. "But it's not a vice! I like to stroke a patient's penis lightly through the sheet for a reason that's got nothing to do with vice."

"What reason?"

"How can I explain? Let's say, it's as if I'm checking with my hand that, despite the illness, life is still always there, present, ready . . ."

"Ready for what?"

As if speaking to herself, she said: "You won't believe me, but my caress is like a question. As soon as I get the answer, that is, as soon as I feel that the caress has the effect I was expecting, I stop. I've never gone on so long as to make a patient ejaculate. Where's the vice in that?"

In my mind I went over and over what she was telling me as if over something dark and impenetrable whose existence, nevertheless, couldn't reasonably be denied. At last I said: "So this is the picture, I don't see how else it could be: the nun on one side, with her cross on her breast; the doctor on the other with his thermometer; and in the middle, covered in his sheet, the patient whose penis you slide your hand over, touch, caress, for just a second when nobody's looking. That's the picture, isn't it?"

"Yes, that's the picture as you call it."

"And that . . . light caress is enough for you?"

"Obviously, seeing as I've never done anything else."

After talking like this for a while we parted, as they say, good friends, having promised each other we would meet again. As in fact we did on a number of occasions, always in the same café. She didn't try to explain why she did what she did now; instead she preferred to tell me stories, though it was always more or less the same things that happened in all of them. You could see that she enjoyed talking about it, not so much to boast as perhaps to try to understand better why she acted in this way. Here's one of her stories, for example: "Yesterday I went to put the bedpan under the backside of a patient who is seriously ill. A small businessman or shopkeeper, middle-aged, ugly, bald, with a moustache and a mean, vulgar face. His wife is one of those sanctimonious types; she sits at the bottom of his bed and does nothing but mumble prayers, counting quick as quick through her rosary beads. I lifted the bedclothes, slipped the bedpan under his lean buttocks, waited till he had done his business, took out the pan and went to empty and clean it in the bathroom. Then I came back to tidy his bed. It was in the evening and his wife was sitting at the bottom of the bed praying as usual. I tidied his bed; but just when I was going to pull up the blankets over the sheet, with a quick movement of the hand, I gave him a squeeze, not very hard, but wide, taking in the whole of his genitals, and I said softly: 'You'll see, you'll soon get better.' Like the vulgar type he was he said with a lewd innuendo: 'If you say so, I know I'll get better.' Then he got angry with his wife who was praying and shouted at her to shut up with all those prayers because they brought him bad luck."

"Did he really get better?"

"No, he died last night."

"But how could you do it to a man like that; seriously ill, and vulgar, mean and gross into the bargain?"

"Where I put my hand he was nothing of the kind I can promise you. He might have been the most handsome young man on earth."

Another time she arrived looking upset. Right away she said: "Last night I had a big fright."

"Why?"

"There's a patient I really like. He's young, thirtyish, and everything about him gives you a sense of rough, simple, country-style vitality. He has a broad, solid face, open, smiling eyes, a curved nose and sensual mouth. He's an athlete, a champion of some sport or other. He had an operation recently and he's in a lot of pain, even though he never complains and never talks about it. He is the quietest of all the patients, never says a word: he lies still and watches television; the set's opposite his bed against the wall and he keeps it on all the time and is always changing channels. Last night, around three, he called me and I found him with the television on as usual and the room dark. I went to his bedside and he muttered in a ghost of a voice – you know how people do when they're in a lot of pain – 'Please,' he said, 'I'd like you to hold my hand; that way I'll feel like I had my mother or sister next to me and it'll make the pain more bearable.' I didn't say anything; I gave him my hand and he squeezed it hard. He was really in pain, at least if that convulsive squeeze was anything to go by. So, hand in hand, without speaking or moving, we watched the television: it was some gangster film. A few minutes went by; every now and then I felt him squeeze my fingers harder, as if to underline the onset of a sharper pain. Suddenly, I don't know why, probably out of a desire to relieve his suffering in some way, I said quietly: 'To help you overcome the pain, perhaps a more intimate contact might be better.' 'More intimate?' he repeated in a strange voice, as if addressing the question to himself. And quietly I said, 'Yes, more intimate.' He didn't say anything. I took my hand out of his, slipped it between the blankets and the sheet and moved it down to lie flat over his penis. It was made like the rest of him. The palm of my hand closed hard around a swelling that was like the stems of a bunch of fresh flowers wrapped in cellophane. I whispered: 'That's better, isn't it?' And from the dark he answered 'yes'. Without speaking at all, still watching the glowing TV, I started to make a slow circular movement with my hand, nothing heavy or insistent, but light and delicate – and do you know the impression I had then? It was as if there was a tangle of freshly caught octopus under the sheet, alive and still moving, all wet and slippery with sea water."

I couldn't help but exclaim: "What a strange sensation!"

"It was a feeling of vitality and purity. What could be more pure and alive than a living creature fresh out from the depths of the sea? I don't know how to express the idea. The impression was so strong that I couldn't help but whisper to him again: 'Nice, no?' He didn't say anything, letting me do as I chose. So we went on for a while longer . . ."

"I'm sorry, but wouldn't it have been better, nicer and more sincere simply to have pulled the sheet away and . . ."

She said stubbornly: "No, I didn't want to lift the sheet, absolutely not. To pull away the sheet would have been like betraying the hospital and everything the hospital means for me."

"I understand. So what happened: did he ejaculate?"

"Definitely not. We went on a while, maybe a couple of minutes, and then suddenly he starts to repeat: 'I'm dying, I'm dying, I'm dying,' and I got scared, pulled out my hand fast and went to call for help. The nun and the doctor on night-duty came and various other nuns and doctors; they pulled back his bedclothes; his left leg was swollen to twice the size of his right and purplish: an attack of phlebitis. Everybody was very frightened, partly because he said his foot was cold and he couldn't feel it. But do you know what? Of course, I was frightened as well and saying to myself how it was all my fault, but I had this touch almost of vanity too, because I thought that the blood that wasn't circulating in his leg anymore had all gone there where I'd put my hand."

"So what happened then?"

"Well, the phlebitis was got under control. This morning I went into his room; he looked at me and smiled and with that smile he freed me from my feeling of guilt."

Another time she told me a story that was quite comic in some ways, though the comedy was always of the slightly macabre kind typical of hospital stories. She said: "Something really incredibly tiresome is going on."

"What?"

"A patient absolutely insists that I marry him and he's blackmailing me: either you marry me or I start a scandal."

"So who is he?"

"An awful man, a brute; he owns a restaurant some place down south. He had an abscess on one knee; looked like he was dying. They amputated the leg and in a couple of days he was blooming again, just like some trees do after they've been pruned; now his face is all red and plump as if he were about to burst with health any second. Taking advantage of a moment when I was tidying the bed – by now there was only one leg sticking out at the bottom – I made the mistake of stretching my hand to where the sheet rose over a truly enormous swelling. I couldn't resist it, the temptation was too strong. I'd never seen a swelling like that. And just imagine what I felt: two testicles as big and hard as a bull's and a sort of floppy tube or sleeping snake. He seemed to be dozing, but he woke at once and murmured: 'Go right ahead, they're there for you,' or something equally vulgar; the kind of thing that should have put me off once and for all. Instead, as I said, the temptation was too strong for me and I did it again; every now and then I would skim my hand lightly, lightly across the sheet just to check that everything was still there, to feel the fabulous volume of the testicles and the extraordinary thickness of his penis. Strangely, he didn't say anything now: obviously he was thinking over his marriage proposal. Then one day he announces that he wants to marry me: he tells me he's rich, that he'll treat me like a queen, that he'll make sure I always have everything I want. Just think, me, married! And to a bloke like that!"

"But you'll have to get married one day."

She looked at me and then replied with profound conviction: "I'll never get married."

"But you're young; you need love."

"Oh, I do that with myself, alone. I don't need to get married. I squeeze my thighs together and rub them against each other and bang, love-making over and done with."

I wanted to ask her a question that I felt was indiscreet. I risked it: "But are you ... a virgin?"

"Yes, and I always will be. Just the idea of love, in the way the restaurant owner thinks of it, horrifies me. And, fancy that, it's precisely my virginity he's after."

"So how will you get out of it?"

A mischievous smile wrinkled her pale, worn, mistreated-little-girl's face: "I told him to go on down to his little village ahead of me, that I'd follow as soon as I could: I swore I'd marry him. Once he's left the hospital, tough luck!"

"And in the meanwhile you'll go on touching him, slipping your hand over him?"

"Yes, I told you, I can't resist it. But I don't see any connection between him and his genitals. He is – how can I put it? – the trustee of something that isn't his, a bit like a soldier who's been entrusted with a weapon to fight. But the weapon isn't his."

"Whose is it then?"

"I don't know. Sometimes I think it belongs to an unknown god, but different from the one the nuns wear round their necks."

"An unknown god?" Surprised, I couldn't help telling her about that passage in the Acts of the Apostles that talks about St Paul's visit to Athens and the mysterious temple dedicated to the unknown god. She listened to me without showing much interest, then said abruptly: "In any case, I only sense this unknown god at the hospital. In the tram the men who rub themselves up against me make me sick."

I said: "If you fell in love, this would all change."

"Why?"

"Because you'd throw away the sheet and look the unknown god in the face."

She looked at me and then replied enigmatically: "God keeps himself hidden. Who ever saw him? I'm not a saint, me."

Strangely enough, after this last encounter, I didn't see her for some time. She'd told me she would telephone me and she didn't. Then one morning she called again and arranged to meet me in the usual café. She was waiting for me, sitting in the shadow; she seemed to have an expression that was at once extremely upset and very calm: an odd combination of moods. Immediately she said: "I killed a man."

"What are you talking about?"

"Just what I said. I killed the man I loved."

"You loved a man?"

"You told me I should fall in love to look the god who hides beneath the sheets in the face. Well, it happened. I fell in love with a boy, twenty years old, with heart trouble. It began with me sliding my hand over him, like with the others, and then something strange happened: for the first time, perhaps because he was an intellectual like you and I continually felt I was being understood and judged, I suddenly saw those caresses as a kind of vice. And so I decided to pull away the sheet."

A little ironically I exclaimed: "What is this? A metaphor? You're speaking in symbols?"

She looked at me, hurt: "The sheet wasn't just the symbol of the hospital; it was also a material obstacle. You try telling me how I'm supposed to make love to a man with a sheet between us. So one night, with the TV screen glowing more intensely than ever in the dark and him teasing me with his soft, sly voice, saying how I'd never have the courage, I was overcome by a kind of fury. I swear, it was like making a great leap into nothingness for me, into the dark; like tearing the veil off the face of that god you told me about. Suddenly I pulled away the covers and threw myself on his naked body. Everything happened in just a few minutes in the flickering light of the TV screen, in that deep, hospital-night silence. As I bent my face over his stomach, I felt I was saying a definitive goodbye to the hospital and to everything the hospital had meant for me in the past. Then a huge glob of sperm filled my mouth; I lifted myself off him and ran down to the bathroom to spit it all out. But I didn't have the courage to go back to his room; I went to my own room and slept there till dawn.

"I was woken by a nun shaking me and demanding to know what I'd done, why I'd gone to sleep when I was on duty. I said I'd felt ill. Perhaps the nun didn't believe me, perhaps she sensed something. Suddenly she said that the boy with heart trouble had been found dead. She added: 'His covers were pushed down to his knees; it looks as though he tried to get out of bed.' "

I was silent for a moment; I was rather horrified and didn't know what to say. Finally I objected: "There is always the possibility that his death wasn't your fault."

She shook her head: "No, it was me, I'm sure. As soon as I stopped being the nurse who knows where to stop if she's not to hurt the patient, and became the woman who puts no limits on her love, I killed him."

She said nothing for a while, then she told me: "I've left the hospital. Now I'm working in a beauty parlour; at least there are only women there." And she concluded philosophically: "I was a good, conscientious nurse, with a vice. I became a sane, normal woman, and a murderess."

The Woman with
the Black Cloak

❦

At table, everything is exactly as it was four years ago when they got married: the blue and white English porcelain dinner service, the crystal glasses from Bohemia, the ivory-handled cutlery, the silver salt and pepper pots, the pewter oil cruet – everything is as it was in those now far-off days. There are even the same roses in the green glass vase, the same tablecloth, the same red napkins with white embroidery, right down to the same ray of sunshine which, entering slantwise through the window, makes porcelain, silverware and crystal sparkle. Yet, at the same time, everything has changed and changed profoundly. So much so that at the moment he feels as if he were the ghost of a memory, rather than a real person of flesh and blood. The problem is that, unlike four years ago, everything is different between himself and his wife. And, in fact, here he is now going back to their quarrel – submerged, discrete, yet all the more painful for being so – a quarrel which has to do with the fact that for more than a year now his wife refuses to make love. With a strange tenderness she says that, yes, she loves him; yes, she knows that he loves her; yes, there was a perfect physical understanding between them; yes, this understanding could return; but, at least for the moment, she doesn't feel like it.

Why? No reason; there is no explanation, that's how it is and there's an end to it.

At this point the cook comes in with the second course: chicken *alla marocchina*. It is a dish which, in a way, is bound up with their relationship: they picked up the idea in Morocco where they'd gone for their honeymoon. The recipe specifies that the chicken must be cut into minute pieces and then cooked at a low heat with pounds of lemons and heaps of olives, so that the meat will soak up the saltiness of the olives and the bitterness of the lemons.

The cook offers the pan first to his wife, then to him; they serve themselves and begin to eat, heads down, while the argument continues. Then, quick as lightning, the unexpected happens. His wife lets out a suffocated shout, lifts her hands to her throat, tries to cough, gets up, throwing her napkin to the floor, sweeps away her plate and cutlery with her hand and begins to run through the flat with him following, still not understanding.

She runs, takes refuge in the bedroom, and collapses on the bed, her hands round her neck. The unexpected is a sharp little chicken bone which has lodged in her throat. But what happens a little while later at the casualty ward of the hospital is anything but unexpected; following her through the flat he had foreseen it with absolute certainty: his wife dies without recovering consciousness.

After his wife's death he stays on in what was previously their home, doing the same things as before: every day he goes to his architect's office, comes home for meals, goes out in the evening with friends, etc. etc. But he sleeps alone, goes out alone and eats alone: no one says goodbye to him in the morning when he goes out to work; no one welcomes him home in the evening when he returns. This loneliness oppresses him because it isn't the sort of temporary loneliness you can shake off with company. It is an irremediable loneliness: the only person who could put an end to it is dead. So he lives alone, all the time asking himself what he ought to do, whether to dismiss the memory of his dead wife once and for all, or to take pleasure in it, letting himself sink slowly down to the depths of grief as if to the bottom of a black, stagnant pool. In the end, infallibly, the second of these alternatives prevails.

So begins a gloomy and at the same time obscurely voluptuous period. His longing for his dead wife expresses itself in numerous ritual activities, like gazing at her clothes stored in the cupboards, or touching her make-up boxes and perfumes one by one; or, more imaginatively, looking with her eyes out of the bedroom window down their avenue. These ritual activities take him beyond the phase of dreamy, fetishistic contemplation and prompt a hallucinatory fancifulness: he pricks up his ears in the silence, almost hoping to hear his wife's voice talking to the cook in the kitchen; or, at night, when he goes to bed, he is almost sure he will see her already in bed, propped up against the pillows, reading.

Imperceptibly, his waiting for his wife's apparition develops and becomes a waiting for her return. He imagines her ringing the doorbell; he goes to open the door and finds her in front of him saying she has forgotten her keys: she was always forgetting dates, things, occasions. Or that she telephones from the airport and asks him to come and pick her up: she never used to warn him in advance which day and what time she was coming back from her trips. Or again, more simply, he imagines finding her in the sitting room, intent on listening to music: she used to do that when she was waiting for him to get back from the office for lunch.

Finally, after the idea of return, comes that of rediscovery. He begins to wander around the streets, going into bars, attending social does, in the obscure hope of finding her again. Yes, suddenly she will be there, in front of him, in the middle of doing something quite normal and ordinary, like somebody who's been around all along, even though for normal, ordinary reasons they haven't put in an appearance for a while. Thus, for example, he imagines finding himself next to her on the underground train, standing, on her way to the Piazza di Spagna to do some shopping.

The rediscovery phase goes on for longer than the return phase; in fact there seems no end to it. Because of course one can return only on certain given occasions; whereas one can be rediscovered any time, anywhere. In reality, any young woman between twenty and thirty, blonde and tall without being exactly thin, could be her, especially if seen from behind and at a distance. So he becomes more and more firmly convinced that, yes, his wife is dead, but that somehow, by reincarnation, resurrection or substitution, she could reappear. One day he will look a woman in the face and exclaim: "But you're Tonia!" And she will answer: "Yes, it's me, why shouldn't it be!" "But you're a ghost." "Not at all. Touch me, hug me, it's me, Tonia, in the flesh."

The morbid nature of these fantasies doesn't escape him. Every so often he thinks, "I'm going crazy. If things go on like this I'll find her again for sure. But that'll also be the moment I have to accept that I'm mad, that I believe in my own hallucinations." This fear of madness, however, doesn't stop him going on hoping he will discover his wife. On the contrary, it adds a certain smack of challenge to the hope. Yes, he will find her precisely because it is impossible to find her.

Finally, to put an end to this gloomy atmosphere, he decides on a change of scene: he'll go to Capri. It is November, the low season: no one will be on the island and he will be left to his memories, his regret. He will take walks, fantasize, reflect. In short, he'll relax and try to recover the energy that's been lost in grief. Because, perhaps, the truth is that his obsession is nothing more than a question of nerves, of physical imbalance.

So he sets off for Capri, where, as he had expected, he finds himself on his own, with almost all the hotels and restaurants closed and no tourists about, just the locals. But it's a different loneliness from the one in Rome. In Rome he was alone of necessity; here he is alone by choice.

Right away he settles down to a very regular schedule: he gets up late, takes a first walk, eats lunch at the hotel, takes a second walk in the afternoon, goes back to his room to read, eats dinner and then, in the near-deserted hotel lounge, watches television. At close down he goes to bed.

Despite this regularity, his longing for his wife doesn't go away; it just assumes a different form. As if death had robbed this kind of evocation of its erotic nature, he takes to recalling more and more often and with great precision and objectivity, certain episodes from the time when he and his wife still used to make love. These evocations are no different from the kind of adolescent fantasizing that frequently ends in masturbation; but he limits himself to fantasizing his wife in action, without adding any physical participation of his own. Besides, he is afraid of getting involved in a sort of necrophilia: in adolescence the women he thought of when he masturbated were all living; masturbation was nothing more than the fantasized continuation of a normal relationship. But if he masturbates over a dead woman, what can it lead to, if not precisely that morbid unreality he came to Capri to escape?

The Woman with the Black Cloak

One episode in particular from the happy period when he and his wife made love comes back to him again and again. They had met by chance one spring morning in a city street where there were a lot of smart shops. His wife was looking for a sweater; he for a record. Surprised and happy at this chance meeting, something had happened the moment they recognized each other, something that, in the form of a look full of desire, left his wife's eyes and headed straight for the centre of his own, as an arrow loosed with skill and a sure aim will go straight to the bullseye. He said: "Do you want to make love?" As if unable to speak, his wife had nodded yes. "Do you want to go home?" To his surprise she answered in a low voice: "No, I want to do it now, right away." "Now, but where?" "I don't know, now." He had looked round: apart from the shops there were a lot of hotels in the street, some of the best in the city. So he said: "If you like we can go to a hotel. But I doubt if they'll give us a room when they see we haven't got a suitcase. Of course, we could go and buy a suitcase ..." She had looked at him hard, and said: "No, not a hotel, come with me."

She took his hand and without hesitating went in through the first door they found. Inside, she went straight to the lift: she seemed to know exactly where she was going. Once in the lift, she explained: "The top floor hardly ever has any doors; it leads to the roof-terrace. If the door to the terrace is open we'll do it there. If not, on the landing; no one goes up there." She had spoken without looking at him, standing facing the door, turning her back to him. He came close to her and she had reached her hand behind, taken hold of his penis and squeezed it hard. The lift stopped; they went out on the landing and found that the door to the terrace was locked, so his wife said between her teeth: "Let's do it here." He had seen her lean forward over the banisters and take hold of the hand-rail with one hand while she used the other to lift up her cloak over her waist. Her buttocks showed white as white in the half-light of the landing; oval-shaped, full, tight and glossy; he had approached her and, despite having a very powerful and purposeful erection, he had wanted to be sure of penetrating at first thrust. So he had bent down to look, from behind, amongst the blonde curls, at the pink and tortuous cleft of her sex. The two large lips were still stuck to each other as if huddled in sleep; he had reached out a hand and separated them carefully with two fingers, like the petals of a flower

35

on the point of opening. Then he had seen the inside of her, bright pink and shining with moisture, made up of different layers, like a shapeless, still-open wound that has cut deep into the flesh. Was it a vagina, or the cut of a sharp knife? He had been left with the sense of having made an irreversible discovery, at once lightning-fast the moment it happened and slow in the effects it was to have. It was the first time he had seen her sex with such clarity and precision; before then they had always made love stretched out on the bed, embracing, body against body, eye to eye. All this lasted no more than an instant; then he had penetrated her deeply and completely with a single thrust of his thighs and his wife had begun to move her hips back and forth, bent forward, both hands on the banisters.

Today, that open, shapeless sex, bloody and shining like a wound, comes back to him again and again, and seems so alive he can't believe it could really have rotted away at the bottom of a grave. He has read, he doesn't remember where, that the first part of the body to decompose after death is the genitals; and his whole mind retreats in horror from this thought. No, he doesn't want to imagine his wife's sex as it is now; he will remember it as he saw it that morning, up there on the landing of the house in the Via Veneto, alive and hungry for all time.

Gradually, this thought gives rise to another. Perhaps he will never meet his wife again (though this can't be ruled out entirely) but he is certain that one day he will see her sex again, the same identical sex. All he has to do, he thinks, is find a blonde woman between twenty and thirty, shapely but not fat, with very white, oval buttocks. They will become lovers: one day he will ask her to stand up against a railing, bend forward and lift her dress up over her waist. Then he will stretch two fingers down between her buttocks and separate the lips of her vulva like two petals of a flower and for just a moment before penetration he will once again have the open wound before his eyes. All this will be simple and easy; no longer the result of a morbid obsession but a happy rediscovery. Because while it's impossible to replace a face, the genitals, on the other hand, have certain physical similarities, are interchangeable.

Yes, he concludes at the end of these reflections, he will stop the first young, blonde woman he sees in the street, here in Capri, and persuade her to make love to him exactly the same way his wife did that morning in Rome in the building on the Via Veneto. With the result that now, without him realizing it, his longing for his wife is gradually being transformed into a longing for something his wife had in common with thousands of other women of the same age and build.

Obviously, he appreciates that this transformation of his nostalgia for a particular person into a fetishistic obsession for one part of that person's body, opens the way to forgetfulness, consolation and substitution: there is probably no one identical to his wife, but it will be easy to find a sex the same as hers. He comforts himself, nevertheless, with the thought that, deep down, his fantasized reduction of his dead wife to her sex also means her transformation into a mysterious and powerful symbol of femininity. Alive, his wife was unmistakable, irreplaceable, unique; now she has become emblematic. In fantasizing her sex, he is fantasizing something which goes beyond the individual; something which his wife held in trust while she was alive, but which now, in their turn, other women are able to offer him.

One night in Capri he has the following dream. Along the quiet, lonely promenade of Tragara, he seems to be following a mysterious woman who somehow resembles his wife. She is wrapped in a big black cloak, just like the one his wife had shortly before she died. Like his wife, the woman has long blonde hair spread fan-like over her shoulders. She has the same way of walking: hesitant, thoughtful, unconsciously provocative. Finally, and this detail is decisive, her legs are bare; he can tell from the colour of her calves above the boots, a luminous white that no stocking can imitate. Then he remembers that when his wife didn't wear tights, this meant that she was completely nude: it was a habit she had. Often, if she wore her fur coat or cloak or a sufficiently large, warm overcoat, she wouldn't bother to put anything on underneath. She said she felt freer and more self-assured. That morning in the Via Veneto, when she had bent forward over the banisters and lifted her cloak over her waist, he had seen that she had nothing on, nothing apart from her high black boots with the red heels and the turned-down tops.

In his dream, he follows this woman who so much resembles his wife, with the determination of a man who knows what he wants and is certain of getting it. Doesn't he, after all, have a short sharp knife gripped firmly by the handle in his pocket? And anyway, she can't escape him this time: the Tragara promenade finishes with the view of the Faraglioni. There the woman will be at his mercy, trapped, unable to go beyond that point. On waking up, this detail of the Tragara promenade seen as a dead end amazes him. In reality the promenade is not a dead end; it goes on around the island, as far as the area of the Arco Naturale. But in his dream he believed it was a dead end, just as previously, in real life, he had believed his wife to be trapped in the apparently blind alley of marriage.

The dream continues: he follows the woman until they both come out into the open space with the view. As if by tacit agreement, the woman immediately goes to lean against the parapet and at the same time reaches her hand behind to lift up her cloak, exactly as his wife had done that morning on the landing in the Via Veneto. Overjoyed, he approaches her, starts to get his penis out of his trousers and prepares to penetrate her. Disappointment! The woman's buttocks and thighs appear to be closed and as if fused together in a dull white covering; where he expected to find her sex he sees nothing but the tight, sealed fabric of a girdle. When he sees this he doesn't hesitate: he takes out his knife and, calm and precise, pushes it deep into the girdle at a point a little below the buttocks. Now he is happy: through the slit in the girdle he sees the wound his knife has made, nicely open, with pale pink edges, and the deeper layers of flesh gradually brightening to blood-red. But just when he moves close to the wound and makes to penetrate it, he wakes up.

The dream leaves, above all, the image of the female figure with the black cloak walking thoughtfully along the deserted little street. So next evening, when he sets off for a walk in the direction of the Faraglioni and sees far away the figure of a woman wrapped in a dark cloak with blonde hair spread over her shoulders, he is sure that it's the woman in the dream. Yes, his wife made him dream of her, to warn him that he would meet her on the Tragara promenade in the form of a woman in a black cloak.

With this in mind, he quickens his pace in an attempt to catch up with the stranger. The night is mild and damp; the sea wind swings the few lamps that hang at regular intervals; one moment the woman is under the full light, the next in shadow. She seems to be walking slowly, yet remains – he doesn't understand how –

the same distance ahead of him, so that in the end he doesn't catch up with her until they are in the open space with the view of the Faraglioni. As in his dream, she goes to lean against the parapet and looks down into the dark drop where the black shadows of the two great rocks rear up, indistinct and enormous. As in the dream, he comes up beside her, very close, almost brushing her arm with his. He realizes that he is acting like a lunatic, but a kind of prophetic assurance assists and guides him: he knows for certain the woman won't reject him. Meanwhile, though pretending to be absorbed with the view, he steals glances at her. She is young, perhaps the same age as his wife: her face isn't so different after all. Her forehead is round and strong and her eyes, a little deeply set, a hard cold blue; her nose is turned up, mouth swollen and chin slightly receding. Yes, she resembles his wife, in all the ways he wants her to resemble her. Suddenly, with naturalness and ease, he says, "You know I dreamed of you last night?"

As he expected, the woman isn't amazed and doesn't reject him. She turns, weighs him up for a moment, then asks, "Oh yes? And what was I doing?"

"If you like, I'll tell you everything," he answers. "But you'll have to promise not to take offence. And most of all not to think that I'm using my dream as a pretext for approaching you. I'd have done that anyway. I've had the misfortune of losing my wife. I loved her very much. You resemble her. Even without the dream I would have spoken to you."

The woman just says, "Okay. So tell me the dream."

He tells her the dream, without any embarrassment, without leaving out a single detail, calmly and precisely. The woman listens carefully. At the end she says, "It could all come true too, except for one thing."

He notices the phrase, "could all come true", and asks anxiously: "What?"

"I don't wear a girdle."

Her voice is intimate, conspiratorial, almost provocative. He looks at her and sees that she meets his gaze with a strange expression of dignity, at once desperate and seductive – as if to let him see that she knows what he wants and won't refuse him; on the contrary is ready to satisfy him. Still leaning on the parapet, she turns to him and says, quietly offhand, as though in casual conversation: "Why don't you tell me about your wife? How do I resemble her?"

He finds he is so distressed that he can hardly speak. Finally he gets out: "Physically you are very like her. But I'm afraid you may also resemble her in another way, something that came between us towards the end."

"I don't understand."

"For a year before she died my wife refused to make love to me."

"Why?"

"I don't know, I never knew. She just said she didn't feel like it. And then she died."

The woman is silent for a moment. Then with unexpected harshness she remarks: "God knows what you wanted her to do. Something like the thing you dreamt last night most probably."

Amazed and pleased with the woman's perception, he exclaims: "Yes, that's exactly what I would have liked her to do. But it wasn't a dream. It was something we really did, about two years ago."

"What! You did it here, against this parapet?"

"No, on a landing in a building in the Via Veneto, one morning when we met by chance."

"On a landing? The top floor, the one that goes to the terrace?"

"How did you know?"

"Because I resemble your wife in some of my tastes as well."

"You like to do it like that too, standing, from behind, like in my dream?"

"Yes."

He falls silent; then decides to use the familiar *tu* form: "And would you do it with me?"

She returns his look, again with that incomprehensible expression of a dignity both offended and conspiratorial. Until her large, sulky lips form the word, "Yes."

"You won't reject me like she did?"

"No."

"And you'll do it now?"

"Yes, now, but not here."

She is silent a moment, then continues more conversationally: "Let's go to the hotel. You didn't realize we were staying at the same hotel, did you? I'd already seen you, that's why I wasn't too surprised when you started talking to me."

He accepts her friendly tone with relief and asks: "But how come I've never seen you in the dining hall?"

She says curtly: "I never go there. I eat in my room." At which he is afraid that for some obscure reason she may have changed her mind and he asks anxiously: "But how will we arrange it?"

This time she is conspiratorial again: "You'll have noticed that every room has a balcony that looks out over the garden. The balconies all have a railing. Tonight I'll come to your room, go out on the balcony, lean forward with my hands on the railing and we'll do what you did with your wife on the landing of that building in the Via Veneto."

With that, she stands up and sets off. He follows her, and can't keep himself from saying: "I'm so afraid you won't come in the end."

He doesn't know why he says this. Perhaps to introduce a realistic note into something that still seems too much like the dream that started it. She says nothing, but as soon as they have left the open space with the view and are walking along the Tragara promenade, she stops, lifts her hands to her neck, undoes her collar and, for an instant, throws open her cloak. And he sees that she's completely naked beneath. The woman asks him: "Do you think my body's like hers too?"

Strangely, despite the emotional state he is in, he can't help but notice some similarities: the same low, firm breasts; the same well-fed abdomen, curving out above the pubic mound; the same thick, short, curly pubic hair of a blonde that verges on tawny. Then a kind of transparent, red flowing of the blood just beneath the skin of the thighs and breasts also reminds him of his wife. In a tone of quiet challenge, closing her cloak, the woman says: "You believe me now, don't you?"

"Do you usually go around nude like that?"

"I was in a hurry. It's warm here in Capri. I wrapped myself in my cloak and came out."

They both fall silent after this, walking quickly some distance apart as if they didn't know each other. She has the same wandering and unconsciously provocative walk, her eyes on the ground as if in thought, while he steals glances at her from time to time, scarcely able to believe in their pact. At the same time his mind is intensely going over and over a bizarre problem: how will she manage to grip the balcony rail while she is bending forward, when the railing is completely covered with a thorny creeper? He ponders over the problem for quite a time, and finally decides he'll have to get rid of the creeper. But how? He'll need some gardening secateurs and he hasn't got any. He'll have to buy some. He sneaks a look at his watch and sees that he has only twenty minutes before the shops close. He says to the woman: "When will you come?"

"Tonight."

"Yes, but what time?"

"Late, around midnight."

He would like to ask her why so late. But he is in a hurry because of the shops closing. He says: "My room's on the second floor, number 11." She replies: "I know. I was behind you this morning when you asked the porter for your key."

They are outside the gate of the hotel now. He takes her hand and says: "You know, you still haven't told me your name."

"My name's Tania."

His wife was called Antonia. "Tonia and Tania," he thinks, "almost the same name." He can't help but exclaim: "It can't be!"

"What?"

He gets confused, then explains: "Nothing, I still can't believe you really exist. I almost don't believe my own eyes."

For the first time she smiles at him; she touches his face in a caress: "See you later," she says and hurries off through the gate into the hotel garden.

Knowing that the shops are about to close, he sets off in a great hurry back up the little road to Capri's main square. He knows where to go: once in the square, he crosses under an arch and walks a short distance along a dark, narrow alley. He finds the hardware shop. He goes in, and heads through all the boxes full of metal objects and racks laden with knives, scissors and other tools, to a woman watching him from behind the counter. "I'd like a pair of garden secateurs," he says.

"Small or large?"

"Medium."

He goes back to the hotel, climbs to his room and immediately goes out onto the balcony gripping the secateurs in his hand. Night has fallen; he examines the creeper in the darkness and sees that it comes up in a fan from a cement pot. To arrange things so that the woman can lean out over the balcony easily, it won't be enough just to cut the branches covering the railing; he'll have to push the cement pot to one side too. Faced with a task that promises to be both tiresome and slightly crazy, he hesitates. Then the image of the woman leaning over the railing with her black cloak hitched over her waist gets the better of him and he sets to work energetically. First he cuts all the higher branches and twigs; then, having stripped the railing, he tries to shift the pot. New problem: where to put the pot so as not to attract attention, so as not to have the woman realize that the bare exposed railing has been prepared on purpose for her and with obsessive premeditation? He decides to push it as far away as possible, to the end of the balcony, and to clear away all the branches and twigs he has scattered over the terrace. He is in the middle of shifting the pot when the telephone rings in his room.

He runs to the bedside table, throws himself on the bed, lifts the receiver, puts it to his ear, and at first hears nothing at all. Or rather, nothing that resembles words. Someone is sobbing into the phone, making an effort to speak and not managing to. "Hello, hello," he says repeatedly, and at last the woman's voice emerges from a storm of sobs and says, all in a rush: "I'm sorry, forgive me, but I'm not coming; my husband died just a month ago and when you told me your wife was dead and that I was like her, I hoped I might be able to take your wife's place for you and you my husband's for me. But now I realize I can't, it's too much. I can't, I can't, I can't, I'm sorry, forgive me, but I can't, I really can't."

She goes on repeating, "I can't," between a new wave of sobs which again breaks up her voice. Then, with a dry click, the line goes dead. He looks at the receiver for a moment and hangs up.

He lies still now, thinking it over. So, the woman was one of those widows conventionally referred to as inconsolable. She had hoped to be able to betray the memory of her husband with him, while he, deep down, aspired to the same liberating betrayal with her. But she'd found she couldn't; the two dead partners had proved too strong, and he and the woman were each left with their own bereavement. At this thought he is overwhelmed by a sense of impotence. He sees himself bound to his dead wife, not out of longing now, but from the impossibility of going on with his own life without her. It isn't love that binds him to her but his inability to love another woman different from her. Just like Tania, he can't betray his dead partner. In the light of this realization, his search for a woman who resembles his wife suddenly takes on sinister overtones. He remembers having read a boy's adventure story where a sailor kills one of his companions and is thrown into the sea alive, lashed to his victim's corpse with a stout rope. He is that sailor. Lashed to his dead wife by the unsnappable cords of memory, he will drown in life's depths, sinking down from one age to the next, right to the bottom of time.

He feels he is suffocating, gets up from the bed where he had taken the phone call, goes to the bathroom, undresses and steps under the boiling hot shower jet. While the water pours down on him, he realizes that he is still hoping that the woman will change her mind and come knocking at the door. The door is open. She could sneak into the room, come to the bathroom and see him turning round and round completely nude in the shower without him seeing her; then she could come towards him and reach out her hand to grab his penis, like his wife did in the building in the Via Veneto. Struck by the power of this image, he abruptly turns off the shower and, standing up, still soaking wet, looks down at his stomach and realizes that his penis is slowly growing erect. Swollen and thick, but not yet hard, it comes up in its own powerful, independent way with little, almost imperceptible jerks, indicating the obscure persistence of desire. He can't help slipping his hand under his testicles which seem to form the source of the energy forcing up his penis. He gathers them hard and wrinkled in his palm, as if weighing them. Then the hand climbs up to the penis, circles it in the ring of two fingers and squeezes. "What am I doing?" he wonders. "Am I going to masturbate now?" He steps out of the shower, puts on a bathrobe, crosses the room, throws himself on the bed and closes his eyes.

What! Suddenly he sees the balcony and the part of the railing where he cut away the creeper. The woman in the black cloak is there. She goes out on the balcony, approaches the railing, leans out, reaches back a hand and lifts her cloak over her waist. But the image of the white buttocks surrounded by the black of the cloak lasts only an instant; it fades and then reappears again, in exactly the same way, with the same gesture: the woman goes out on the balcony, leans over the railing and reaches her hand behind.

Another fade, another identical apparition. The scene repeats itself again and again, but never goes beyond the gesture of the hand lifting the cloak. At that point it is as if a bank of fog came down between him and the woman; the image blurs and vanishes. He jerks himself free from the torpor of this obsessive repetition, opens his eyes and sees his penis totally erect, sticking rigidly out of the flaps of his dressing gown. Almost without realizing what he is doing, he goes to the window, lifts the shutters and goes out on the balcony.

In front of him the huddle of trees in the garden is silhouetted black against a black sky with just a hint of shapeless, sciroccotorn, white clouds hanging motionless in the still air. He moves his hand down to his penis and takes it in his palm, his fingers tracing the jutting, branching veins. Slowly, he frees it from its sheath of skin and sends the swollen, purplish head up and out into the air. He looks at his penis as it quivers imperceptibly, raising itself at a sharp angle from his pubic hair; then he squeezes it at the base, brings his hand back up as far as the head, strokes down, comes up, and goes down again. His hand moves up and down with a slow, hard rhythm now, stops occasionally as if to test the resistance of the head, which – dark-red, swollen, polished as satin – seems about to burst; then starts stroking up and down again. The orgasm finally comes while he gazes at those whitish, indistinct clouds, and it is pleasurable to the point of pain, or rather, it is a burning pain which becomes pleasure. At every throb of the orgasm, a violent, copious jet of sperm gushes up from his penis, runs down his hand and dribbles onto his stomach, and he can't help but compare this ejaculation to a minimal but nonetheless deep eruption. Yes, he thinks, it is the eruption of a vitality too long repressed and finally liberated; it has nothing to do with his wife, nor with the woman in the black cloak, just as a volcano has nothing to do with the fields and houses it buries. Finally, just as with an eruption, a last spout of sperm gushes from his penis and at the same moment the spasm of the orgasm bends him forward over the railing and the sperm falls away from him, cast outwards, into the dark of the night. He feels, then, that he has made love not with a woman of flesh and blood, but with something infinitely more real, even though intangible.

He stays standing there, looking at the trees and the sky. Now the meaning of the night's events unfolds in his mind: his wife is dead and their love is dead; he has freed himself and risen again. From now on he won't be trying to rediscover his wife or a woman like her; the widow in the black cloak has healed him, her absurd faithfulness has cured his morbid faithfulness. Wrapped in these thoughts, he looks at the white clouds hung indistinctly in the black sky, while at the same time his fingertips are peeling away the film of congealed sperm from his stomach.

The Devil Can't Save
the World

I am an old devil, very old, it's true, but I'm not a good devil and
even less a poor devil. If you think that in the last hundred years I
have dedicated myself above all to the progress of science and that
the discoveries which led to Hiroshima were prompted by me,
suggested little by little, one by one, at the price of their souls, to
all the major scientists of the century, starting with Albert Einstein,
then you will have to admit that I am a devil of no small importance.

Someone, perhaps, will want to know how on earth a man like
Einstein, who in some ways was quite angelic, could have sold his
soul to a being generally marked out as the enemy of humanity.
To respond to a question of this kind, one has to consider the
psychology typical of the so-called creative spirit, whether or not
inspired by the devil. Have you ever heard of a poet who renounced
publication of his own poetry? Of a painter who tore up a painting
he felt was successful? It's the same with scientists. None of those
who made the pact with me felt they could renounce the discoveries
that I had them make, even though they were all perfectly aware
that these discoveries were diabolical.

Einstein was not, sad to say, an exception to this rule: he knew very well that his inventions would lead directly to something terrible and unspeakable; but I can assure you that not for a single moment did he let this knowledge count for anything on the eternal scales of good and evil. At most he tried not to think about it, to throw the responsibility for the foreseeable and foreseen catastrophes onto the backs of the other scientists who would develop his discoveries and the government leaders who would, and in the event did, make use of them.

Not everything goes smoothly, however, in these diabolical contracts. There are those who, when the moment comes, refuse to pay the debt; there are others who ask for a supplement of success, power and glory; and finally there are those who try to cheat me, who think they can put one over on the devil. Last of all there was the unique case of Gualtieri, whose debt I would like to have cancelled. This is the true story of that attempt.

Who isn't familiar with the name of Gualtieri? Who hasn't seen at least a photograph of him? An old, yet at the same time youthful-looking man: tall, thin, and elegant, with a charming face at once severe and smiling; penetrating eyes set in the shadow of thick black eyebrows; silver hair; a large, hooked, imperious nose, and a proud, noble mouth. Along with this somewhat intimidating appearance, he has the gentlest voice and the most persuasive manner imaginable.

This extraordinary man was already extraordinary when, still a student, I approached him for the first time with the intention of getting him to sign the fatal contract. I already knew of him from his physics professor, Palmisano, another one who had sold me his soul, though without achieving anything because of his incredible, pathological laziness. On the verge of death, Palmisano had said: "So much the worse for me; I've damned myself for nothing. But I want to recommend Gualtieri to you – my best student, a real, potential genius. If he decides to make the pact with you, you can rest assured he will revolutionize modern science and cause havoc in a field that's still so dull even today."

This recommendation filled me with a burning desire to approach Gualtieri, but I hesitated quite a while over the method. What form should I assume to appear to him? That of a fellow-student? A businessman in search of new talent for his laboratories? A woman in love? I settled on this last option. The disguise I like best is the female character. If for no other reason than because it combines the temptation of success with the often irresistible temptation of desire.

I started to follow Gualtieri wherever he went, appearing sometimes as a girl studying at the university where he taught, sometimes as a married woman at some social gathering or club he used to go to, sometimes as a prostitute at the corner of the street where he lived. The women I appeared as were all remarkably beautiful and they all did everything possible to have Gualtieri see that they were ready to do whatever he wanted. But Gualtieri, then a young man of about thirty, didn't spare them so much as a glance; he displayed an indifference that somehow was both relaxed and effortless. He simply didn't seem to be interested in women.

I was beginning to despair of ever finding a way to approach him, when one day, towards the end of a particularly sultry summer, I came across Gualtieri in the last place I would ever have thought of finding him, the public gardens. He was sitting on a bench with a book in his hand, but the book was closed. He seemed to be watching something very intently. I disguised myself as a shapely brunette and went to sit opposite him. I stared at him insistently; but soon realized that his eyes were directed elsewhere. With an air of profound attention he was watching a group of twelve- to fifteen-year-old girls a little further on who were playing that well-known game that consists of hopping in and out of squares drawn on the gravel. The devil, as everybody knows, is very intuitive. From seeing Gualtieri staring at those little girls, as the game they were playing lifted their skirts bit by bit above their knees, to deciding that I had discovered not only the disguise in which to approach him but also the way to make him sign the infernal pact immediately, was the work of a second.

I got up from the bench, went into a thicket of trees, and transformed myself at one go (oh yes, the devil can do all that, and more) into a little girl around twelve years old with a thick head of hair, slender bust and long, muscular legs. Then off I go to join in the game and, whoops, I hitch up my dress to help me jump better. I am the devil and I appreciate that my methods are often brutal and crude; nuances and ambiguities aren't my style. So you won't be amazed to hear that to help me jump I lifted up my dress a great deal more than was necessary. What's more, when disguising myself I'd decided to put on nothing underneath. Gualtieri immediately notices this nothing. I get that from the speed with which he suddenly buries himself in his book, gripping it tight in his hands. A few moments later I leave the group and go towards him. I am perfectly sure of myself now; I know I've hit the bullseye of his most intimate target first shot.

I go up to him clutching a regular exercise book, on the first page of which, as I well know, written in gothic letters (old habits die hard, I'm afraid, it's those German origins) is the familiar contract. With a typically cheeky little girl's voice, I say: "I'm collecting signatures. Will you sign my book?"

He raised his eyes, directing them first at my bare legs, then at my face. He looked me hard and long in the face, as if to make sure what I was up to. Then he asked: "What do you want from me, my dear?"

"I'm collecting signatures. I want you to sign my book."

"Let me see."

I handed him the exercise book, open on the page of the contract. He took it while I, as if to make clear what I wanted, pretended to have an itch in my crotch and began to scratch myself through my dress. He flashed me a sharp glance, then went back to examining the exercise book. At that moment the letters must have been near-blazing beneath his eyes; but I must admit he didn't so much as move a muscle. He read and reread those few words, then said: "So, you want me to sign?"

"Yes, please."

"And what will you give me in exchange?"

At this point you're probably thinking it would have been easy, and logical too, to answer that I was willing to do just what he liked whenever, wherever, and however he liked. Oh no, not a bit of it! I wasn't there to encourage his perverse inclinations; anyway, he could perfectly well satisfy those without selling me his soul. No, I was there as part of an extremely ambitious plan, to make Gualtieri one of the arbiters of the world's destiny. This idea was clearly, albeit briefly, outlined in the contract (it's not a standard document, every contract is personalized) and doubtless he had understood everything the instant he set eyes on the exercise book. Something like an abyss must have yawned open before him at that moment, in the sultry heat of that summer day, in the banal setting of the public gardens. Then he plunged headlong into that abyss, eyes closed, determined to explore its unplumbable depths. He repeated: "So, are you going to tell me what I get in exchange?"

"Everything you want."

With extreme coldness, he replied: "Then all that remains is for me to ask you for a pen to sign your book."

I had a bag over my shoulder. I rummaged around, took out my schoolgirl's pen and gave it to him. He signed with decision, gave me back the exercise book, then raised his eyes and said in a cutting voice: "It's no good your standing there in front of me now. Go away and play, go on. And from now on, don't forget to put your knickers on." It was exactly what you say to the devil when he disguises himself as a little girl. I didn't wait to hear it twice. Hurriedly I said: "Thank you for the signature, see you soon." And I ran off to rejoin my fellow-schoolgirls.

So, Gualtieri signed the pact which, over thirty years' hard work sustained and inspired by myself, was to make him one of the most famous scientists in the world. Despite his fame and consequent wealth, however, he continued to teach at the University of Rome. And I thought I knew why: because of his insatiable curiosity for femininity. A lot of girls attended his lessons, charmed by what I have already described as Gualtieri's at once severe and gentle manner. Yet I never heard even the vaguest rumour of his having a love affair with a student. Again, I thought I knew the reason for this propriety. The truth is that Gualtieri should have been teaching not at the university, where the girls are all over eighteen, but in a secondary school, in a classroom packed with twelve-year-olds like the ones he had been ogling in the public gardens. His ability and fame made this secret desire impracticable. But how many times, I thought, must he have bitterly envied his more modest colleagues who worked amongst the pre-pubic lassies of the secondary school!

One inviolable rule in the relationship between the devil and whoever has made the pact with him, is that the demonic creditor appears only twice: when the pact is signed and when the debt must be paid, that is, at the moment of the debtor's death. The devil may, however, if the fancy takes him, keep a watch on his victim, spy on him, check on him from close up, using any disguise he feels is suitable. I must confess that quite apart from his profession

Gualtieri intrigued me as a man. There was a stubborn pride about him that seemed rather out of keeping with the condition of inferiority he had put himself in by signing the pact with me. I shall tell you a revealing anecdote.

At the beginning, feeling very proud of my conquest, I kept in close contact with Gualtieri as he went from one great success to the next. One evening, disguised as a waitress, I was standing near him in a restaurant where his colleagues were giving a dinner in his honour. Suddenly somebody says: "Gualtieri, you wouldn't by any chance have made a pact with the devil, would you?" Perfectly calm, he replies: "I haven't, no, but I'd be ready to." "Why?" "Because by now the devil is a step or so behind man. So I'd be making the pact with him, not him with me. That is, it wouldn't be him dictating the conditions to me. I'd be dictating them to him."

Get it! He wanted to dictate the conditions to *me!* Such presumption irritated me. So I made it a point of honour that I would find the weak spot of this man who didn't seem to want to accept that he owed his tremendous success to me and to me alone. I wanted to trample on that pride of his. Every now and then I caught myself thinking that of the two of us it was he who was the devil. Once I'd found his weak spot it would be easy to put him back in his miserable, human-being's place.

It may seem strange to you that I didn't realize that Gualtieri's weak spot was nothing other than his overreaching ambition. But the particular erotic inclination I had exploited to have him sign the pact, was obscuring the truth of the matter – namely that, yes, he did like little girls, but not so much as to put them before success. In short, even though sex had been useful in getting him to make the pact; the pact, once made, had to do with science, not sex. Still, I hadn't forgotten the long, sharp gaze Gualtieri had directed at the bare legs of the girl I had disguised myself as, nor that remark of his: "And from now on, don't forget to put your knickers on." I felt the right thing to do would be to disguise myself on the basis of that first encounter, which, in reality, had established a certain relationship between us that would never change.

One evening, there I was waiting for Gualtieri in the university gardens after his regular lesson. I was disguised as a middle-aged woman, fiftyish maybe, wearing modest, conventional dark clothes – an appearance I then belied by adding the garish, provocative make-up typical of a certain profession. Gualtieri was walking with his head down, immersed in his thoughts. Suddenly I block his path and say, "Professor, just a word." He stops, sizes me up and says, "I'm sorry, I'm afraid I don't know you and I'm in a hurry, so . . ." I interrupt fast, lowering my voice rather exaggeratedly and using the familiar *tu* form: "When you know what I've got to tell you, you won't be in such a hurry." He frowns and says, "Who are you?" I have my answer ready: "Someone who knows you and wants to do you a favour. Wait, listen. She's eleven years old, a virgin, her mother's in on it, she's all yours if you call this number." I hand him a piece of paper with the number.

It is as if a sharp pain in the heart had suddenly taken away his breath and paralysed his legs. He stands still, mechanically takes the piece of paper, opens his mouth, hesitates, then says: "The mother's in on it?" "Sure." "And she's a virgin?" "Of course. You come along and you get in first with your big cock." All at once a dark blush climbs up his face, like someone who feels insulted and wants to hit back. He says, "And this is the phone number?" "Right, you can get me at this number twenty-four hours a day. You call, come along, in ten minutes the girl is there." "With her mother?" "Of course, with her mother." Like a man possessed, he keeps coming back to the idea of the mother selling her daughter, as if to something fascinating and incomprehensible. Finally he goes off without saying goodbye, slipping the piece of paper with my phone number on it into his pocket.

This time I was quite sure of success because I knew that in certain cases a few unexpected, decisive words, spoken at the right moment, can break down the fiercest resistance at a single blow. But I was wrong. Gualtieri didn't phone, not the day after, nor the following days. So, it had all been a waste of time and energy because, even if the devil can do anything, still, assuming the form of an old, seasoned pimp and hanging around in the university gardens to offer one's wares to a famous and respectable professor – these are hardly things to be taken on lightly.

Nevertheless, Gualtieri's so visible and profound uneasiness when confronted with the pimp's proposal convinced me that I was on the right track: it was simply a question of persevering. I decided on another transformation, more direct this time. I knew that

Gualtieri parked his car near his house in an old part of the city. One evening, disguised as a thirteen-year-old girl, I opened the car door and crouched down on the back seat. Want to know how I looked? Nothing easier: apart from a triangle of panty over my crotch I was completely nude. Gualtieri gets in and starts the car. I pop up, put my hands over his eyes and say: "Guess who!" Neither startled nor surprised, he accepts the childish game immediately. "Who is it?" he says. I answer in a drawling, vulgar, lower-class voice: "Mummy threw me out because I was too naughty. I didn't know where to go so I hid in your car. Anyway, I know you, I know who you are, I see you go by every day. I'm sure you won't throw me out like she did."

Without a word, he lifts his hand to the rearview mirror and directs it at me. "But you're a boy!" he exclaims. In reply, I climb to my feet and pull down my pants: "A boy, me! Just you look and see if I'm a boy!" He looks, hard. Then, in a voice I hadn't expected, says: "True enough, you're a little girl. Okay, get out." At once I protest: "Mummy threw me out naked. She said, 'Go and get one of the men who pay you to give you a dress.' Don't you want to buy me a little dress?" "No, get out." "I'm not getting out, not naked like this. It's embarrassing." Without a word he gets out of the car, opens the door, grabs me by the arm and simply extracts me from the car like you extract a shellfish from its shell. Then he gets back in and drives off.

At this point I realized I'd have to think of something different: a man like Gualtieri wasn't going to fall for a common pimp or a little prostitute. I had been too crude, too self-confident; I'd have to think of a temptation that was more complex, more criminal, more out of the ordinary; in short, more diabolical. I thought it over for a good while, then was amazed not to have had the idea before – it should have been the first thing to occur to me. Gualtieri had married late in life, to a woman younger than himself. They had had a daughter, and then separated. The daughter was now eleven years old and lived partly with her mother and partly with her father. This girl was what is commonly referred to as a real beauty; her childish yet curiously mature body had the charm of a sensuality all the more provocative for being unconscious.

So, what I had to do was have Paola (that was the girl's name) lead her father into temptation; and, in turn, have Gualtieri fall in love with his daughter. In other words, incite incest, a proposition that not even the devil undertakes with much enthusiasm, since, unless there are some particularly promising special conditions, sexual relations between parents and children are so completely taboo that there's very little to be achieved. But for once those particularly promising, special conditions were there: Gualtieri loved little girls. What's more, this was the kind of temptation a proud character like his would go for; for him the taboo itself could, at a certain point, become an incentive rather than an impediment.

Then there remained the problem of the girl. Perhaps you will want to know how the devil can unleash sexuality in an eleven-year-old girl. In this case it was very simple. One morning that summer, very early, I transformed myself into a common cabbage white butterfly. I fluttered in through the open window of the daughter's room and found the beautiful little Paola fast asleep, stretched out completely nude, with the sheet pushed away because of the intense heat and her legs apart.

Circling here and there, I finally land on the sleeping girl's pubic mound, right where a light fold of flesh marks the beginning of the vulva. I stay there just an instant, but in that instant I manage to instill in that eleven-year-old girl all the cunning, determination and desire of a woman of thirty. My "injection" begins to take effect. Late that very afternoon, as if inspired, Paola takes her maths book and her exercise book and goes determinedly to her father's study. She enters without knocking and says to Gualtieri, who is sitting at his desk reading: "Daddy, you promised you'd check my homework. Here I am." Unsuspecting, Gualtieri says he's ready and points to the seat next to his own. But Paola answers: "I'll sit on your knee. That way I'll see the corrections better." And without more ado she climbs on his knee and settles herself there as best she can. I take advantage of the wriggles of the thighs she makes in this process to have it seem as if she is trying to use her buttocks to get a kind of grip on her father's penis.

But this still isn't enough: thinking that his daughter is doing what she does without meaning to, Gualtieri could still reject the temptation and make Paola get down from his knee. So I set about having Paola make it clear that she has done it on purpose.

This is one of the most difficult undertakings of my long career: to have Gualtieri understand that Paola is doing it on purpose and that, at the same time, she doesn't realize she is doing it on purpose. This is how I go about it. Paola moves, settles herself on her father's knee and at last manages to grab hold of Gualtieri. At which point she suddenly freezes, as if alert to what she is feeling; and the lesson can begin, but in a very different atmosphere from that which usually surrounds a good father who checks his young daughter's homework. Distracted and thoughtful, Paola stays still, unnaturally so, given her usual extreme vivacity. For his part Gualtieri's voice is inexplicably hesitant, sign of a deeply felt uneasiness.

While the lesson proceeds, I don't stand idly by with my hands in my pockets. To create an atmosphere in keeping with the tragic transgression of the incest taboo, I arrange for a fearful thunderstorm to gather over the city.

A dark bank of cloud hangs motionless over the bell-towers and cupolas, over the roofs of Rome, like a forehead screwed into a threatening frown. In the study it is almost dark. Instinctively father and daughter press closer to each other, and as if his hands were not his own but another's, the incredulous Gualtieri realizes he is hazarding a timid caress. Paola leaves him be for a few moments, then snorts with impatience, takes his hand and guides it unashamedly to the right place. Gualtieri has a last flutter of resistance; with his other hand he turns on the lamp. So Paola slips down from his knee and says: "I'm fed up with homework. Let's play. I'll go and hide. As soon as I've hidden, I call you and you come and look for me." Gualtieri agrees: by now he would agree to go and look for her in hell. In response to a suggestion from me, Paola adds: "If you find me, there's no point in laying your hands on me. Shout my name, there's only the two of us in the flat anyway." With this provocative piece of advice, she disappears on tiptoe.

Gualtieri remains seated at his desk and puts his head in his hands. But despite this gesture of despondency, a minute later, as soon as Paola's expected call echoes through the house – "I'm hidden. You can start looking" – he jumps to his feet and hurries out of the study.

At this point I intervene again, via the thunderstorm. I black out all the lights in Gualtieri's part of the city; at the same time I have a harsh, cavernous and exceptionally long thunderclap explode in the distance, while a blinding flash of lightning illuminates the hall where Gualtieri is already hunting through the folds of the curtains. The flash is intense and vibrant, filling the space with a light as brilliant as it is unreal. The lightning stops, the thunder dies away in the distance; in the dark and hush of the flat only the vast, thick pattering of rain falling on the city breaks the silence. But, with a little tinkle, there is Paola's voice: "Why don't you look for me?" she cries.

Amidst thunder and lightning, apparently resigned now to what is about to happen, Gualtieri gropes his way out of the hall and goes into the sitting room. Now the structure of the sitting room suits my plan, which consists in having the incest taboo violated in a witches'-coven atmosphere. The room was once a roof terrace. the old arches having been closed with large windows. If the incest takes place – as it must – the flashes of lightning, the thunderclaps and the rain which form the background will convince Gualtieri that nature itself is rising up in revolt against his horrible crime. And the fact is that while another in his place would be daunted by this, Gualtieri, being truly possessed, may well draw further courage from it.

Gualtieri gropes his way into the sitting room. I have my reasons for believing that Paola has now put the finishing touches on her preparations, so I let fly a super-intense flash of lightning. The livid light lasts at least half a minute. At the far end of the sitting room, Gualtieri sees Paola stretched on the sofa in the same pose of seductive expectation as that found in Goya's celebrated *Naked Maja* (oh yes, I'm a cultured devil, I am): that is, with her hands together behind her neck, her breasts pushed out, stomach pulled in and legs well closed. She is completely naked; the only divergence from the famous painting being that I have taken care to see that the plump, hairless, white slit of her sex is highly visible and constitutes the focal point.

The lightning flickers out; darkness takes its place. Now I wait for Gualtieri to throw himself on his daughter. I already know what will happen: at that very moment Paola will dissolve like a mist in her father's arms leaving him with nothing to do but bite at the upholstery of the sofa. This is the norm with diabolical spells of this kind; they are only real up to a certain point, up to the breakpoint, as it were, like dreams. Beyond that point they become phantoms evoked by a disturbed mind.

But I'm in for a surprise. In the dark I hear an explosion of wild, sarcastic laughter, followed by Gualtieri's voice shouting: "A Goya! A Goya in my own home! Oh, but I'll have to keep a record of this apparition. I'll have to get a photograph of my little Duchess of Alba. Stay still now. Daddy's going to take a photograph. And instead of a magnesium flash I'll use one of these magnificent flashes of lightning!"

No sooner said than done. Before I can recover from my amazement, Gualtieri fishes out a camera from the bottom of a cabinet and, between persistent bursts of truly diabolical laughter, using, just as he said, *my* flashes, he takes a whole host of snaps of his daughter stretched naked on the sofa. It would be time wasted to describe what followed; how with all his photographing Gualtieri overcame his incestuous lust and how in the end he ordered his daughter to get dressed and go off back to her homework. Furious, I call off the thunderstorm. Gualtieri goes back to his study and I retire defeated.

Understand? At the last moment, instead of giving vent to his feelings in action, Gualtieri had chosen the way of contemplation. He had resorted to the age-old trick of artistic – or almost – reproduction. And he had also made me look stupid by using the lightning of my thunderstorm as if it were a magnesium flash. Thoroughly bad-tempered, I defused Paola's charge of precocious lust and returned her to the torpor of childish innocence. As far as Gualtieri was concerned, I decided not to tempt him any more. Our pact was due to end in two years' time: there was little for me to do but wait until midnight of the fatal day and collect my debt.

A few days later I heard that Gualtieri had accepted a teaching post in an American university and had left for the USA.

Someone will probably object that for the devil I was too quickly daunted. And here I feel I owe the reader an explanation. As I have already hinted, precisely the fact that I had fulfilled Gualtieri's ambitions prevented me, after the evening of the thunderstorm, from tempting him again via his inclination for young girls. You can't serve two masters. The lonely young man I had met in the public gardens had still been uncertain of his destiny, wavering between ambition and sex. When I asked him to sign my exercise book, I had, yes, used sex as a way of achieving my end, but at the same time I had made him establish ambition as the number one priority in his life. Incapable of dominating his secret inclination, from that moment on Gualtieri had finally found in his ambition the obstacle that his conscience refused to pose. A great scientist can't while away his time seducing little girls. Thus Gualtieri had saved himself at exactly the moment when, by signing my exercise book, he had damned himself for ever.

For almost two years I lost interest in Gualtieri. From America, news of his extraordinary successes filtered through, but I wasn't especially pleased, which was odd, given that, after all, they were my own doing. While I'm waiting to send those who've signed my pact to eternal damnation, I usually follow their successes attentively and can't help feeling a certain satisfaction over them; the way a good craftsman does when he looks at something he has made. Instead, in Gualtieri's case, I realized that a sort of peeved sense of frustration had replaced the usual craftsman's self-congratulation. Why? In the end, after long reflection, I came to the only conclusion possible: I had fallen in love with Gualtieri.

Someone will imagine that this must have been a homosexual love, seeing as the devil is male. But it's not like that. The devil can be either male or female, heterosexual or homosexual as he chooses. And how could it be otherwise given that, amongst other things, he can transform himself into a butterfly? In Gualtieri's case, I was female, irremediably female. Despised and rejected by him, in a disguise which had been dictated by his perverse inclinations, I had now fallen in love with him, as though that self-same disguise had turned into a second nature. I was female and I loved Gualtieri, and his being wildly ambitious and successful didn't mean anything to me now: I wanted him as my lover. Before presenting him with that fatal exercise book, I wanted to make love to him, whatever the cost.

The second of the two years was almost up when, quite suddenly, I decided: I'd go and see Gualtieri in the USA and try to tempt him one last time before presenting myself in my real devil's shape to demand observance of the pact. But there was the problem of how to disguise myself. Gualtieri taught at the University of A; I realized that I wouldn't be able to go to his lectures – as I must – if I disguised myself as a twelve-year-old girl. Yet it was crucial that Gualtieri find in the adult me something of the little girl who had seduced him years ago. I racked my brains: a round face with wide-open eyes maybe; a little fringe, tiny features, a girl's face on a woman's body? Or little hands and little feet? Barely budded breasts? A smaller stature than usual? One by one I rejected these ideas for the very good reason that almost all women have at least one of these features without as a result being mistaken for little girls.

Then I remembered something. That night when I had pushed Gualtieri to the point of incest, I had noticed in his study, hung on the wall right opposite his desk, an enlarged, framed photograph. It must have been a photograph Gualtieri had taken himself on a trip to the Far East. There was a young woman, Cambodian, Malay or Japanese, holding a little girl's hand in her own, while her other hand supported a large basket full of fruit that she carried on her head. The motion of lifting an arm to hold the basket had made the material wrapped round her thighs that formed her dress come apart in front so that you could see her naked sex. It was a little girl's sex, a simple white crack, with no hair and plumpish edges; but the length of the crack was that of a grown woman; in fact it began not far below the navel – a naked, healed, sabre slash, all the more striking since it formed a marked contrast to the woman's maternal attitude. While Gualtieri had been checking Paola's maths homework, I had looked at this photograph and reflected that that sex was similar to her own and that Gualtieri had doubtless had it enlarged and framed solely because of this highly abnormal detail of a child's sex on the body of a woman. One could see that the rest of the picture held no interest for him, partly because there was nothing else interesting about the scene – it was one of those snaps that tourists take by the thousands on their trips to the Orient.

There remained the, albeit unimportant, problem of whether the photograph had been taken by chance, or arranged, set up. I was inclined to think the latter; I could just imagine Gualtieri paying a fair sum of money and then getting the Malay girl to pose with a baby girl in one hand and a basket of fruit on her head. I could see him, opening the dress material like a tiny theatre curtain, just the chink it needed to have the whole of her naked sex visible, a sex so extraordinary and surprising with its childish form and adult size. For such a man, discovering this anomaly – a woman with a girl's sex – must have been like a stamp collector discovering a rare, hitherto undiscovered specimen.

So for the first time I realized that it wasn't so much little girls that fascinated Gualtieri, as a little girl's sex, and only her sex, with its colours, its shape and its mound. Paradoxically, it might well be that it was precisely this contrast between an adult body and an infant sex that he was after. Perhaps he would have loved even an old woman if she had had a sex like that. Besides, this explained one of the many photographs he had taken of Paola the evening of the thunderstorm, from very close up, kneeling on the floor, with the lens clearly aimed at the middle of her body.

I hesitated no longer. I created a character for myself following the observations set out above: a woman, not even especially young, around thirty, tall, her whole body formed like an adult's apart from the sex. This I made just like a young girl's, but monstrously large: white, hairless, plump around the edges. I added a low, full bust, decidedly maternal in its shape and softness, narrow thighs, a small backside and very long, attractive legs. At the end, remembering the photograph of the Malay girl, I decided on Eurasian features: eyes a little oblique though without the folded Mongol eyelid; a tiny nose and mouth, and straight black hair. Besides, I was counting on the fact that Eurasians are common in the USA: I would thus be able to remind Gualtieri of the Malay girl without at the same time being too obvious. A last detail: I would be very well versed in the subject that Gualtieri was teaching in his seminar. That way I counted on being able to fascinate him with two monstrosities: my abnormal sex and my unparalleled knowledge.

Very pleased to be who I was, I took a plane and after a long journey landed at A airport in the middle of the desert. The state in which A is located is famous for its nuclear power station where experiments are constantly being carried out on the atom. In fact the university is nothing more than an appendage to this nuclear station.

The seminar was meeting for the first time when I turned up in the lecture room and went to sit in the front row. At exactly the same moment Gualtieri was announcing the theme of the seminar: long-term possibilities for future developments of the most recent discoveries. It was a promising title. After the lesson, which had dealt with general topics, I went up to Gualtieri and introduced myself. I saw that he considered me of no importance at all; for him

I was just one student among many. So, taking advantage of a moment when he was alone, I shot him the dart of a scientific observation that required an infinitely superior knowledge to that of his students: all in all an observation whose significance perhaps only three or four people in the whole world really grasped. I saw Gualtieri start and stare at me surprised from under his thick black eyebrows. Then he asked me what University I'd been studying at till now and I told him I came from the University of Tokyo. I was very pleased with the amazement I had aroused: from now on he wouldn't get me mixed up with his other students. But it was only the beginning. Next I would have to get him to fall in love with me, and by now I knew for certain that I could only manage that by showing off my incredible, unique, monstrous, little-girl's sex.

It wasn't an easy business: it's easier to demonstrate your knowledge than exhibit your sexual abnormality. At the beginning, partly because – at least at first – I had to play the rôle of the intelligent and innocent student, and partly because I still hoped to avoid having to exhibit myself, I chose to resort to the normal methods a woman uses to try and attract the attention of the man she loves. I sat, as I said, in the front row and, never taking my eyes off him, tried to make my expression convey the love I felt for him without any reserve. But right away I was forced to accept that Gualtieri wasn't at all interested in me, or at least, not in what he was able to see of me. For him I was an attractive Eurasian girl, one of his many students. True, I was very knowledge-able, surprisingly knowledgeable even, but that was all. So, what to do?

I tried to approach him again with the pretext of talking about what he had been teaching in the lesson. But now that he had got over his first surprise at my exceptional knowledge, I very soon realized that instead of being more interested in me, Gualtieri tended to avoid me. I wondered a great deal what the reason behind this behaviour might be. Was he embarrassed by the emotion that I allowed to shine clearly through my eyes? Or by my scientific knowledge? After long reflection I came to the conclusion that Gualtieri must be fairly used to his female students getting crushes on him, a fact that would be flattering to his vanity. On the other hand there was something about the way he tried to avoid my learned observations that I couldn't understand. I was definitely his best-informed and most brilliant student, so why did he try to keep away from me? In the end it was Gualtieri himself who provided the explanation.

It happened halfway through the seminar course. Gualtieri's lessons had been getting more and more difficult and obscure; at the same time, a strange mood, somewhere between violence and melancholy, visibly oozed out of him. He was at once brusque and sad, impatient and gloomy. He gave the impression of being tormented by one dominant, unspeakable thought, and that this torment was growing greater and greater as time went by. Naturally, I knew perfectly well what that thought was: in a short while, just a few weeks, our pact would expire and I would appear before him with my real face to claim the price of my not unselfish favours. But strangely, I got the impression that it wasn't only the pact that was haunting him: there was something else. But what?

Quite suddenly, the lectures on future scientific developments took on a note that was both fantastic and catastrophic, at least for me, I being the only student there capable of understanding what Gualtieri was driving at. A lot of the students stopped coming to the lessons, partly because by now Gualtieri was speaking more in enigmas than anything else and partly because he refused to give explanations when they were asked for. His brusque manners, obscure teaching, and the generally dazed atmosphere of the seminar baffled most of the students. In the end there were hardly any of us left in what was quite a large lecture room. I was the only person in the front row. Then there were no more than a dozen or so students scattered around two or three rows behind.

At last, during one particularly thorny lecture, I had a revelation. Gualtieri was speaking like this because – everything pointed to it – he was alluding to a particular discovery he had made that he hadn't as yet made public. So no one knew anything about his discovery except him; hence no one could understand its importance except me. That day I took a lot of notes. Once back at home, I tried to put these scattered fragments together. When finally I understood, I was stunned. I remember lifting my head from the table and staring for a moment through the window at the barren desert outside where the sun was dying in a blaze of red. Then I bent back over my papers, went through my notes again and in the end was bound to accept that my first impression had been correct: Gualtieri was talking about the end of the world. It was to this and nothing else that the future scientific developments to which he had dedicated the seminar were leading.

Now I understood, or at least could sense, darkly, Gualtieri's drama. He had come to catastrophic conclusions; at the same time he was threatened by a personal catastrophe. One catastrophe was connected with the other. If Gualtieri hadn't sold his soul he wouldn't have made the discovery; and it was precisely this discovery, achieved at the cost of his personal catastrophe, that was now threatening to provoke a universal catastrophe.

This very human intuition brought me, once more, to a realization that my diabolic nature was tending to keep hidden: I was no longer there to tempt Gualtieri and exploit his perversion to humiliate him; I was there because I loved him. I understood this from the feeling of affectionate and totally feminine compassion I experienced while watching him speak from the lecturer's desk and seeing him so gloomy and desperate. I wanted to be close to him, to smooth his forehead, hug him tight, whisper words of love.

But this feeling of love was inhibited by my awareness of the limits that my being a devil put on the possibility of love. I have already said that I knew very well that the moment Gualtieri embraced me, penetrated me, I would vanish like mist in the sun. When I was still thinking of punishing Gualtieri for his arrogance by playing on his taste for little girls, I had thought that this vanishing in his arms would confer on his punishment a sense of mockery very much in keeping with my diabolic nature. But now I had discovered that I loved him, I realized that of the two of us it would be me, not him, on the receiving end of the mockery. I would disappear exactly at the supreme, ineffable moment, and then all I could do would be to reappear before him in my horrible demonic form to demand payment of his soul according to the usual, merciless ritual – a meagre consolation which I would happily have done without. I didn't want his soul in another life, I wanted it in this life, here, that we were living together! Still, it's typical of the human nature into which I had transformed myself to go on hoping with the body even when the mind despairs. Hence the certainty that I would dissolve in smoke the moment we came to intercourse did not affect my feeling for Gualtieri at all. Even though I knew I could never have sex with him, I still felt driven towards him by a powerful impulse of physical devotion, and I had an obscure hope that at least in this case the infernal limit might be crossed. But what was this hope, in some sense desperate and in any event quite unfounded, if not love? That love which at the beginning was to serve as a trap for Gualtieri and into which I felt that I, and not he, had now fallen? So I decided to use what my intuition had told me, to force Gualtieri to agree to a meeting with me outside the university, if possible at his house. At the end of the lesson after the one that had brought my revelation, I went up to him and said, quietly and confidentially: "One understands, from the way you present them in the seminar, that scientific developments are leading directly to the end of everything. That is what you meant, isn't it?"

I was struck by his appearance. Thin and emaciated, with hawk-like eyebrows hung over sunken, feverish sockets and a beakish aquiline nose, he looked like a bird of prey, ruffling hostile feathers, ready to attack whoever dared come near him. In fact it was almost in a rage that he replied: "'One' doesn't understand anything at all. Say, if you must, I have understood."

"Still, it's obvious. Given certain premises, there's only one conclusion to be drawn."

"Which is, pray?"

His voice was so harsh that I preferred to answer: "I would like a meeting with you, if possible at your house, to discuss all this."

His voice still distorted, he exclaimed, "In my house? That's not possible."

"But why isn't it possible? Everything's possible for men of good will."

"Look," he said brutally then, "I long ago understood what you're after. Unfortunately, however, I am not in love with you and don't imagine I ever will be."

"Are you quite sure?"

"Find yourself a lover from the boys in the seminar, seeing as you're so hot for it. And leave me in peace once and for all."

He spoke these last words very loudly; luckily the other students had already left and we were alone. I looked at the lecture room where all those rows of empty benches seemed to encourage a move towards greater intimacy. For a moment I felt a wild temptation to pull up the mini-skirt wrapped tight as a sheath round my legs and have myself fucked then and there, under the desk, from behind, like any old cat or dog. It was an instant of violent, craving desire. Then, with more human moderation, I decided to restrict myself to declaring my love. But my soft, quiet, humble voice as I said, "I love you and no one but you," must have betrayed something of that innocent animal craving, because Gualtieri, moved perhaps, suddenly calmed down. He lifted a hand, touched my cheek and asked: "Do you really love me?"

"Terribly," I said impetuously.

With decision he said: "Forget it. I'm not available. It's impossible."

I took courage and began to explain boldly: "I have reason to believe that there is one particular part of my body that you would like. Next lesson I'll arrange things so that you get to see this part of me. If I'm right and you do like the thing I show you, please, let me know by lowering your eyes, like this," and I demonstrated, slowly. He looked at me for a moment, perplexed and perhaps already stirred. Then in a fatherly voice he said: "You're a strange girl."

I took his hand, raised it to my lips and kissed it with passion. Then with a hurried, "See you tomorrow," I quickly left.

The following afternoon, before going to the lesson, I got a Cambodian outfit out of the cupboard, a jacket and trousers made of black cotton. Using scissors, needle and thread, I widened the fly opening at the height of the crotch, then reattached the zip I'd taken off. Now, with my trousers on, the zip could barely close: all I had to do was to pull down the tab and my plump, supple, young woman's abdomen would pop out of the too-tight trousers showing off my incredible little-girl's sex. My idea was to sit in the front row as usual, wait for a propitious moment, pull down the zip and at the same time open the flaps of my jacket like a theatre curtain on the spectacle of my sex. So that for the whole remainder of the lesson that rare and, for Gualtieri, irresistible physical attribute I had boasted of the day before, would be right under his nose.

Immediately the lesson began I noticed that Gualtieri seemed agitated. He spoke in a tired voice, alternating hurried sentences with excessively long silences: rather than someone who doesn't know what he's talking about, he gave the impression of not being able to concentrate on what he was saying because his mind was elsewhere. I didn't listen too carefully but spent the lesson watching him more than anything else: I wanted to surprise him with my exhibition the moment he looked towards me. His head propped on one hand, Gualtieri looked away to the back of the lecture room while he spoke. Then – here goes – he straightens to pour himself a glass of water. I pull down the tab of the zip, the trousers fly open, my abdomen pops out and I throw aside the flaps of my jacket, lying back with my legs wide apart, thrusting out my crotch. In this near horizontal position I know that the plump, white slit of my sex is visible in all its abnormal length from the base of my open thighs right up almost as far as my navel. It is the same, little-girl's sex that thirty years before persuaded him to sign my exercise book in the public gardens; that the old pimp woman offered him at the university; that the little eleven-year-old prostitute pulled down her pants to show him in his car; and, finally, that his daughter let him photograph so long and with such relish during the thunderstorm I unleashed over Rome. It is the sex he has dreamed of all his life, and that his ambitions have prevented him from enjoying except in dreams. Now, this precious object, the obsession behind his most secret desires, is there on show in front of him, thrust forward, offered, at a moment when he has nothing left to lose by accepting and enjoying it.

I was sure that none of the few students scattered around the back of the lecture room could see me, so I didn't think twice about keeping the theatre curtain of my jacket flaps open as long as possible. At a certain point I even had the idea of stroking my crotch with my hand, the way little girls do sometimes, unconsciously immodest and provocative. While I was distractedly stretching my hand down over my stomach, I glanced round and saw that the door to the room was ajar and that two bright eyes were spying on me through the crack. At the same time I turned back to look at Gualtieri: he was drinking the water he had poured; over the top of the glass I distinctly saw that he was lowering his eyes in the sign of agreement.

How impressionable the female nature is, even when it's a disguise for the devil! After seeing those two eyes snooping on me, I felt more dead than alive: my usual confidence was replaced by a confused sense of fear and shame. No matter how much I told myself, "but remember, you are the devil", I still experienced the feelings of a young woman who knows she's been caught out while indulging in too bold a piece of flirtation. This feeling of fear turned to panic when the door was pushed wide open and a boy in blue jeans and a checked jacket, with red hair and bright sky-blue eyes, came to sit next to me. Of course, as soon as I'd seen Gualtieri make the agreed signal, I had hurried to zip up my trousers. But I realized I'd been too late. My neighbour scribbled a note and then passed it to me without even trying to hide the gesture. I could hardly get out of reading it. In typical students' slang it praised the thing I had shown Gualtieri; then, somewhat abruptly, it invited me to wait for its writer outside the lecture room.

I put the note in my pocket and with my heart racing looked at Gualtieri: the lecture was over and he was getting to his feet. So I jumped up from the bench and went to stand a step away from the dais, just as Gualtieri was coming down. Under my breath I whispered: "I'm lost, the boy with the red hair saw me." Gualtieri took it in at once, glanced round at the student who was now getting up from the bench, and said: "We'll go out together, take my arm and try to talk to me."

With fake enthusiasm, I exclaimed: "What a magnificent lesson, professor. Can I ask just one question?" At the same time I passed an arm under his and had the joy of feeling him give it a conspiratorial squeeze of understanding. Then he replied without looking at me, his voice offhand: "I'm the one with a question to ask. Are you really made like that down there, or ..."

"Or what? I've been like that since I was a little girl. At thirty I'm exactly like I was at eight."

"It's not that you shave it or something?"

"Shave it? Why should I? I've never had even the suspicion of a hair."

By now we were in the corridor outside the lecture room. Suddenly, the boy with the red hair and bright sky-blue eyes blocked our path: "Professor Gualtieri, this is my girlfriend. Please, we have a dinner date this evening."

A little hysterically I exclaimed: "It's not true. We don't have a date at all."

The boy was embarrassed but resolute. Reaching out a hand and taking me by the arm, he said: "Come on, come on, I know we had a bit of a row, but it's all over now, come on, say goodbye to the professor and let's go."

He was gripping my arm tight, staring into my eyes with his own bright, slightly lunatic pupils. I said: "All lies. I never saw you in my life."

On top of a thick, muscular neck, his small triangular face was motionless as if carved out of stone. Finally, as though to exclude Gualtieri from the conversation, he said in a low voice: "I, on the other hand, saw you perfectly clearly."

This time Gualtieri intervened with feigned authority: "Come on now, there must be some kind of misunderstanding. This is my daughter and she really doesn't know you. And nor do you know her if it comes to that. What's she called?"

The boy with the small face perched on the big neck said nothing. His eyes spoke for him. You could see he wanted to shout out the truth, that he had seen me with my crotch naked, pushed out at the man who said he was my father. But he was a boy in the end, and well-educated at that; not a thug. He just muttered, "Some father!" while Gualtieri pulled me away, almost at a run, towards the entrance.

A few minutes later and we were in his car racing across the desert towards a horizon still ablaze with the sunset. Gualtieri drove with intense concentration, as though thinking fiercely about something without managing to reach any precise conclusion. Finally he said: "By the way, that student didn't know your name. But it's just occurred to me that I don't know it either."

I was taken aback. Of course I had a name in the passport I'd shown to the police at the airport on my arrival. But I realized I'd forgotten it. I said at random: "Call me Angela."

After all, it was a name that told the truth: the devil is a fallen angel, chased from heaven, thrown down to earth. He answered, but seemed to be talking to himself: "No, I'll call you Mona."

"Why Mona?"

"In Venetian dialect it's the word for what you showed me in the lesson. But at the same time it forms the second part of De-mona. Anyway, there are plenty of women called Mona here in America."

"Demona," I repeated. "Why Demona?"

"Or Mephistopheles."

He had understood then. Or more exactly, he was hazarding a guess, prompted by a suspicion that by now was more than legitimate. In an instant I imagined what would happen if I were to admit I was the devil. At the very least, Gualtieri, horrified by the idea that such an attractive exterior could hide the old, repugnant, infernal goat (thus humanity has depicted me since time immemorial, though in reality I am a spirit and, as such, can be anything I want), would refuse to make love to me – that impossible love to which, despite everything, I aspired with all my strength. So I decided to deny it immediately, to deny everything.

"What kind of idea is that? Why Mephistopheles? I don't understand."

After a moment's silence he answered through his teeth: "Because you are the devil. Admit it and everything will be simpler."

What did he mean by "everything"? The fatal, now imminent, midnight revelation? Or love? I said: "I know why you think I'm the devil. In your place, frankly, I'd think the same myself."

After a long drive we had now arrived in a large tarmac-covered space in the middle of the desert. Powerful lamps at the top of terrifically high pylons made this immense, completely empty space as bright as day. There were a few cars parked about, plus a crane and a couple of American army trucks. At the far end you could make out the closed gates of a barbed-wire fence whose posts marched off in both directions to be lost in the now complete darkness of the night. Gualtieri made a half-turn and went to park in some shadow away from the blinding light of the lamps. He switched off the headlights but turned on the courtesy light inside the car, before turning to me: "Why, according to you, do I think that you're the devil?"

"Because you think that only the devil could tempt you in such an unusual way."

He looked at me from the corner of his eye below thick eyebrows: "It wasn't so much the way that seemed diabolical to me. It was the thing you showed me."

I pretended not to understand: "What's diabolical about a woman's genitals?"

He replied thoughtfully: "The truth is that only the devil could have known about my particular erotic tendency."

I felt a sincere thrill of love for him. I threw my arms round his neck and whispered in his ear: "If it makes you happy, go ahead and think I'm the devil. The fact is I'm just a poor girl who's so, so happy to be with you right now and have you like me."

I was kissing him on the ear, the temples, the cheeks, my tongue searching for his lips. But he turned stubbornly away. So then I whispered: "You want to make love here, in the car? Look, I'll show you again, the thing that turned you on so much in the lesson. There, look at it, go on, touch it; it's all yours, yours."

In my excitement I didn't know what I was saying. At the same time I felt both a violent desire and an equally violent desperation, because I knew it was impossible for me to make love with Gualtieri: at the moment of intercourse I would dissolve in smoke. But the desire was stronger than the desperation, and it was with a strange hope of being able to break the law which until now had governed me that I reached my hands to my trousers, pulled down the zip and opened the flaps of my jacket as wide as possible. At the same time I stretched out as much as the confined space of the car would allow, opened my legs wide and whispered, craving: "There, see, you like it, now get on top of me, get it in."

I was expecting, with a strange, desperate hope, that he would jump on me. Instead, he pushed me gently away, then reached a hand to my crotch, not, as I had thought for a moment, to stroke it, but to pull up my zip again. He didn't manage though, because my stomach, which had burst out of the very tight trousers, prevented him. Suddenly he said: "Okay, don't cover yourself. I'll look at you while I'm speaking and it will give me courage."

So, he did have an insatiable appetite for what lay at the origin of his tragedy. I sat crosswise a little on the car seat so that he could look at me whenever he wanted and answered: "Look away. But what have you got to tell me? Why do you need courage to say it?"

He was silent for a moment, then he began gesturing, with a wave of his hand, towards the deserted tarmac. An animal, a dog maybe or a jackal, was crossing the space at a quiet trot. "You know where we are here?" he said. "Outside the fence that surrounds the area where the last nuclear weapon was exploded. Now, whether you're the devil or not, you must understand that I brought you here to tell you something that is very closely related to what they use this place for."

Once again, I pretended not to understand. In a light voice I said: "But how on earth can you, a great scientist known all over the world, believe in the devil?"

His reply was strange and ambiguous. "Of course I don't believe in him. How can you believe in the devil? But there are a lot of elements in the real world that lead one to think that he does exist."

I decided to play things down: "What elements? The fact that I knew you liked a hairless fanny? Come on, I took a guess and as luck would have it I guessed right."

"First of all, yes, it is pretty diabolical your guessing my, let's call it, erotic speciality so exactly. And to be precise, that speciality is not for a hairless sex but for an infant one. Still, it's not a question of sex anymore now, but of something very different."

"What?"

He looked round at the tarmac space: the dog, or jackal, or whatever it was, had gone; everything was light, loneliness and silence. "That," he said finally, pointing to the gate in the fence, "even if that is inextricably related to this," and he pointed to my naked crotch. "But to have you understand this connection, this confusion, I'll have to take you back thirty years."

I encouraged him in a friendly voice: "Okay, let's go back."

As if talking to himself, Gualtieri said: "If you're the devil, as I still believe you are, you'll be able to confirm that I'm telling the truth: only the devil knows, only he could contradict me. If you're not the devil, if you're just a girl in love with me, you'll appreciate my confidence: you're the first person in the world I've told this story to."

So Gualtieri began to tell what soon turned out to be his whole life story, from far-away adolescence right to the present day. He told it in an orderly, calm, rational way; it was the famous scientist speaking, except that this voice, accustomed to the cold exactness of scientific demonstrations, was now striving to throw light on a life that had nothing calm, orderly, or rational about it. It was the life of a man who from childhood had had to deal with two equally demanding masters: ambition and sex. With time, the latter had, as it were, become specialized, in the way you know. Gualtieri told me that his most secret inclination had first shown itself with his doorman's daughter, a far from diabolical twelve-year-old who would sometimes come up to his flat to bring the post. Between the twenty-year-old student and the twelve-year-old girl, a love affair developed, which, according to Gualtieri, had nothing perverse about it at all: his taste for paedophilia was yet to come. The affair with the girl had lasted a whole winter long without either remorse or scruple and to the complete satisfaction of both. Then the girl had been sent to her grandparents in the country and he was left with nostalgia for something which, in his own words, must have been very similar to the love between Adam and Eve before they were banished from Eden.

Of course, he had tried to repeat the experience, but the results were so disgusting he'd sworn to himself he would never succumb to the temptation again. How many times had Gualtieri tried to return to the Eden of infant love before renouncing it for good? He didn't tell me, only hinted, rather vaguely, at two or three "procured" encounters, which came about not directly like the first relationship but through dealing with one of those pimps I myself had appeared as, to waylay him near the university. These so-called encounters had plunged him into such a profound state of self-abasement as to have him toy with the idea of suicide. But he did not kill himself: he continued to live with his two passions; that of his ambition, still far from finding an adequate outlet, and that of the flesh, already rejected and repressed, even though still there in the form of temptation.

This was how things stood when I surprised him in the public gardens in the act of ogling the little girls' legs, behaviour which eloquently demonstrates how in certain cases rejection and re-pression can add incentive and spice to temptation. Curiously, Gualtieri's version of our first encounter was very like my own. The little girl's provocative behaviour, he told me, had roused him so profoundly that quite suddenly he had decided that if the temptress approached him he would forget his scruples and abandon himself to his fatal passion for ever. He realized that this would mean the end of his ambitions, but, as he said himself, at that particular moment the sight – now you see it now you don't, depending on the game – of the girl's naked crotch was more important to him than all the marvellous discoveries of Albert Einstein. At the same time he was perfectly aware that this would ruin him for ever, so when the girl had stuck the formula of the infernal pact under his nose, he had experienced an immense sense of relief: better damned in the next life for the sake of ambition than damned in this one for a bit of bare groin.

This explanation, as I said, agreed with my own: I too was convinced that ambition had won out over sex chiefly because the pact had supplied him with the absolute certainty that ambition could be satisfied beyond his wildest dreams. But Gualtieri added: "The fact remains that I signed in a moment of weakness, of breakdown almost. And this weakness, this breakdown, was provoked not by the prospect of scientific success at all, but by the sight of that child's sex, so similar to your own."

At this point I must explain an important detail about the way the infernal pact is signed. The devil informs his victim of the terms of the pact, presenting them to him written clearly at the top of a page which he, the victim, will sign. But, and this is one of the many mysteries in the dealings between the devil and men, once the pact has been read, the writing disappears, as if it had been penned in erasable ink; so that in fact the victim signs a blank page. If anyone wants to know why this happens, I can offer this reply: probably the plan is that the victim damns himself with complete freedom of choice, while retaining, right to the end of his life, the doubt that this may have been a hallucination or a dream. So it was with Gualtieri. He told me that when he came to sign, he realized that the writing, the pact, had vanished from the page. But he had immediately thought that this disappearance must not alter his decision. If it had been a hallucination brought on perhaps by what he called his breakdown, then so much the better. Yes, so much the better: at least, putting ambition above sex, he would save himself from a destiny he found repugnant and wanted to avoid at all costs.

At this point I asked him why, given that he wasn't entirely sure he had signed the pact, he now believed so firmly in the devil as to imagine that he was capable even of hiding himself behind the innocent appearance of a Eurasian girl like myself?

He pretended not to have heard the allusion to our relationship and said that the proof that the devil existed and that he really had signed the pact lay in the present nature of scientific research as analysed and interpreted by himself in thirty years of constant and rising success. True, the fact that in the end the demonic child had got him to sign the pact, not with the promise of success and glory, but with the exhibition of that naked girl's crotch, did seem to demonstrate that the devil still counted on the old and traditional means of sex. But this wasn't so: these days the strength of the devil lay in scientific research. He went on: "If you want to understand this business of proof of the devil's existence, I'll tell you my life story from the beginning, that is, from the moment I decided to become a scientist, because as a boy I didn't feel I had a vocation for science, but – and this will seem strange to you – for poetry. I was very ambitious; I wanted to become another Leopardi, another Hölderlin. All the same, since I did have a lively interest in science, I enrolled in the physics faculty at the university. This was partly because I didn't think there was any contradiction between poetry and science: in ancient times the poets were scientists too and the scientists poets. And in fact it was through writing poetry that I came to understand very early in life some fundamental things about creativity. Every time I felt I had written a poem that was less mediocre than usual, I realized that this had happened because I had not been alone while I wrote. With absolute certainty I sensed beside me the presence of that mysterious entity once known as inspiration but which I prefer to call by the name of demon. It was he who dictated the words inside me; it was he who had me make that leap in quality from cold thought to what you can only call poetry. At this point you'll want to know, were these poems really good? My answer is that they were the best I could write. Though my best was certainly the worst of a real poet. In short, every poet, good or bad, has his demon. It's a question of presence, not of poetry. If he is present, the demon will make you write exactly the poetry you're capable of writing, nothing more."

"So, they were bad?"

"Probably, yes. At least one has to think so, because at a certain point I gave up poetry for physics. Still, as I've already said, poetry helped me to understand the existence and the function of the demon."

"Or rather, the devil."

"Slowly does it: for the moment let's keep it at demon. I'm coming to the devil now. So, I dedicated myself passionately to physics;

poetry disappeared from my life. I got a scholarship to go to the United States and became the best student of the famous Steingold. Steingold was already very old then and, being a Jew, a great reader of the Bible. One day, when we were talking about our profession, he came out with this striking remark: 'By now God is powerless; that's clear from all kinds of evidence. The devil's got the power now.' I asked him why he made a remark like that, him a believing, practising Jew. And he said: 'Because if God were powerful he wouldn't for a moment allow the progress of science to go on, especially not in the field we're working in.' I insisted on hearing more, but he just made this one, final remark: 'Even God's powerlessness may be a sign of his power. God has decided mankind is lost, he feigns weakness and lets the devil have his way.' "

"Very pessimistic, this Steingold."

"Not really; after all, he still believed in God. Whereas I don't believe in God or the devil, only in myself. Anyway, I never spoke to Steingold about God or the devil again. When the university year was over I went back to Rome and continued to dedicate myself passionately to experiments in nuclear physics. I thought no more of Steingold and what he'd said, but I had to think about it again the day I made the first of the many discoveries that were to make me famous. And here's why. While I was working, I realized that every time my mind made the leap forward from thought to invention, just before it happened I would find myself thinking with nostalgia and desire of my girlish lovers of so many years before. Then, strangely, as I forced those ghosts from my mind and got back to concentrating on my work, I realized that somebody, the demon that is, or rather, the devil, had had me make the creative leap. Yes, no doubt about it, the demon intervened, rarely at first, then more and more often and always in connection with my erotic speciality. At this point, how could I fail to see the relationship between renouncing sex and scientific creativity? Between what could have been my ruin and what seemed to be my glory?"

I interrupted here: "You still haven't told me why this demon has become the devil, though."

"Simple. I was already well advanced in the research that later was to culminate in the discovery I've been speaking about, albeit enigmatically, in this seminar, when I was struck by this reflection: all the scientific progress of the last century, when seen from the point of view of its usefulness for humanity – which, when all is said and done, is the only thing that matters – is absolutely, completely negative. In themselves and for themselves our discoveries are marvellous, but their technological application is entirely directed towards man's final destruction. When these discoveries seem useful, as, for example, with the creation of new sources of energy, you can be sure that precisely the same results could have been achieved by other means. The self-destructive nature of scientific progress, however, is made very much more palatable by the moral value the conscience attaches to the process of getting closer and closer to the truth. Hence many scientists have completed their research without caring about the practical applications. They felt justified by the certainty that they were following the high road of scientific progress, and beyond this certainty they would not go. The effects of their inventions held no interest for them; that was a problem for heads of state, ministers, generals, etc., etc. But I couldn't help remembering Steingold's remark about the now proven powerlessness of God and consequent power of the devil. From which I was forced to draw the only conclusion possible: that is, that given the totally self-destructive nature of science today, the demon who stood beside me during my experiments could be no other than the old devil himself, the enemy of humanity so often described in a past which, after all, is fairly recent. Yes, a scientific development which leads directly to the end of the world, can be none other than – though always with God's approval – the work of the devil. So, and I repeat, I don't believe in the devil; but I believe in the evidence which demonstrates his existence." He was silent for a moment, then added unexpectedly: "The devil has lavished his favours on me. According to the diabolic logic, everything points to his putting in an appearance quite soon, at midnight tonight."

I wasn't expecting this abrupt conclusion; I was shaken: "Excuse me," I exclaimed, "but what has midnight tonight got to do with it? Why should the devil turn up this midnight and not midnight next year?"

He replied soberly: "Because, at midnight tonight exactly thirty years will have passed since I met the devil and sold him my soul in exchange for his favours."

"But you can't be serious. First you say you don't believe either in God or the devil but only in yourself. Then you come out with this absurdity about having sold your soul to the devil. Where's the logic in all this?"

"And yet that's how it is. In those few lines on the little girl's book in the public gardens, it said the pact would last thirty years. Tonight the thirty years are up."

It was true. The pact said thirty years: time enough to make a career. I exclaimed: "That girl was just a girl! And you imagined it all, the pact, the thirty years, midnight, the lot."

He gave me a strange reply: "Even if I did imagine it, what does it matter? It would mean that the devil isn't outside me objectively, but inside me subjectively. The result would be the same."

Without realizing it, at that moment Gualtieri was touching on the greatest problem of my diabolical existence: the fact that at the moment of intercourse I vanished in smoke. Like dreams conjured up by desire. Like the images which preside over masturbation. Impetuously, I said: "The devil is neither outside nor inside you. Don't think about the devil anymore; enjoy life."

"That is, enjoy your love, no?" He sighed, then went on: "Anyway, if the devil were to appear disguised as a girl again, this time, damned as I am, I wouldn't hesitate to make love with her, on one condition."

"What?"

"First of all that the pact be extended for a further thirty years. And then that the devil let me make a career in the opposite direction to the one he has pointed me in so far."

"What direction?"

"How can I explain? In the direction of a discovery that would save humanity from the now inevitable catastrophe. But one can't speak lightly of things like this. Even if I did deliberately bring you here to speak about them, to the gates of the fence around the nuclear test site."

At this point I felt terribly agitated. I realized what he was after and with my heart beating fast I told myself he was blackmailing me: either you accept my conditions or I don't make love. Pretending not to have noticed that "deliberately", which was meant for me, I said: "Maybe. But don't you realize that the devil can do anything except what commonly goes under the name of good? You must see that saving humanity is exactly what the devil can't do."

He stared at me; he seemed excited by the prospect of being about
to do what he had denied himself all his life. "Come on," he
exclaimed, "the devil can do anything, even good."

"Who says?"

"You say."

"Me? What have I got to do with it?"

He suddenly pointed his finger at my chest: "Because you are
the devil, no doubt about that now – only the devil could have
known I go wild for that monstrous thing of yours. But now I've
got the knife by the handle. You love me and I'm telling you, either
the pact is extended and I get a career pointed in the right direction,
or no love, I stay with the pact, you take my soul and humanity
heads for catastrophe."

A thousand dreams were exploding like fireworks in my mind.
Yes, it was true, I told myself, the devil can only do evil, yet by
being in love, through the immense power love has, perhaps the
devil could do good too? It would be a miracle, but the devil has to
believe in miracles, otherwise what kind of devil is he? At once
desperate and hopeful, I said: "I'm not the devil, I'm a poor girl
who, as you say, is in love with you. Let's try and make love, and
then you'll see that I'm not the devil."

"Why, how will I see?"

I didn't want to tell him the truth, that is that the devil can't
make love because, at the moment of ecstasy, he vanishes in smoke.
I answered: "You'll see at midnight, when you realize that no devil
has come to take your soul."

I was speaking sincerely now. I would make love with him, grant
him an extension of another thirty years, live with him for those
thirty years and inspire him to make positive discoveries for the
benefit of mankind. What did it matter to me? To satisfy my burning
desire, I was even ready to do good.

With a strange fervour he replied: "No, not that. I want to make
love with the devil and nobody else. The idea that the stinking old
goat is there inside such an attractive body turns me on. I want to
make love with him and only him. I wouldn't know what to do
with a poor girl who's fallen in love with me. I'll make love and
then go to hell."

I looked around across the immense expanse of tarmac in an
agony of uncertainty and fear. Then I made up my mind. I threw

my arms round his neck and shouted: "I am the devil, yes, I am the
devil and I love you. And now you know, let's make love, yes, for
the love of God let's do it. I feel this time there'll be a miracle and
then we'll be happy and live together always."
Gualtieri says nothing. Our two mouths meet, our tongues
tangle, our hands go where they have to go, mine to pull out an
extraordinarily thick, hard penis from his trousers, his to separate
the naked lips of my little girl's sex all swollen with desire. He
whispers: "Get on top of me," and shifting myself as best I can, I
climb over him with my legs astride in the cramped space of the
car. Panting in his ear, I say: "Squeeze me, fuck me. Can't you feel
that I'm a woman of flesh and blood, not a ghostly shadow."

So saying, I thrust my hips forward so that my sex is an open slit
in front of his erect penis. One more push while our mouths melt
in a kiss, and his member penetrates deep into my vagina. I heave
a sigh of relief, sensing that I have a real belly made of flesh not
smoke and that a real penis of flesh not smoke is going right up into
it. I begin to wriggle furiously, my thighs tight round his hips, my
arms round his neck, cheek on his shoulders, eyes turned towards
the tarmac space seen through the rear windscreen. Then my eyes
fall on my arm around his shoulders and I see from my wristwatch
that it's midnight.

At that very moment, with unspeakable horror, I feel myself
vanishing. Against my will, in spite of my frenzied desire to stay
real, I realize that I am becoming the same impalpable stuff that
phantasms and dreams are made of. Piece by piece I dissolve: first
my head, neck, arms, breasts; then my feet, my legs, my pelvis. In
the end there is just my incredible little-girl's sex, white and hairless,
still swollen with ungratified desire. Like one of those smoke rings
that expert smokers can curl round the lighted tips of their cigars,
the oblong slit of the vagina hangs suspended for a moment at the
end of Gualtieri's penis; then, slowly and softly, begins to dissolve,
to vanish. Now, between my lover's arms and on his knees, there
is nothing but a tenuous, trembling puff of smoke that could quite
easily have come from the overheated engine of the car. And
Gualtieri watches amazed and sorrowful as, sticking straight out
of his trousers, his penis erupts with violent, intermittent tremors,
throwing up gush upon gush of sperm, one after the next.

Yes, that's how it is: the devil can do and have others do anything but good. And whoever is so deluded as to think he possesses him, ends up embracing emptiness.

The Sign of the Operation

Marco sat up on the bed and looked in the half-light at the back of his still-sleeping wife. It was a white back, too white, a fat, sleek whiteness you often find in mature, blonde women. She slept curled up, her curved back giving an impression of both force and constriction together, like a spring bent to the limit of its resistance. But it was also, he went on thinking, a beaten, despondent body whose sleep seemed to signify humiliation and defeat.

Carefully, he got down from the bed and just as he was, in trousers, his chest bare, tiptoed barefoot into the studio, a huge room with a slanting ceiling and large windows. The light from an overcast sky was right; with scrupulous and professional attention he immediately set about examining three paintings mounted on three easels. He was painting all three at the same time and all three showed the same thing: a woman's torso cut at mid-thigh and a little above the waist. The abdomen was prominent, plump, tight as a drum; the pubic mound was swollen and oblong, plum-shaped, and seemed to be divided by the cyclamen-pink slit of the vulva. In two of the paintings it was completely hairless, but in the third painting, the hairs had been painted in, one by one, black, sharp and clear against the sleek celluloid-like whiteness of the skin. All three stomachs had, to the left, the white scar of an appendix operation.

His examination of the three paintings left him dissatisfied. He had wanted to change something in the same old female torso he'd been painting in the same old way for years; he had added the pubic hairs and the result was disappointing: black and bristling as they were, those hairs introduced a note of realism into a painting that absolutely must not be realistic.

Quite suddenly he picked up a razor-blade that he used to sharpen his pencils and slashed the canvas from top to bottom twice so as to make two intersecting cuts. How much money had he lost destroying the already finished painting? He couldn't work it out, he didn't know the latest prices his work fetched on the market. He threw away the blade in anger and went to the sitting room.

Rather than looking out over the dunes as his studio did, the window here faced directly over the beach. You could see some spiky, yellow bushes shaking in the wind and beyond them the sea under a cloudy sky, wearily piling up its green and white waves. At the horizon, though, the sea was an inky blue of parallel bars shifting and dissolving into each other. Marco watched the sea for a while, drumming his fingers on the glass: while he watched it he asked himself why he was watching it; then he went and sat on the couch and began to stare, without impatience but with determination, at the closed door in front of him. He didn't think anything; he waited, knowing for certain what was about to happen. And in fact, a few moments later, with a punctuality that was significant, the door slowly opened and the little girl appeared in the doorway.

She asked cautiously: "Where's Mummy?" Marco couldn't help thinking that it was exactly the same question that a woman who wanted to be alone with her lover might ask. He answered: "Mummy's still asleep. What do you want her for?"

As usual, the reply was evasive and ambiguous: "I don't want her to see me getting a biscuit" – where biscuit might either stand for the food or, instead, for anything else equally forbidden and equally tempting. He watched her walk with little steps to the far end of the sitting room, to the cupboard on top of which her mother usually put away the biscuit box. The girl pulled over a chair, climbed on it and, raising herself on tiptoe, reached up an arm. In this position, her very short dress came up over her stomach to reveal her long muscular legs, almost out of proportion with the rest of her body. He wondered if the girl was showing him her legs on purpose, and couldn't decide. Perhaps she wasn't showing them deliberately, but she was deliberately not avoiding showing them. In the end he decided that it was a question of unconscious provocation. But what wasn't unconscious in a girl of her age?

The girl, who had now managed to grab the big round box and hold it pressed against her chest, was taking off the lid. She took a biscuit, put it between her teeth, closed the box, and lifting herself on tiptoe again, once more showing her legs, tried to put it back in its place. In his paternal voice Marco warned: "Be careful, you could fall." Once again the girl's reply was ambiguous: "You're watching me; if I fall, it'll be your fault."

She finished pushing the box on top of the cupboard, got down with a little jump and, still holding the biscuit between her teeth, pulled the chair over to the table. Only at this point did she take a bite of the biscuit, breaking off a small piece. Then, without hurrying, she came to sit opposite Marco and said: "So, are we going to play the game?"

Marco pretended not to understand and asked: "What game?"

"Come on, you know perfectly well what game, so don't pretend not to. The Russian mountains game."

Marco said: "First finish your biscuit." He wanted to make her say why she was in such a hurry to play the game: there must be a reason. But the girl answered evasively: "I'll eat the biscuit after the game."

"Why don't you eat it right away, before the game?"

"Because Mummy might come in any minute."

"All the more reason to eat the biscuit quickly, no?"

The little girl looked at him amazed: "You know you're thick, you are. It's the game that Mummy doesn't like."

Marco was astonished by the realism of this reply. And yet one couldn't be absolutely sure that the girl knew what she was talking about. He insisted: "But Mummy doesn't like you to steal the biscuits either."

"Mummy doesn't like anything."

Marco saw that he couldn't go too deeply into what his wife did or did not like and said, offhand: "Okay then, we'll play the game."

He saw the girl stand up quickly, put the biscuit on the table and come towards him. But suddenly she stopped, as if doubtful: "There's a way of playing you've got that I don't like."

"Which way?"

"This game is called the Russian mountains game because I let myself slide down along your legs right to the bottom. If your legs were, I don't know, a hundred metres long, I wouldn't say anything. But you've got short legs, like everybody else, so what Russian mountains game is it, if you go and put a hand in front of yourself? My slide stops in a second and goodbye Russian mountains."

It was true: she would climb on his knees and Marco would lift them up. Then with a cry of joy she let herself slide down, down along his legs until her genitals collided with the genitals of her step-father. The collision itself was inevitable and in a certain sense involuntary, but it was followed by a second and different kind of contact which, on the contrary, was not inevitable and probably was voluntary: he felt quite definitely that during the collision the little girl tried and managed to get hold of his sex with her own. There could be no doubt about it: her lips closed round his penis like a sucker and squeezed it for a moment; the squeeze was confirmed by a sudden, simultaneous contraction of the thigh muscles.

Then she would get off his knees like a horseman climbing out of the saddle and, lifting up her dress to feel freer, would say enthusiastically: "Let's do it again." He would accept and the whole thing was repeated without any change: her triumphant cry as she slid down his legs, her lips closing round his penis, the muscular contraction of the thighs. The game was repeated over and over: it would finish only when the girl said she was tired.

And she really did look tired, with two dark scratch marks of fatigue under blue eyes that were narrow and treacherous as two fortress loopholes.

The game had gone on like this for some days. After the first shock, he had got used to it and would certainly have stopped playing if he hadn't been intrigued by the question of how far the girl's behaviour was conscious and intentional. Was that physical contact of the two genital areas unconscious, originating, that is, from an obscure instinct; or was it conscious, the product of an already well-developed sense of flirtation? He didn't know why himself, but the question had become an obsession over the last few days. Thus he had played the game over and over again, always with the hope of arriving at an answer, but without ever being quite certain he had managed it. The girl escaped him with the unconscious capriciousness of a butterfly that flutters off just when a hand is about to grab it. In the end he realized that as long as they went on, in tacit agreement, pretending to play, he would never have his answer; and, what's more, that such an answer could never be formulated unless and until the game were replaced by a direct and irremediable relationship.

So yesterday he had decided to renounce once and for all an investigation that threatened to make the material being studied more and more obscure, and the moment the two groins collided he had interposed his hand, flat, between his own crotch and the girl's.

Now she was presenting him with a dilemma: either play the game her way, with her lips closing round his penis; or not play it at all. To see how she would respond, he said: "But from now on I want to play the game like this, with a hand between you and me."

The girl's reply was immediate and resolute, like a prostitute dealing with a client: "Then I won't play any more."

Marco said reasonably: "I put my hand between you and me because if I don't, you bang into me and it hurts."

With her usual ambiguity, the girl took his justification seriously. "Hurts? How?"

"It's a delicate place," Marco said. "Don't you know that? The slightest thing hurts."

With unexpected, brutal sincerity, the girl suddenly said: "The truth is you haven't got the courage."

Marco thought: there, she's fallen for it, she's going to give herself away. He asked gently: "For what, in your opinion, haven't I got the courage?"

He saw her hesitate a moment, then reply with sarcastic evasiveness: "To be hurt a bit in that place that's so delicate." She paused a moment, then said in a falsetto voice, mimicking him: "Be careful, you could hurt me in my delicate place." She paused again and then, unexpectedly, said right to his face: "You know what you are in the end?"

"What?"

"A sex maniac."

It was an insult, Marco thought, and what was worse, meant to hurt; and yet he sensed some kind of uncertainty in the girl's voice. Quickly and persuasively he asked: "And, in your opinion, what is a sex maniac?"

The girl watched him, confused; clearly she didn't know what to say. Marco said very calmly: "You see, you don't know."

"Mummy's always calling you that, how should I know? If Mummy says it, it must be true."

Marco realized he would never get anywhere: the girl was smarter than he was; she would always elude him. In a conciliatory tone, he said: "Okay, we'll play the game your way. But it's the last time. After this I won't do it any more."

"Good, that's fine," she said happily. "I won't hurt you, you'll see." She lifted her dress and straddled his knees, raising first one leg, then the other, without modesty, but without showing off either. Once in the saddle, she settled herself with her hips, then said: "Ready then?" Marco answered: "Go."

The girl let out a cry of triumph and let herself slide down his legs.

In that fraction of a second her slide lasted, Marco had time to see his whole future right up to old age stretch out before him like a view seen from a tower: they would become lovers, the girl would grow up alongside him and become a woman, with what was about to happen any moment forever and irrevocably between them.

He saw now that the truth he had been hunting for for so long was that of a lure and a temptation, each going on forever, as boundless as they were elusive. Yes, perhaps the girl did just want to play; but the game relied on the fact that he must behave as if it weren't a game. These reflections, or rather realizations, decided him. At the very moment the girl's crotch was almost touching his own, he slipped in his hand, flat. She got down immediately shouting: "It doesn't count, it doesn't count. I'm not playing with you any more."

"Who will you play with then?"

"With Mummy."

So she continued to elude him, even when he thought he had her trapped. Annoyed, he said: "Play with who you like."

"Yes, but you're a scaredy cat."

"Because I'm afraid that you'll hurt me, right? Okay then, yes, I'm afraid. So what?"

But the girl was already thinking of something else. Suddenly she said, "Let's play another game."

"What?"

"I'll go and hide and you look for me. While I'm hiding, you cover your eyes with your hands and don't take them away till I tell you."

Relieved, Marco said: "Okay, we'll play that."

The girl ran off shouting: "I'm going to hide. Don't look." He put his hands over his eyes and waited. Time passed, he didn't know how much; it could equally well have been a second as a minute. Suddenly he felt two lips brush across his mouth and a light breath mingle with his own. Then, while he still kept his hands over his eyes, the lips began to rub slowly along his own, going back and forth, in an even, calculated way, from left to right and back again, growing more and more moist and open each time they passed. He thought this time there could be no doubt: the girl was a precocious, perverse sensual monster and an affair with her now seemed not only inevitable but legitimate. Meanwhile, her lips were moving back and forth, and now her tongue darted at his mouth, as if to find an opening. There, the tongue easily forced its way through his teeth, penetrating right inside, thick and pointed, and he reached his arms forward, still keeping his eyes closed. Beneath his hands he felt, not the delicate shoulders of the girl, but the fat heavy bulk of his wife.

He opened his eyes, pulling back sharply: his wife was standing in front of him with her dressing gown open and her belly pushing out of it, a belly exactly similar to those he painted in his pictures – white, plump, tight, with the pubic hair shaved and the white scar of the appendix operation on the left side. He lifted his eyes and looked up. His wife was bending over him with a generous look: her head had the air of a flabby Apollo, with blonde hair hanging loose, a large nose and wilted, capricious mouth. After a moment, she said with a hint of severity: "What were you doing with your hands over your eyes?"

"I was playing with the girl."

"You had a strange expression on your face that made me want to kiss you. Did I bother you?"

"On the contrary," Marco said. He reached out his arms and plunged his face into her stomach, kissing her at the level of the navel, with eager violence. He felt his wife's hand come to rest on his head, caressing him gently; then he broke away from her and pulled back. His wife closed her dressing gown and asked: "Where's the girl?"

"I've no idea," Marco replied. "She went to hide and now I'm supposed to look for her."

At almost the same moment a faint, distant cry was heard from another part of the flat. Marco made to get up. His wife stopped him. "Let her stay where she is. I want to talk to you. What were you doing a moment ago? Playing the Russian mountains game, no?"

Marco was astonished: "How did you know?"

"I heard you. I was behind the door. Now, if you don't mind, you must promise me not to play that game ever again."

"Why?"

"Because it's a game that inevitably involves physical contact. You know what she told me?"

"What?"

"She told me: 'Marco always wants to play the Russian mountains game. I don't want to because he touches me. But he insists and so I accept to make him happy.'"

Marco was on the point of exclaiming: "What a liar!", but then stopped himself, thinking that his wife wouldn't believe him. In spite of himself, he said huffily: "Don't worry, I won't play with her again, not that nor anything else either."

"Why? You've got to play with her. She doesn't have a father. You have to be a father to her."

Resigned, Marco said: "You're right, I'll play father."

Putting her hand on his hair, his wife said: "You know, that kiss has made me want to make love. You haven't kissed me like that for ages. Want to do it?"

Marco thought he could hardly get out of such a direct invitation. "Yes," he said.

His wife took him by the hand and led him across the sitting room as far as the door, then down the dark corridor and into the bedroom, still in shadow. She took off her dressing gown, threw herself on her back on the unmade bed, immediately opened her legs and, in that position, with her legs bent and open, waited for him to take off his trousers. He told himself he must simulate the passion of a desire he didn't feel, or at least not for her, and he threw himself violently between those legs, so graceless and so white. Suddenly, the girl's shrill voice sang out from right nearby, in the room: "You didn't find me, you didn't find me."

His wife pushed him off forcefully, got up off the bed completely nude and ran out of the bedroom.

Marco turned on the light and looked at the corner where the shout had come from. There was a screen. The girl suddenly popped out from behind, shouting: "Cuckoo."

Marco asked: "But where were you?"

"Here, behind the screen."

"And . . . did you see us?"

"How could I see you? There was the screen."

Marco looked at the girl, uncertain. Then he said brusquely: "Well, let's go, come on, let's go somewhere else. Mummy still has to get dressed."

He took her hand and she let herself be led gently out of the room and across the corridor to the studio. Marco shut the door and went to the picture he had slashed that morning. "Look," the girl cried, "someone has cut your painting."

Marco said drily: "I did."

"But why?"

"Because I didn't like it."

"Why don't you do a portrait of me like you do of Mummy?" she demanded.

Marco answered: "I don't do portraits. This could be any woman's body."

The girl pointed at the painting: "But Mummy has a scar on her tummy, just like this woman. Don't you like doing Mummy's portrait any more? If you don't, why don't you do one of me?"

She was silent for a moment, then added: "I have a scar too."

Marco was amazed: how could he have forgotten?

It had happened a year ago. He had been abroad and while he was away the girl had been operated for appendicitis. With an effort, he got out: "I know you have."

The girl said chattily: "When I had the operation I said to Mummy, now I have a scar like you. So, will you do my portrait?"

The Belt

❦

I wake with the sensation of having been offended, hurt, insulted, sometime yesterday. I'm naked, tightly wrapped in the bedclothes like a mummy in its bandages. I'm curled up on my left side, with one eye squashed against the pillow and the other open, looking in the direction of the chair where my husband laid out his clothes before coming to bed yesterday evening. Where is my husband? Without shifting position, I reach out a hand across the bed behind me and find the space empty: he must have got up already. From a muffled sound like splashing water, I deduce that he is already in the bathroom. I put my hand back between my legs, close my eyes, and try to get back to sleep, but that anguished sensation of having been deeply offended prevents me.

I open my eyes again and look at my husband's clothes. His jacket is draped over the back of the chair; his trousers hang, neatly folded, under the jacket. He took them off without unthreading the belt; it is held there in the loops and the part with the buckle dangles from the chair. With just one eye open wide and staring, I can see a bit of the belt's leather and the square-shaped, yellow metal of the buckle. The leather is thick, smooth, brown and stitchless and long use has given it a greasy look. I gave this belt as a gift to my husband five years ago, soon after we were married. I went to a high-class shoe shop in the Via Condotti and spent a long time choosing it. At first I thought of getting him something black, crocodile skin perhaps, for evening. Then I decided that if I got brown he'd be able to wear it during the day as well as in the evening. It was too tight for him: he's not fat exactly, but fairly hefty, so I had them make three more holes. Often, after meals, he loosens it, because he eats and drinks a lot. I had them engrave a kind of dedication on the buckle: "to V from his V": that is; to Vittorio from his Vittoria. Oh, how delighted I was then by this similarity between our names! It even seemed a good reason for getting married. I used to say to him sometimes: "Our names are Vittorio and Vittoria; we're bound to be victorious."

Here he comes. My husband opens the door of the bathroom and his big body, thick-limbed and heavy, but not really fat, already in vest and underpants, steps between me and the chair. And suddenly it comes back to me and I remember how, where and by whom I was offended yesterday: by him, by my husband, by him of all people, after dinner at the house of the businessman he works for. Somebody asked what was everybody's ideal type of woman. And with complete spontaneity my husband replied that his ideal woman was the English blonde, with a fair complexion and generous curves. The sporty, tomboy type, childish and cheerful. Whereas I, on the other hand, am dark, skinny, and completely flat except for my backside. And my face hasn't got anything childish about it, let alone cheerful. My face is drawn, devoured, you might say, by a feverish passion: my eyes are green, my nose hooked and my mouth big and swollen. I always wear too much make-up, like some provincial prostitute. I don't know why; I just can't resist the temptation to paint my face like a violent mask, with a cloudy, threatening severity.

Thinking over my husband's reply, I feel once again and with the same intensity what I felt yesterday evening – a mixture of humiliation and jealousy. Plus the impulse that yesterday evening, in the presence of so many people, I had to control; the impulse to express what I feel as soon as possible, no matter what.

My husband bends down now and brushes a kiss across my ear. Right away, without moving, in my worst, deep, growling voice, I say: "Watch it. Don't kiss me. Today's not the day." You'll notice that I say, "Today's not the day," when what I should say is:

The Belt

"Today is the day." Yes, because I feel it. I'm sure that today is one of those days when what I secretly call "the calamity" happens. What is "the calamity"? It is something casual, insidious, negative – a banana skin, a patch of oil or ice: something you want to avoid and instead end up slipping on, fatally. It is the word you let out in spite of yourself, the blow you can't hold back. It is violence. In short, "the calamity".

I hear my husband's voice, quite dumbfounded, asking: "What's got into you, what's wrong?" And I answer: "Yesterday evening you insulted me in front of everybody."

"You're crazy."

"No, I'm not crazy. If I was crazy I'd have got up and left, there and then."

"But what's got into you?"

"This has got into me: when we were talking about the ideal type of woman, you said yours was the English tomboy type, blonde, generous curves, sporty."

"So?"

"You also said you imagined her having pubic hair like foam on champagne: blonde, transparent and curly. Whereas you're always telling me that I have a friar's grizzly, black beard."

"And so?"

"So you offended me, you hurt me. Everybody was looking at me, seeing perfectly well that I wasn't your ideal type. I wanted the ground to swallow me up."

"But it's not true. Everybody thought it was hilarious: they were all laughing precisely because you're not blonde and curvy."

"Don't touch me, please: the slightest touch of your hand gives me goose pimples." I say this because, while we've been talking, he has sat down on the edge of the bed, pulled down the bedclothes as far as the dip at the small of my back and tried to stroke my bottom. I put myself face-down and add: "I'm not just saying it, look." And I show him my lean, dark arm. As though from cold, or as if a gust of wind had blown across the still, calm surface of a lake, goose pimples are visibly spreading across the skin. He says nothing. He pulls the bedclothes down further to uncover my buttocks. Then he bends down to kiss me right there, beneath the coccyx. So I reach back my arm – I've got a heavy bracelet on my wrist, the kind with studs – and I give him a hard thump in the face. So hard, it feels like I've broken his nose. He cries out in pain and shouts: "What's got a hold of you, you bitch!", and he throws me a punch on the right shoulder. Furious, I say: "Now, on top of everything else, you hit me. What next? Why not get the belt out of your trousers and beat me, like last time? I'm warning you, though, just so that you know, the moment you go to get your belt I'm leaving this house and you'll never see me again."

To understand this threat, you have to realize that "the calamity" has recently taken the form of my husband's using his belt to punish me for my sharp tongue. I provoke him, insult him, invent cruel, mocking, scornful jibes which hurt and offend him; then, short on answers, or rather insults, he gets the belt out of his trousers, jumps on me, and holding me still, face-downwards, with one big hand pressing on my neck, he grabs the belt with the other and beats me.

He does it systematically, despite being genuinely furious, with well-distributed, criss-cross blows, under which my thin brown buttocks are soon zebra-striped with dark red weals. Beneath these blows, which have an even, slow rhythm that seems to be the same as the rhythm of his breathing, I don't struggle and I don't try to escape. I stay still, face-down, patient and alert, the way I do when a nurse gives me an injection. Except that I betray the fairly complex sensation I'm feeling by letting out a thin, querulous moan, almost a yelp, very different from my normal voice, which is warm and hoarse. Even while I'm making it, this sound amazes me because I sense in it a whole part of myself that I feel I don't know. I moan, I shift my backside, not so much to escape the blows perhaps as to make sure they are evenly distributed. Finally, he throws himself on top of me, panting, and, still with the belt in his hand, slips it under my chin. Then he lets go of the belt, there, on the pillow and moves his hand down to my crotch to help himself in. At which point, just like a dog, I bite the leather of the belt hard, close my eyes and moan again at the new and different sensation he's inflicting on me.

I can already hear someone exclaiming: "Nice discovery! Sado-masochistic love! Old hat, hashed and rehashed." And yet, no, it isn't like that. I'm not a masochist and my husband isn't a sadist; or rather, we only become so for those five or ten minutes of sex; and we become so, I want to stress this, as a result of "the calamity":

that is, we slip over on it, like you slip over on a banana skin, without either of us wanting or even less expecting it. It's like a brawl between drunkards, or a crime of passion; like a fit of violence that pounces on you in a moment of happiness, lightning from a cloudless sky. So much so, that afterwards we are both ashamed and we won't talk about it; or, as happened last time, we promise each other never to fall into the trap again.

Now, for example, while I am defying him to beat me, I search through my mind and don't find the slightest hint of desire there. No, I don't want to be beaten, just the thought of it provokes a sense of boredom and sadness; and yet, and yet . . . Still repeating, "Go on, get your belt, go on, beat me," I look at the strip of leather I can just see between the loops of his trousers, and I'm not at all sure that I am seeing it with the foreboding and indignant horror my words might suggest. On the contrary, I see it as a familiar object with which, when all's said and done, I am not on bad terms.

But this time, I don't know why, absolutely nothing happens. Yes, I see him go to the chair; I see him take the trousers, but instead of tearing out the belt, like the other times, he goes and puts the trousers on. I try to provoke him, *in extremis*: after all, the belt is there, in his hands, all he has to do is pull it out of the loops instead of tightening it round his waist. Angrily, I say: "So, come on, what's stopping you beating me like you usually do? What are you afraid of, come on. I'm right here with my bare bum, at your service, ready to take the brunt of your sadistic impulses. What are you waiting for?" And so saying, scarcely realizing what I'm doing, as though crazed, I put myself in a better position to take the blows, and push down the cover which has ridden up over my waist. But he looks at me as though stupefied and doesn't move. I go on: "Admit it, you're afraid, you coward, you're afraid that I'll really leave you this time, that I'll go. And I'm telling you, you're right, dead right: the moment you make a move, I mean just a move, to beat me, everything is finished between us, for ever."

I see him now, looking at me, with the staring, searching, amazed eyes of someone who suddenly thinks he's understood something important; then he lifts his shoulders in a violent shrug and leaves, slamming one door after the other; first the bedroom door, then the door in the passage and finally the front door.

I'm left with nothing to do but get up, wash, make up and dress:

95

paralysed by frustration, my imagination can offer me nothing but this minimal programme. But once out of the bathroom, as I move to the mirror to put on my make-up, I'm alarmed by the sight of my face: it's haggard; beneath staring eyes my thin, panting cheeks seem to have been sucked in by a big mouth that's pushed out as if in a thirsty, voracious pout. It's the face of a hungry, greedy, lustful woman; but hungry, greedy and lustful for what? I finish putting on my make-up, and I say to myself: "Well, to be getting on with, I'll go and see my mother and tell her I've decided to leave Vittorio."

My mother lives in the same building, on the floor below mine. It was me who wanted this arrangement, out of affection I thought, at the time of our marriage. Now I realize that it had to do with my instinctive and fatal need to surround myself with slave-drivers, torturers and sadists. What is my mother in the end, if not precisely the chief of all the slave-drivers who have tormented me my life long, reduced me, as a few minutes ago, to the shameful provocation of the very tortures I pretend to rebel against?

While I'm going down from my flat to hers, I make a mental list of all the things that I, along with every other human being on this earth, had a right to, and which my mother robbed me of. Yes, robbed, with her disgraceful, inhuman behaviour. I had a right to an innocent, untainted childhood and my mother robbed me of it, destroying my innocence by making me a witness to her indecent behaviour with my father. I had a right to a serene and happy adolescence and my mother robbed me of it by involving me in the various affairs she consoled herself with after splitting up with my father. I had a right to a hopeful, unselfish youth and my mother robbed me of it by pushing me into what, in the end, is a marriage of convenience. And this morning, I can hardly help concluding, I had a right to be belted by my husband, and instead he pulled up his trousers, tightened the belt round his waist and left. I sense there is a connection between my childhood frustrations and this frustration of married life, a humiliating, sordid connection. Once I used to expect so many fine, good and honest things from life, and because of my mother I haven't had them: this morning I would have settled for being beaten, and instead I didn't even get that. So, there's been a profound degradation in my life. How did I come to sink so low? And who is directly responsible, if not precisely my mother?

I ring at the door and wait impatiently, biting my lower lip, always a sign of distress with me. The door opens and my mother appears in a soft bathrobe, her head turbaned in a towel. She exclaims: "Oh, it's you! Just the person I needed."

I look at her without a word and go in. My mother's face always has the same effect on me; I mean, it always prompts the same thought: when on earth will she decide to get old? Really old, with wrinkles and wobbly yellow teeth, watery eyes and wispy, untidy hair? Because my mother has managed, I don't know how, to elude time; at fifty she has the same smooth, enamelled, doll-like face she had at thirty. True, the affectedly charming oval of this face has been completely reconstructed and stitched up in Switzerland by expensive plastic surgeons, but, all the same, every time I see her, I can't help attributing this physical immutability to an analogous immutability on the moral plane. Yes, my mother has remained so young because she is serene, self-confident, without nerves. And she is serene, self-confident and without nerves because right from the start she was convinced, let's put it like this, that the arseholeries of bourgeois piety constitute the *non plus ultra* of moral perfection. To me it seems the height of injustice that at twenty-nine my face is scored with deep wrinkles because I believe in nothing, starting with myself, while my mother's face is smooth and syrupy as a doll's for the opposite reason: because she's a cretin who believes in everything.

Thinking over these things, I sense that I am winding up my anger, like an alarm clock. I follow my mother into her fifties-style sitting room and here too, as when faced with her false youthfulness, I can't help but think what I always do: is it really possible that all this pseudo-antique furniture, made up of so many new and old bits glued together; this stuff she bought from the swindling antique dealers who were all the rage when she was young – is it possible that these pseudo-Spanish, Provençal and Tuscan pier glasses, cabinets, chairs, tables and stools still haven't disintegrated; that they're still there to fool the gullible visitor with their fake solidity and authenticity? "You need me?" I ask my mother curtly. "What do you want?"

With the artlessness of a mistress addressing her slave, she stretches a leg out of the bathrobe and, showing me a bare foot, says: "I haven't got time to go to the chiropodist. And you do it so well: there, look, you'll have to get rid of that small corn on the little toe. I don't know why, but it keeps growing back."

Suddenly I explode: "Look, go right on out to the chiropodist. Today's not the day. And then, if you want to know the truth, your corns make me puke."

My mother immediately reacts as I expected: like the candid egoist who thinks the whole world revolves around herself. She shuts the bathrobe smartly and asks, almost amazed: "So what did you come for?"

"Not to cut your corns, that's for sure."

My mother pretends to busy herself with a big bunch of flowers in a vase on the table in the middle of the room. She tidies the petals and pulls out the wilting flowers. With a sigh, she says: "How unpleasant and crude you are. You're unbearable."

Improvising then and there a decision I haven't taken, I announce: "I came to tell you that I'm leaving Vittorio."

My mother replies with indifference: "You're always saying that and you never do it."

"But this time I mean it. He doesn't love me; our marriage is a failure."

"You should have children. Not that I care for the idea of becoming a grandmother, but it's the only remedy."

"I don't want them, what am I supposed to do with children?"

"So, tell us what you do want."

I watch her hands as she lifts them to arrange the flowers in the vase. They are the big hands of a big woman, opaque magnolia-white, fleshy and smooth with big fingers and thick oval nails: they move with sluggish, involuntary slowness. I know those hands; most of all I remember how ruthlessly and systematically brutal they could be when, at the end of an argument that had gone on too long, she would suddenly decide to hit me. This was when I was a child; but the pattern of what I call "the calamity" hasn't changed: the fatal and obscure pretext, neither desired nor created by myself, which used to provoke my mother's violence in the past, is the same as that which today drives my husband to beat me with the belt. My mother would tell me off in a particularly stupid, irritating way; I would answer back, giving as good as I got; then she would tell me off for answering back; I would get more aggressive; and, with one insult leading to another, the moment of "the calamity" would be reached: I definitely didn't want the argument to end in blows, and at the same time I felt I was doing everything I could to make sure that it did. And, of course, my mother would hurl herself on me and beat me. Or rather, she tried to beat me; but I fled the threat of her big, accurate, brutal hands. I ran all over the flat till in the end I would take refuge in the cupboard room, the room where, between four walls of wall-cupboards, our maid, Veronica, used to do the ironing, standing in front of a big table. I burst into this room and threw myself into Veronica's arms. My mother caught up with me and began to beat me, with calm and precision. At the first blow I would begin to yell; and just as today the dog-like yelps I come out with during my husband's lashings in some obscure way amaze me because they seem to reveal an unknown part of my character, so, then, the piercing, stuck-pig shrieks my mother's blows tore out of me would astonish me. Was it really true, was it really me yelling like that?

I pressed myself against Veronica and yelled. My mother, mean-while, not at all impressed, continued to beat me systematically; she even went so far as to take me by the chin to make me turn my head so that she could land her blows better. This beating lasted quite long enough for me to come to my senses and to try to push my mother off somehow; but the remarkable thing was that I never did this, that my only reaction was to yell. In the end, panting, though always maintaining her self-control, my mother would stop and walk out, saying: "That'll teach you a lesson for next time." An ambiguous remark which seemed to promise that there would be other times. For my own part, I would hug myself to Veronica, who – note this – like the cold, even disdainful person she was, hadn't lifted a finger to defend me; and sobbing I would say: "I hate her, I hate her, I don't want to live in this house any more, not a minute longer."

Looking at those hands now, I tell myself that my mother would be perfectly capable of beating me again as she did in the past; just recreate the atmosphere of "the calamity" between us and she would do it. Prompted by this idea, I say brusquely: "I don't want anything. The only thing I want is for you to give me back what you robbed me of."

"Robbed? What are you talking about?"

"Yes, robbed. Isn't it robbery to cheat a human being out of the happiness he or she has a right to?"

"And who would this human being be?"

"Me. I had the right to a happy childhood, but you took it from me, having me watch your filthy sex with your husband."

"Who is also your father, if I'm not mistaken, no?"

I know perfectly well that what I've said isn't true. It was me who as a little girl, urged on by I don't know what irresistible curiosity, would spend all my time spying on my mother and father, while they, as sometimes happens, weren't overly worried about being seen while they made love. But I don't think twice about lying now, because my aim is not to tell the truth but to provoke "the calamity". "Yes, I saw you jerking him off. I saw you put it in your mouth. I even saw you have him get it in from behind."

She doesn't get worked up, but takes a wilted flower out of the bunch and says: "Have you finished?"

"No, I haven't finished. After a peeping-Tom childhood, you turned me into an adolescent pimp. You got me involved in your affairs; you used me to make it up with the lover you'd scared off with your jealousy. You even suggested, as if it was nothing at all, to try a little petting. Very nice, mother and daughter – what man would resist such a juicy temptation?"

This isn't true either, and I know it. In reality it was me, and then only on one occasion, who offered myself as peacemaker between my mother and one of her lovers, and this because I liked the man and in my bright and delirious, ambitious, little-girl's mind I foolishly hoped to steal him from my mother and take her place. But he wouldn't play along with me and after a little sparring he rejected me in a particularly humiliating way, something I've never been able to forgive my mother for. I watch her to see if this malicious lie has got her angry. No, nothing. Once again, with a wisely patient voice, she asks: "Have you finished?"

"No, I haven't finished. I could go on for ever. You even robbed me of the happiness of being a young woman. It was you who practically sold me to Vittorio; you started a sort of white slave trade in your own family. And the price of the slave I am was no more nor less than this flat which he gave you when the deal was done, right after our wedding."

The Belt

This is not only untrue; it is the exact opposite of what really happened because, as I've already said, it was me who insisted that my husband give my mother this flat, because I wanted her near me, always at hand, in the same building. For the third time I look at her, hoping to catch some sign of anger, a trembling of those hands, for example, once so ready to punish me. But again she doesn't react. It's obvious: with the instinct of the torturer she has understood that I want to provoke her and she refuses to satisfy me. Unflinching, she says: "Now go away, because I've got work to do. And don't come back until you've got over it."

I go. But at the door I can't resist the temptation to shout: "I'll never get over it."

I find myself on the landing again, with an atrocious feeling of frustration: my whole body is trembling and my eyes are clouded with tears. Then, through this mist of tears, an image takes shape, one that by now we can call symbolic of my brief and anguished existence: an image of a sea wave, high and green, topped with white curls of foam, arching threateningly over me with its sparkling, glassy weight.

This looming wave is not just a figment of my terror-struck imagination; I saw it in real life many years ago in the sea off Circeo when my father and I had foolishly gone out for a swim. We had left the beach to the north of the promontory where the sea was calm; but as soon as we rounded it, with deceptive slowness, the sea became rougher and rougher. With the result that, all at once, without understanding how it had happened, we found ourselves in a chaos of waves colliding, crashing and breaking against each other without any apparent order or direction. My father shouted to me to follow him and began to swim through the waves that danced frenetically around him, heading for the point of the promontory. Right at that moment, as I was struggling to stay close to him, I saw a wave rear up from the total disorder of the sea not far away, an inexplicably compact, well-formed wave that seemed – how can I explain it? – conscious of where it was going and why. To put it bluntly, that wave threatened me and only me: it had the obvious intention of catching and destroying me. At once I shouted: "Dad!", and then a moment later the wave was there, rolling towards me, all by itself in the middle of a sea that in comparison now seemed calm.

Again I shouted desperately: "Dad!", and at the same time, the wave arched over me. But my father wasn't far away; he came out of the water close to me before the wave broke on us. With a third cry of "Dad!", I threw my arms round his neck and clung tightly to him.

The wave crashed on us. After a frantic struggle in the dark we came to the surface again, him trying to swim to the shore and me clinging tighter than ever to his neck. So then he pulled back and tried to get free from my arms. But I didn't leave go; I clung to him. The last thing I saw was my father trying to prise my arms from his neck and then, when he found he couldn't, biting his lower lip between his teeth, taking aim and throwing a fierce punch at my face with all his strength. I passed out. He freed himself from me and dragged me to the shore by my hair. I came round to find him crouched over me giving me mouth-to-mouth resuscitation.

From that day on, that high, purposeful wave became a symbol of everything that threatens me in this chaos of existence; and likewise that punch of my father's has become the symbol of everything which, albeit with violence, is trying to save me and can. The wave is over me now and I decide to go straight to my father – the only one who can save me from that ancient threat.

My father is a sculptor and lives in an old studio at the bottom of an overgrown, neglected garden beneath the Gianicolo. I park outside the gate and press an antique bell. Two or three minutes go by, then finally the gate unlocks with a buzz and I head for the studio which is right at the bottom, under the Gianicolo hill. I walk fast along an overgrown path between flowerbeds full of lush weeds. What am I coming to visit my father for, I wonder, seeing his sculptures emerge here and there amidst the high June grass, expressing so clearly the man's creative impotence. They are enormous monolithic blocks of pink, grey or pale-blue stone, crudely sculpted in an Easter-Islands or pre-Columbian-Mexico style with hints of monsters or equally monstrous human heads. In reality, I think, glancing at them as I pass, they are nothing but enormous paperweights or ashtrays; their size doesn't alter their fundamental futility. So, what am I doing, coming to see the designer of these paperweights? And I answer my own question: obviously to ask him to smash that saving punch right in my face again.

The Belt

I lift my eyes: there is my father in the doorway to his studio – a dilapidated, tottering giant in a light-grey linen shirt and cord trousers. But as I come up to him, I realize, not for the first time, that he won't give me that punch I long for with such ambiguous nostalgia: I must count on myself alone to escape the wave that threatens to overwhelm me. Yes, because for two years now my father's face has been grotesquely disfigured by paralysis: it's as if two cruel fingers had grabbed his left cheek and were pulling it hard away from the nose, forcing him into a permanent wink, a doltish grimace of dubious and equivocal complicity.

He gives me a hug, mumbles something indistinct and goes on ahead of me into the studio. The barely cut outline of one of the usual monoliths is standing in the middle. There are other finished examples around the walls. For form's sake, I walk round the sculptures, pretending to be interested; I play the part of the respectful, understanding visitor. But at the same time, my distress is crushing me. Suddenly, with a strangled voice, I announce: "I've come to tell you that Vittorio and I are splitting up."

At which the following dialogue takes place, with him mumbling away inarticulately and me speaking with a choking lump in my throat: "Why?"

"Because he beats me."

"How does he beat you?"

"He gets me to lie face-down, naked, and he beats me with his trouser-belt."

"And you're leaving him for that?"

All of a sudden I see that high, black wave again, looming and arching over my head; I see my father bite his lower lip between his teeth to concentrate on his punch, and then I forget his paralysis and cry: "The truth is I'm leaving him because I want to come and live with you."

My father is visibly frightened. He stutters that he hasn't got room here in his studio; that there is a woman in his life (his maid, I know); that I must try and make it up with my husband, and other such things. But I don't listen and suddenly I throw my arms round his neck just as I did that day in the sea, and shout: "You remember fifteen years ago at Circeo, when you saved me from drowning? You remember how I clung to you, just like now, and you punched me in the face so as not to drown along with me?

"Oh father, father, with all these people wanting to beat and hurt me, you're the only one who loves me, and I remember your punch as the only violence that was ever done to me for love."

I clutch at him madly. Frightened, he pulls back and mumbles: "But who wants to hurt you?"

"Mother, my husband, everyone."

"Everyone?"

"Mother beat me just a few minutes ago. I wanted to talk things over with her and that was how she reacted."

He gapes, takes my wrists in his hands and frees himself, but without punching me. He mutters: "Your mother loves you."

I shout: "But can't you see the marks her awful hands have left on my cheeks? And right after my husband had already beaten me with his belt. You don't believe me? Look then, look."

I don't know what exhibitionist frenzy has got a hold of me. I lean up against the monolith in the middle of the studio, bend over with my head down and lift up my skirt over my behind. I have a masculine behind, tight and muscular, with two quivering dimples, one on each buttock. I shout: "Look, look how my husband treats me."

What's happening? I must admit there does seem to be a great silence behind me as I try to push down the top of my knickers. Then my father puts his hand over mine and stops me, moves my hand away. And that same hand of his pulls down my skirt. I turn. He is standing in front of me, shaking his head. He mutters: "Don't do that kind of thing."

I rush at him, grab his hand, lift it to my lips, kiss it, saying: "Only you can save me."

He frees his hand, looks at me and, with a visible effort, finally manages to say what he's been thinking since the beginning of my visit: "You're mad."

"No, I'm not mad. It's you that's changed. You used to be terrifically handsome, now you're a wreck, with your face all twisted. You used to be a man who could throw a punch at his daughter; now you're afraid of seeing her buttocks!"

This time he gets angry; the allusion to his paralysis has cut him to the quick. Strangely, his anger allows him to overcome the impediment caused by the paralysis and he says fairly clearly: "Look, you're in a state over your husband. You'd better leave."

The Belt

I shout: "Coward, come on, punch me, let's see if that hand of
yours is good for anything apart from those idiotic, monolithic
paperweights."
Some hope! He slowly lifts his enormous hand, but keeps it open,
as if to have me measure its size. Struggling to speak, he says: "Go
away. What do you want me to do? Start beating you up? I'm sorry,
but I'm not in the habit of hitting women."
And with that, there really is nothing left for me to do but go.
Just like with my husband and my mother. I go. My father doesn't
take me to the door. He has already picked up a tool to sculpt: he
waves goodbye from a distance, tool in hand. The fact is, I tell
myself, he doesn't care about me at all and he'll forgive me even
my insults so long as I go away.
So here I am, rejected and frustrated again. Mechanically, I walk
back along the path, between the flowerbeds thick with tall grass
and my father's monoliths sticking out from amongst it. I go out
into the street, get in the car, start up and put it in reverse. But with
the terrible state I'm in, I get the wrong gear. The car leaps forward
and smashes against a lamp-post which, God knows why, is right
there in front of me; if it had been a yard further away, nothing
would have happened. I brake, open the door, get out, go and look.
The radiator grille is smashed and a headlight is shattered; the
bumper is stove in. But I don't feel the impotent, miserable anger
that usually grips me on such occasions. This disaster has given
me an idea: I'll go and see Giacinto.
Giacinto is the only man I have betrayed my husband with in
five years of marriage. I say I've betrayed my husband with him,
but it's not true; because the fact is that Giacinto doesn't count.
I often ask myself: "What does 'betrayal' mean in such cases?
Giacinto entered and withdrew, that's all, and then only once. Is
that what betrayal is?"
It happened like this. I had an accident, just like today's: instead
of putting the car in reverse, I put it in third. Like today, the grille
got smashed, but there the similarities end. It was my first car and
I didn't have a mechanic. Suddenly I remembered that there was
a repair place not far from my house in a backstreet I used to drive
down every day. On the left side of the street in front of this
workshop there was always a car being repaired with a mechanic
on his back on the ground, half under the car and half out. That

mechanic was Giacinto. Even before seeing his face, I had noticed his genitals: with him being on his back with his legs apart, they formed a visible swelling you could see even from a distance. Then I saw his face too: he was a handsome, middle-aged man, with ancient-Roman features, thin and severe, an aquiline nose, a proud mouth: finger smears of grease gave him a curiously wild expression. I swear, I didn't think of making love with Giacinto at all the day of my first accident; I was just furious because it was my first car and there it was, ruined already, and I didn't have any money either.

I went straight to the backstreet. It was May, a nice warm day, and as usual he was mending a car, on his back, with half of his body under it and half sticking out. Heaven knows how, but I had what they call an inspiration. I bent down and, without a word, gave him a pat right there on the swelling of his jeans. Then, naturally, I said: "Excuse me. Could you take a look at my car?" The pat had been so light that when he came out from under the car and stared at me, his blue eyes all dazed, I thought he hadn't noticed and I didn't know whether I was sorry or happy. He went to look at the car and told me right away in a brusque, business-like voice how much it would cost to put it right. It was a lot, much more than I'd feared. I had a sudden fit of miserliness and almost without thinking I said: "That's a lot for me, really a lot. But mightn't there be some other way of paying?" He looked at the car and then at me exactly as if I were an object up for barter, and with his working man's seriousness, he said: "There is another way, of course." And then after a moment's reflection: "Get in, we'll test the car, see if there's anything wrong with the engine." So, with him driving and me sitting next to him, silent and stunned, we went to a suburban street that runs parallel to the Tiber. He swung the car into a track that ran into some brushwood. Then, still driving along the track, he said: "Only this once though, because I'm a married man and I love my wife." I said warmly: "Okay, just this once, because I really don't have the money." God knows what was making me so miserly that day!

Three years have passed since then: I've already changed my car twice and I always go to him for repairs because he never makes me pay and every time I reach for my purse he invariably says: "It's on the house," which is his way of telling me that those ten minutes when he entered me and withdrew were important for him, so important as to have him repair my car free for the rest of my life. But, as if by agreement, we have never spoken about making love again.

Now I go to Giacinto as to the only person who can help me survive this tidal wave in my life. I'm not going out of miserliness this time: I'm going because that day when he entered me and withdrew, seeing as a few moments before he had volunteered the information that he was married, I asked him: "If you found out that your wife, who you love so much, was betraying you, just like I betrayed my husband today, what would you do?" "I don't even want to think about it." "But come on, what would you do?" "I think I might even kill her."

"Kill her!" Oh yes, a likely story! All bark and no bite. Yet now it would be very convenient for me, if this dog really did bite. Strangely, perhaps because Giacinto is a worker, a prole, a man of the people, I keep thinking of that cruel, gloating word "execute" that the terrorists use so often in their communiqués: "We have executed . . ." and then a name, surname, profession and perhaps one of those definitions of theirs, full of contempt and hatred. To the ear of someone like myself, predestined victim of every kind of violence, that word has a good sound: "Yesterday we executed Vittoria B, typical bourgeois housewife, unworthy of dragging out her miserable inveterate-masochist's existence any longer." It's true that Giacinto isn't the ideal executioner; in the end I suspect he's just a petty bourgeois like any other; but when it comes down to it, he is the only working man I ever made love with in my life, and if someone has to kill me, I'd like it to be him.

So I go to the backstreet not far from my house where he has his workshop. I find him as usual, half under the car he's repairing and half out. So I crouch down, look around, see there's no one about and give a hard squeeze to the swelling in his trousers. He comes straight out, frowning, and you can see he's angry. "Just look what I've gone and done," I say.

He says nothing, goes to my car without a word, walks round it, then says in a businesslike manner: "Quite a mess. It's going to cost fifty thousand lire."

"So, you'll fix it for me."

"But no credit this time."

"Which means?"

"Which means you pay me fifty thousand lire, madam."

He calls me madam! He makes me pay! I'm seized with rage, a complex rage which includes something of everything: miserliness, frustration, the idea that I don't want to go on living, the word "execute", and so on. In a low, conspiratorial voice, I say: "Let's go to the track. I have to talk to you."

He is silent again. But he gets in the car. I climb in next to him and we set off. While we're driving, I say through clenched teeth: "I don't want anything for free. I'm ready to pay for the work the way I paid the first time."

Without turning, he answers: "No, I want the money and that's that. I already told you: I'm a married man. I've got a wife."

I come back: "You've got a wife, eh! Well, your wife's betraying you. I made you come here on purpose to tell you. She's betraying you with Fiorenzo."

I swear that, however unlikely it may seem, as little as a minute before I hadn't even thought of telling Giacinto that his wife was betraying him. And least of all with Fiorenzo, one of his workers. It came to me off pat to tell him that, a sudden inspiration. Of course it's a lie, but just the lie I need to provoke his violence. I see his whole face go red under the smears of car grease, a dark, nearly black red. He says: "Who told you?"

Is there a threat in his eyes already, or am I mistaken? I hurry to step up the pressure. "You look like an ancient Roman with that stern face of yours, and instead you're a modern Roman, a loser, with a wife who cheats on you without your realizing. No, you don't realize that while you're lying under cars, Fiorenzo is lying on top of your wife."

Nice, eh! Exactly one of those poisonous phrases that sink right in and hurt. And immediately he loses his head; he turns and grabs me by the neck with both hands. Just what I wanted. I let out a strangled sob, gasping for air, then cry from between those hands that are squeezing me: "Kill me, yes, kill me, execute me!"

Alas, my invocation has the opposite effect to what I had intended. Perhaps the word "execute" has made him suspicious, frightened him. He lets go of me, opens the door, jumps out and heads off down the track at a run. The last I see of him is his back as he runs off through the bushes.

The Belt

Amazed and stunned, I stay still a few minutes in the car. The door is open and through it I can see the undergrowth of this piece of brushwood, full of litter and rubbish. Finally I tell myself that in reality all these disasters stem from the fact that, like any self-respecting wife, I want to be loved by my husband, that's all. The disappointment with him this morning was the source of all my other disappointments: the argument with my mother, the tussle with my father, the break-up with Giacinto, which, when you think about it, is where the real damage has been done in this whole affair, since from now on I'll have to pay for my repairs. These down-to-earth reflections cheer me up somehow. I'm not a lunatic after all, looking for someone to beat, trample and kill me; I'm just a woman in need of love. I shut the door, start up and set off for home.

A few minutes later I'm on the landing outside my flat. I open the door a crack, slip in like a thief, making sure to make no noise. I tiptoe from the hall into the corridor and from here, still on tiptoe, as far as the bedroom. It has been tidied; the woman who comes has done the cleaning and gone. The room is empty; the shutters are half down; there is a clean shadowiness, discrete and quiet. I have the impression there is something unusual about the room; perhaps it's just a sense of the contrast between this order, this silence and calm, and the scene that took place here this morning between my husband and myself. But no, there is something else, something new and different that I can't put my finger on. Then, with a glance in the direction of the bed, I suddenly realize that on the side where I sleep, to the left of the bed, hanging by the buckle from a nail I don't remember seeing before, is my husband's belt.

I go and take it down, and gripping it in my hands I sit on the edge of the bed. I'm both excited and afraid. So far, all the beatings I've got from my husband have been provoked by that unforeseen, unforeseeable fatality, both feared and unconsciously desired – "the calamity". We would fall into the trap together, he and I, despite ourselves, without realizing what was happening. But now, this belt, hung near the head of the bed, like an instrument of torture in the inquisitor's cell, ready to hand for use the moment it's needed – this belt which will hang over my head while I sleep and be there before my eyes when I wake – terrifies me, because it's a sign that both he and I have set out once and for all along the path of a lucid, knowing yet, for all that, enforced complicity. From now on we will know in advance, the way you do with organized pleasures, that at a certain moment I must lie face-down, must push back the bedclothes to uncover my buttocks, and that then my husband must unhook the belt from the nail and beat me thoroughly while I let out my strange yelps of pain.

Since all this is bound to happen now, it is consequently repugnant.

But perhaps that belt hung on the nail is an affectionate warning. My husband has banged in the nail and hung the belt there to inspire precisely these reflections, this repugnance. As if to say: "Look, this is the abyss we're falling into."

Who knows? Perhaps, like me, he wants it and he doesn't want it. But one thing's sure: it was he who put the nail there and hung the belt on it.

I hesitate, looking at the belt I've got in my hands across my knees. Then I make up my mind. I get up and go and hang it back on the nail. Now I look at my watch. It's almost one. He'll be back for lunch soon; it's time to get something to eat. I cast a last glance at the belt hanging over the bed and leave the bedroom. He'll come and we'll talk about it all over lunch. At least a complicity like ours is good for one thing: we can talk about it.

The Owner of the Flat

❧

Everything is ready. I've converted the sitting-room sofa into a bed. I'll sleep there. He (or she) will sleep in my bed. I've bought a bit of tinned food, a few kilos of pasta and a fair amount of cheeses and cold meats in case he (or she) doesn't want to or can't leave the house. Finally I've emptied my clothes out of the cupboard which should serve him (or her) as storage space. Now there's nothing for me to do but wait: judging by yesterday's phone-call, he (or she) should arrive within an hour at the most.

But we must be clear about the words we're using. Before, they had what we can call a normal sense; now they have a sense that I will call "organizational". For example, in my case, the verb "to wait", in an organizational sense, doesn't mean to wait for somebody or something; it means to stay in the place I've been assigned to and not to move for any reason whatsoever. In short, if it's true, as I believe it is, that in every wait there is a personal element at stake, then this is not waiting. Hence we have this strange contradiction: while I am waiting for something precise to happen in a Utopian future, in my immediate, day-to-day, common-man's existence, I don't really know what I'm waiting for, and perhaps I'm not waiting for anything. Unless I decide to transform the means into an end: that is, to make of myself – no more than a

III

means – the end of everything. But in that case, how could I believe in the ultimate end, the only one that offers satisfaction, even if it is exceedingly remote?

Anyway, even the term "common man" has taken on a different meaning since I joined the Organization. Before I was convinced, with a tinge of self-satisfaction, that I really was nothing other than a man like all the rest. Now I know for certain that it is precisely to the fact that I'm a common man that I owe the rather unusual rôle I have been called upon to play. Thus "common man", in my case, means a common man who pretends to be a common man so as to do something uncommon: pretty complicated, no?

But even while waiting for nothing, I still have to pass the time and unfortunately I can only pass it the way I did before, when I was waiting for a woman, for example. This is the kind of waiting that a man like myself, middle-aged, not exactly ugly, who has a reasonable salary and lives alone in a two-room flat plus kitchen and bathroom, knows well. This is waiting *par excellence*, the most typical; the kind which, even at the humdrum, day-to-day level, sums up all the other kinds, even the most sublime and Utopian. Of course, given that the Organization empties words of their substance, leaving only the husk, I won't so much "live" this wait for the arrival of a woman, as act it out: that is, I will act as if I really were waiting for that most privileged of moments which separates desire from satisfaction.

The first thing I do is go to the window, throw it open and stand by the sill. I live on the second floor, an ideal place for observing without being observed, and even less involved. Evening has come after a day of spring rain that has left the tarmac wet and the air smoky and damp. From my window my gaze goes directly across to the other side of the street, a block very like my own, with row upon row of windows, all the same, one above the other right up to the sky, and a line of shops at ground level to the right and left of the main door. From the block my attention shifts down and backwards to the cars parked herring-bone fashion along the pavement and from here to the big plane trees planted at regular intervals and already covered with tiny spring leaves. Closer still there's the tarmac surface where two rows of cars come and go incessantly in opposite directions.

The Owner of the Flat

Finally, I can see a pavement exactly like the one on the other side of the street, with plane trees and cars parked herring-bone fashion. The only difference being the newsagent's kiosk. As for the façade of my own block and the line of shops at ground level, obviously I can't see them, but I "sense" them; I know they're there and that they are exactly like the façade and the shops opposite. That's right, you don't imagine the things that are common and normal, you "sense" them.

As I look out over this urban landscape I realize it has changed. Once I felt I was part of it myself; and I wasn't simply aware of this – I was pleased about it. Sometimes, especially towards evening, after a day spent at my desk, I would get up, go to the window, open it wide and, with a sense of luxury, light a cigarette, looking down at the street. In reality, I didn't so much observe all those things, already familiar and observed a thousand times before, as savour the grateful affection they stirred in me: it was like rediscovering kind, friendly presences who helped me to live. What was strange about that anyway? I was a common man living in one of the most common parts of town and doing the same things everybody else did. It was right, as well as inevitable, that I should feel pleased when I opened the window and looked out.

But it's not like that now. I realize that from the fact that instead of lighting a cigarette, I am almost embarrassed to look out over the windowsill. I don't know what to do and at first glance I feel as though I were excluded from the reality stretched out beneath me. No, I no longer recognize myself in the street; it's like a mirror that's misted over and doesn't reflect me any more. What I was resembled the street; what I am merely needs the street. After being for so long the place where I lived, the street has now become the place where I pretend to live.

Suddenly the streetlamps go on all together and instantly the street passes from the confused shadow of the evening to the deceptive visibility of a night lit up with city lights. Then, from nowhere, a woman steps off the pavement opposite and comes towards me. She is young, very young perhaps, big and majestic, as if bathed in a halo of beauty. She is wearing a long sweater and blue jeans and the jeans are so tight round her groin that they form a host of little wrinkles about the crotch, making me think of a sun shooting its rays above the horizon. She walks with the charming awkwardness of a woman who is graceful only when naked, her breasts pushed out and her hips drawn back. She has a round, strong neck and a serious face, a little full around the cheeks and narrower at the temples, with high cheekbones and large, clear eyes.

Where have I seen that face? Perhaps in the reproduction of a female figure by Piero della Francesca that I have hanging in my bedroom.

This very beautiful woman sheds the dark of the night, stepping forward erect through the parked cars, her eyes lifted towards me. It's her. No doubt about it. It's the person the Organization is sending me. It's her, and I'm the luckiest man on earth. Now she's reached my side; in a moment she'll disappear. I can't help it, I lift my arm, making an expressive gesture with my hand which says: "Come on up, I live on the second floor." She sees me, acknowledges with a nod of the head, disappears. With my heart beating fast, I turn away from the window, run to the hall and put my eye to the peep-hole.

It's something I've done hundreds of times in the past when waiting for girls. I'm not a man who's had lots of affairs; I know for sure that even in this field my experience is normal, i.e., negligible and limited. Everybody has done everything, that's the truth. But just for once I have the feeling that something rare and unique is happening to me: the person the Organization is sending me is also the woman I will love, no, whom I already love. This thought makes me happy, like a gambler who, from the first stake on, has swept the board at every play.

Looking through the peep-hole has always had a strange effect on me. You see things as if they were far away, when in reality they are right under your nose. Perhaps because they seem so far away, people have a meditative, funereal, unreal look about them: they look like figures seen in dreams, or even ghosts of the dead; they instill in me a sense of guilt, as if they were there, calmly waiting for me to chide me for who knows what failing. Once again I experience the two combined sensations of dream and guilt. I see my little landing transformed into a long, long corridor with the invitation of the stairs at the end, where, in a few moments, the figure of the woman with the long sweater will appear. That invitation seems a million light years away, but at the same time I know that when I open the door, she'll be so close she'll walk right into me.

The landing stays empty for what seems an infinity. Perhaps the woman is taking time looking at the names on the doors, searching for mine. At last her head appears at the bottom of the corridor, coming up the stairs.

At once I realize there must be something wrong. She's much thinner than the woman I saw in the street. Her neck isn't round and strong but thin and nervous. Her face doesn't have that expression of angelic gravity that Piero della Francesca's women have; it's a triangular, foxy face, with a blank look. Her hair hangs straight and wet-looking down her hollow cheeks; her sweater doesn't bulge at the chest but much lower, as if her breasts had slithered down towards her waist. She approaches, and then I discover that she isn't looking at the names to find mine, like somebody in the Organization would, and after hesitating a moment, she sets off up the stairs to the third floor. So I open the door, look out and say: "Hey, you, where are you going?"

She stops and turns. She has a rash of red between one nostril and the corner of her mouth; she sketches a smile: "I didn't know where to find you. You waved and then disappeared."

She has an ugly voice which manages to be both hoarse and shrill at the same time. She comes back down to my landing; in a moment she'll come into my flat. Quickly I close the door again. "Hey," she exclaims in an unpleasant voice, "what's up with you?"

Through the door, I say: "Excuse me, I mistook you for somebody else."

"I should have known," she says meekly. "It's always happening to me, people mistaking me for somebody else. Still, you'll give me something at least, won't you?"

"What do you want?"

"Give me five thousand lire, to eat."

I suddenly remember that a few days ago I found a syringe in the entrance hall to the block, the disposable kind. Obviously someone had been too impatient to wait and injected themselves right there, instead of doing it on the street. "Eat, eh!" I say angrily. "Shoot up more likely."

"Are you going to give me the five thousand lire or not?"

I take a note out of my wallet and slip it under the door. Through the peep-hole I see her bend to take it; and at that moment, behind her, still far away, the figure of a short, stocky man appears, his face very white, beard very black and two round eyes like chestnuts under his bald forehead. His hand holds a fairly large suitcase. He flashes a questioning glance at the girl. She turns her back on me and goes off with an awkward swinging of thin hips. I open the door and he comes in.

My Daughter Is Called
Giulia Too

Here I am all alone on August Bank Holiday, after one of those
bogus strokes of fate: a bolt from the blue, as they say. We were
supposed to go away, Giulia and I, to a seaside town near Rome.
At the last minute I find out that we won't be alone. A certain
Tullio, who Giulia's been getting to take her to the cinema lately,
will be coming too. According to Giulia, Tullio is a friend, pure and
simple – okay, let him be – but on August Bank Holiday too!
She answered my protests with the usual psychoanalytic jargon:
"You'd like to make me think you're jealous. The fact is that in
your subconscious you want me to betray you." I don't know why
but I flew into a temper when she said this. "Oh, it's like that, is it?
Well then, it'd be better if we didn't see each other any more." And
she, with disconcerting calm: "I think that would be the best thing
too." "So, goodbye." "Goodbye."

I ask myself now why I broke off with Giulia. Or rather, why I
didn't break off with her before. Why did I allow such a sterile,
irritating relationship to drag on for two long years? I ask myself
the question stretched out on the couch in my study in the silence
of the summer holiday. But I ask it without enthusiasm, lazily.

The truth is that instead of stimulating and intoxicating me, the sensation of finally being free after two years' sentimental servitude has a soporific effect. As if freeing myself from Giulia gave me the right to sleep, rather than providing the answers to certain questions. Yes, I say to myself, thinking of *Hamlet*, "to sleep, perchance to dream", but in any event to suspend reality for a while, the way they suspend a play when something goes wrong with the lights.

I push off my shoes with my toes and kick them away with a sense of luxury. I unbutton my collar, loosen my tie, unbuckle my belt. Then, having cast a glance around at my beloved books, so numerous and so useless, as if to thank them for watching over my liberated intellectual's sleep, I doze off.

I don't sleep long though, ten minutes maybe, and while I sleep I have the sensation that I'm regretting Giulia and would like to be woken by her. Then, still half-sleeping, I hear the phone ring, a loud aggressive ringing, like in a film. I think to myself: "Let it ring; she'll get bored sooner or later." And I know I'm thinking of Giulia. But the telephone doesn't get bored, so I jump up from the couch and pick up the receiver. I hear Giulia's voice asking: "Is the professor in?" I have a feeling of joy mixed, naturally enough, with impatience. And I answer: "This is the professor. What do you want now?"

"We have to talk."

"You know perfectly well," I say in the patient voice I use with ignorant students, "that in these last two years we have done everything but talk. There is no communication between us, you should have appreciated that by now. It must be a question of the generation gap or culture or whatever, but I get the same thing with you that I get with my daughter: we don't understand each other, we are two perfect strangers. So why go on?"

"No, this time we have to talk properly, to understand each other, to stop being strangers."

"But talk about what?"

She is silent for a moment. Then, with some hesitation, she says: "I know you think I express myself in, what do you call it?"

"Psychoanalese."

"Yes, psychoanalese. But all the same we have to talk about our relationship, about ourselves that is. I mean about the fact that while I know for certain that you are simultaneously my father and my son, you insist on ignoring the fact that I am simultaneously your daughter and your mother."

"And you call this talking?"

"And so, while I ask for nothing better than not to change anything, because you can change your boyfriend but not your father or son; you, on the other hand, would like to change everything because you don't realize that you can change your girlfriend, but not your mother or daughter."

"And you call this talking?"

After a short pause, she asks cautiously: "Are you with someone?"

"No, no one, why?"

"Then I'll be round in a moment."

"Hang on, what are you coming for?"

But the line is dead. I look at the receiver, then go back to lie on the couch. She said she'd be here in a moment; what does a moment mean? An hour? Two? Ten minutes? Twenty? Of course, I'm both happy and unhappy, relieved and oppressed, lustful and indifferent. All this is normal. If anything, it is Giulia's phrase – "We have to talk" – which stirs an echo in my memory – an echo as undeniable as it is mysterious. Who, in my most immediate past, said that? Doubtless somebody who meant the phrase not in Giulia's psycho-analytic, prefabricated sense, but literally. And in fact, together with the phrase, the echo recalls the tone in which the phrase was spoken, painful, desperate – to talk, that is to explain ourselves, to understand each other. But who said it?

Another ring on the phone interrupts these reflections. I imagine it's Giulia. This time I decide I'll tell her with the utmost firmness that I absolutely don't want to talk. I lift the receiver and ask violently: "Who on earth is it?"

A subdued, inarticulate voice gets out: "It's Giulia." So right away I shout: "Listen, Giulia, I've changed my mind. It'd be better if we didn't see each other. Everything really is over between us."

Naturally, with my usual cowardice, having made such a drastic declaration I don't bang down the phone; I wait for an answer. The voice says: "No, it's Giulia, your daughter. Don't you recognize my voice?"

I look at the receiver for a moment, the way you look at the hands of a conjurer at a magic show. The fact that the two Giulias have the same name seems exactly that kind of mischievous, inexplicable trick. Still carried away by my decision to break with the other Giulia, I say: "Oh, it's you! And what do you want?"

My daughter's voice doesn't have the provocative, didactic tone the other Giulia's has; she is affectionate, daughterly, but with a hint of formality and forcedness. "Dad, really, we haven't seen each other for two years and this is how you speak to me! When I left home you went on and on saying, 'We have to talk, us two.' So, Daddy, I've come to talk. Do you mind?"

"No, but I was expecting someone."

"A woman called Giulia, like me! Oh Daddy, really!"

"What's strange about that? Giulia is a very common name."

"A Giulia you can't bear, who you don't want to see any more. Okay then, I'll come instead of her. That way I'll be giving you a good excuse to send her packing. You can tell her: I've got my daughter here, I can't see you now."

"But she'll be arriving any minute."

"I'll get there before she does. I'm down here, in the bar in the square."

"Are you alone?"

"Of course. I'll come up."

I feel so overwhelmed I can't button my collar or do up my tie. So it was me, me of all people: my eighteen-year-old daughter wanted to leave home and I said: "We have to talk, us two," and, stubborn and contemptuous, she replied that she wasn't the least bit interested in hearing what her father had to say. It was me; and now it no longer seems such a coincidence that just a month after my daughter's leaving I should have met the other Giulia, also eighteen and also running away from home.

I throw away my tie, go to the window and look out over the square four floors below. It is a little square in Rome's baroque style, with its *palazzi*, its trattoria, its bar and its shops closed for the Bank Holiday. From up here you can see the deserted cobbles, usually hidden by parked cars. There is just one car in a corner in the shade. Suddenly my daughter appears from the bar and walks diagonally across the square to where a typical youngster, sporting the inevitable beard and long hair, is leaning against the car. My daughter speaks to him and he answers. I withdraw from the window and go down a narrow corridor lined with books to the entrance hall, just in time to hear the lift down on the ground floor starting to come up.

Who will ring the doorbell now? Giulia or Giulia? Giulia, my girlfriend – call her that – who said: "I'll be round in a moment," or Giulia, my daughter, who said: "I'm in the square, I'll come up." Which of them will get here first? And then, who do I want to see arrive at my door?

I hear the lift stopping at my floor. Someone gets out, closes the doors and gives my bell a short, reticent ring.

I go to open the door with the strange hope that it will be a third woman, perhaps my wife who I haven't lived with for years; or a third Giulia, who isn't my daughter and at the same time doesn't consider herself my daughter. Who doesn't have a bearded young man waiting for her down in the street; nor a certain Tullio to take her to the cinema.

I pluck up my courage and open the door. It's Giulia – my girlfriend Giulia – as deep down, I had hoped. She's small, with a big head and tiny body, enormous eyes, capricious mouth, and that indefinable gracefulness short women sometimes have.

Automatically, I say: "I was expecting my daughter."

"Who? Giulia? I saw her just now in the square chatting to some guy. Well, you can tell her you're busy, that she can come back tomorrow. Don't worry, she needs you, she'll come back."

She walks ahead of me down the corridor, swaying lightly, as if pleased with her own gracefulness. She adds: "Anyway, how many daughters do you want to have? Aren't I enough?"

There Was a Basket
Down by the Tiber

❦

Some years ago, upstream from my block, the road which runs along the Tiber collapsed, eroded by the river. They put up barriers, stopped traffic and began work on stabilizing the situation – work which is still going on today. So the road by the river became a quiet place, the only cars coming and going being those of the people who live here. Kids practise with their skates; lovers do their love-making openly; mothers bring their babies out for walks. Of course, it wasn't the collapse of the river bank which opened my eyes to the fact that by now I really am nothing more than a pensioner, but somehow the closing of the road to traffic has taken on a symbolic meaning for me. Yes, my life too has become closed to traffic. To continue the metaphor, I am safe from any accidents here, but at the same time I know for sure that nothing new will ever happen to me.

Inevitably, the very lack of novelty tends to make me attribute novelty value to the most insignificant things. I spend hours looking out of the window. What do I look at? Anything that's even slightly different from what usually goes on there: a dog running and barking; two lovers kissing, leaning against the parapet; a group of lads inspecting a motorbike; a jogger running in a blue tracksuit bunching his fists against his chest. For want of anything better, I watch the leaves of the plane trees changing colour. Nature, now there's something that never stands still, that's always new. The leaves of the big plane trees that stretch away in a line as far as the eye can see along the Tiber, change shape and colour every day. Bright buds, of an almost livid green in spring, become dark green leaves as big as hands with their fingers spread in summer; they grow red in autumn and finally, shrivelled and yellow, they fall to the ground at the beginning of winter. But each colour and each grandeur has its nuances, its many phases. Oh yes, even a plane-tree leaf can be perpetually new, if you know how to look at it.

Today, for the first time for a long time, it seems that something really new is happening. I should explain that beyond the parapet, the river bank is thick with trees that lean their branches down towards the water. Unfortunately, since the parapet is fairly low, the undergrowth here has become a dumping ground for everyone who wants to get rid of any kind of rubbish, especially the bulkier sort. They arrive in small vans, jeeps or cars, throw the stuff over the parapet and drive away. So that between the dark green of the brambles the undergrowth is turning white with piles of rubbish, with the larger objects that haven't been completely broken down sticking out of the piles: ruined armchairs, rusty fridges, gutted mattresses, legless chairs, and various other carcasses of the like. Along the parapet, particularly when the sirocco blows, you can't breathe for the stench. Sometimes, from my pensioner's window, and with nothing to do but look out of that window, I've shouted down: "Pigs!" In reply I get derisive gestures, or maybe the usual warning to "Mind your own business, old man."

Today, though, the thing that deep down and unconsciously I've been waiting for for so long, suddenly happens. A small, green-and-brown estate car turns into the street by the river and stops near the barrier by the parapet. A blonde girl in blue jeans and a red sweater gets out. I watch her carefully. She is small, a little squat, well-built, with very prominent breasts – a wet-nurse's breasts I suddenly think, heaven knows why. Over one arm she carries a big, woven-reed basket like the ones housewives use in country markets. I watch her approach the parapet and climb lightly over it, and as she does so I notice that she has big, powerful thighs. Now she walks carefully on the other side of the parapet, big-breasted and thick-set, her head with its pageboy-cut blonde hair bent forward to scan the ground scattered with refuse and thick with brambles.

I take a pair of binoculars which I always keep to hand and point them at the girl. I watch her pick her way about fifty yards behind the parapet, and then stop in front of two small heaps of refuse. Perched on one of these heaps is an armchair with its legs in the air; on the other, nothing. The girl glances round: it's siesta time, the early afternoon, so the street is completely deserted; there is just one man walking along the pavement with a dog on a lead, but he turns away from her. So the girl makes up her mind and quickly places the basket on the heap with nothing on top of it. Then she climbs lightly over the parapet and runs to her car. Just a few seconds later – the time it takes to start up and get into gear – the car does a U-turn, drives off along the river and disappears.

I have followed all the girl's movements through my binoculars; the last thing I saw of her was her bare back where her sweater rode up as she climbed over the parapet. Now I direct the binoculars towards the heap of refuse again. The basket is still there, on top. I get up quickly, put on my sailor's jacket, press a beret on my head (two things I like to think I look young in), shout to the maid from the passage that I'm going for a walk and slip out of the flat.

Going down in the lift, the suspicion that first arose when I noticed the odd behaviour of the girl with the wet-nurse's breasts crystallizes in my mind. There's a new-born baby in that basket; I'm sure there is. The girl has abandoned it by taking it to a rubbish dump where, all the same, it can't help but be seen fairly soon. In short, she has unloaded the so-called fruits of sin on a heap of refuse, a bit like the way people used to leave babies on the church steps. But this thought prompts another: what should I do if my suspicion proves correct?

Strange to say, it doesn't occur to me that I might hand the baby over to some institution: the first and only idea that comes to mind is that this baby has been put there for me, and that, in my old age, I will have to take it into my home and bring it up. I don't want to be misunderstood here. I'm a widower and I have three children, two boys and a girl. All three are married though, for the moment, without children. What I mean is that I know perfectly well what it means to have a family. It means just that – to have children. How long does a family last? If the children are the rebellious kind, not more than fifteen years; if, on the other hand, they are the more traditional kind, as many as twenty or twenty-five years. Mine were the second type, but they left all the same. So, taking this baby into my home, I would in a certain sense be making a family for myself again, prolonging family life for another fifteen or twenty years. The baby would grow up, would become an adolescent, a man. What kind of man would he become? That's easy: one of the many. A man like all the rest.

I stop on the street by the river to get my bearings, although, in fact, I know perfectly well where I'm going. Then with my hands deep in the pockets of my seaman's jacket and my beret thrust down over my eyes, I take on the street with a brisk, bold pace. Alas, having reached the parapet, I'd like to do what the girl did a moment ago when she went over almost without touching, and with the basket over her arm too. But my leg can't make it and I bang my knee and hurt myself. Then I start to walk, limping and rubbing my knee, across the uneven ground full of litter, tins and rags. There is a sharp smell of decomposition, so strong that I take my handkerchief out of my pocket and bury my nose into it. Meanwhile, in my old head, numbed by I don't know what anxiety, the usual clichés circle like bats. What an idea, abandoning your child in a dump! In the past these kinds of women were called unnatural mothers. Still, it's an ill wind that blows nobody any good; one thing leads to another, etc., etc.

Here's where the girl stopped; here are the two heaps of rubbish, one with the armchair on top, its legs in the air, the other with the basket. How attractive the basket looks – whole and clean with its reeds neatly woven – on top of that filthy heap of rubbish. It seems a symbol of everything alive in comparison with everything dead. And yet, perhaps precisely because the basket is so alive, at the last moment I'm almost afraid to lift the lid and see what's in store for me there. I look round, towards the street: the man with the dog has finished his walk and is coming back now. I'll soon have him on the other side of the parapet. So I make up my mind. I stretch out a hand and lift the lid.

I start with fright: two enormous blue eyes stare at me from the basket, wide open, astonished. Then I see the tiny nose and cute mouth between two chubby cheeks and at last I understand. It's a doll, a very ordinary doll. The girl certainly wasn't more than eighteen years old. Abandoning her doll at the river's edge, she obviously intended to act out some initiation ceremony, or rite of liberation. She wanted to free herself from her girlhood, symbolized by her favourite doll. The delicacy with which she placed the basket on top of the heap of rubbish indicated a surviving, affectionate attachment.

I press my beret on my head and leave without touching the doll. What use have I got for the propitiatory rites of a silly little girl infatuated by her own interior development? Here's the parapet to get over again. This time I take precautions; I press both hands on the top, lift my leg, and in three stages get myself over onto the pavement on the other side. Now the street. Proud and dignified, I cross without hurrying, my hands deep in my jacket pockets.

But in the hallway another novelty awaits me on this afternoon of novelties. A dog comes towards me with its tail between its legs and whines very expressively. It's a medium-size dog with long, variously coloured fur: grey, black, white, brown and red. I try to remember what this colour made up of so many colours is called and finally I have it: roan. Meanwhile, the dog, though still with his tail between his legs, begins to make a bit of a fuss of me, jumping at me and sniffing me. It's obvious: the animal is miserable because he has been abandoned by his old master; but at the same time he is happy because his instinct tells him that he has found a new master. And in fact he's right. "Let's go, come on," I say in a resigned voice, and the dog follows me into the lift.

Of course the dog is very well received at home. The maid discovers a collar round his neck with a big "C" hanging from it made of a whitish metal that looks like silver; and there and then she christens him "Chestnut". Hearing himself called Chestnut, the dog seems finally reassured: he wags his tail and follows me into my study.

I go to sit on my regular chair near the window. The binoculars are there where I left them a short while ago on the windowsill. The dog curls up at my feet and half shuts his eyes as if to sleep. Then I take the binoculars and point them towards the street along the river. The basket is still there, on top of the heap of rubbish – whole, clean, alive.

A Bad Memory Block

CAMO

Has it happened or hasn't it? An ambiguous blank has formed in my head, a blank that could equally well be due to the trauma resulting from what has happened, or to the repression of what is about to happen. And yet the thing in question concerns me directly and immediately: if it didn't happen fifteen minutes ago, it should happen in fifteen minutes' time. But both possibilities prompt the same feeling of near-frenetic impatience which makes it impossible for me to wait for the facts that would supply me with the definitive explanation I need. I can't wait so much as a minute, not only because I must prepare myself to face two very different situations – that is, the one where it has already happened and the other where it hasn't – but also and above all because I absolutely must, as soon as possible, overcome this block which is preventing me from doing something fundamental for myself: taking stock. Right, that's what the problem is, and everybody appreciates the enormous difference between taking stock before the action and taking stock after the action. But how can you take stock when the action is, so to speak, on the tip of your tongue, and can't make up its mind whether to assume the form of the already seen, the already done, the already suffered; or that of the not yet seen, the not yet done, the not yet suffered?

I slip a cigarette into my mouth one-handed, taking it from the pack in the dashboard and then lighting it with the car lighter. Meanwhile, with my bent left arm I continue to tug at the zip of my jacket which has somehow jammed and is still undone, so that the butt of the gun is sticking out and can be seen. It occurs to me that since my memory is blocked, if I want to know whether the thing has already happened or is still to happen, I could look for the answer in the real world, search there for the clues to the already happened, or the not yet happened. For example, the jammed zip. Yesterday it was working, so it must have jammed this morning. But did it jam with everything done, or with everything still to do – as a result of too brusque a tug due to the shock of the already happened, or because of the nervousness of the not yet happened?

I give up with this dilemma because I recognize in it the same indecipherable ambiguity which lies at the origin of my amnesia, and I tell myself I have only one way to check whether the event has already taken place or not: look at the gun, see if it has been fired. The relief with which I welcome this plan tells me that the idea is right. Why on earth didn't such a simple, logical solution occur to me before?

But the relief doesn't last long. Yes, the gun can give me the proof I was so desperately seeking, but it is a proof from outside. It is as if I were to ask the clothes I'm wearing or the shoes on my feet for the proof of my existence. And instead this proof must lie in the certainty that I exist without any need for proofs; in the very fact that I don't go looking for proofs. What is more, the proof of the pistol frightens me because it would confirm this fateful, unbearable disassociation. After the proof I would know for certain that the thing has happened, or hasn't happened; but at the same time I would be faced with another disturbing certainty: that it has happened or has not yet happened to somebody else, given that inside myself I will go on not knowing whether the event has taken place or not.

And yet I must know. I can't wait. It is as though I had dived to the bottom of the sea and my oxygen mask had got something wrong with it and I were suffocating, knowing I had only a few seconds to get back to the surface. Besides, my urgency to know is justified by a traffic jam my car is now stuck in, irremediably, to all appearances, forever. I'm in a big, suburban street I'm unfamiliar with. The cars are at a standstill in four lanes, on both sides, ahead and behind. Right in front of me the view is blocked by the yellow-and-black rectangle of a huge transport van. To the right of the van, way down the street, the traffic lights have already turned green and red three times without the cars moving. There must be an accident, or one of those inexplicable hold-ups that can last for hours. And before the jam unjams I absolutely must, unaided – that is, with my memory alone and not with the clues offered by the real world – find out if the thing has happened or is still to happen.

At this point I remember (my memory works better the further back the events I try to remember are) that some years ago we crossed the Sahara from Tunis to Agadès, and that on a number of occasions we got lost and ended up off the track. So what did we do to find the way again? Following a rule learned from experience, we would go right back to where we'd set out from. We'd start again from there and, in fact, after a more or less long stretch we'd find the exact place where we'd gone off course. Once we had to go back three or four times before discovering where we had gone wrong. We would always get lost in the same way, always at the same point. In the end, though, on the brink of desperation, with the sun going down and the prospect of running out of petrol – in the end we suddenly found the track again. It was behind a bush no taller than a small child, buried for no more than three or four yards. It is easy to lose yourself in the desert.

Now, I'll do the same. I'll go back as far as the point where my memory stopped working, the moment where the blank – I was about to say the desert – begins. But I must hurry to get on with this memory-prompting operation, because the jam in the street could start moving any moment now, and in that case it is quite likely that in a few minutes I shall find out for certain whether the thing has happened or is still to happen. But I won't find out by myself, unaided, but through the collision with reality, something I'd never be able to forgive myself and which would resolve nothing, since my problem is not that of knowing, but of remembering.

So, let's see, at what point during the morning (it's about twelve now) did my memory stop working? With a sudden sense of amazement I discover that I don't remember anything since ...

since the moment I woke up. This means that I only remember waking and nothing more, because before waking there is the blank of the night spent in sleep, and after waking there is the blank of the mental block. But waking, those few or more minutes I spent in the dark this morning before getting up, that I remember perfectly and can describe in every detail. I shall describe it now: through this description, I'm sure, I shall rediscover the thread of my memory; discover, as in the desert, the small bush that hides the track.

So, here goes. I woke at more or less the arranged time, but by myself, before the alarm went off. I turned on the light, looked at my watch and saw that there were five minutes to go. My first impulse was to turn out the light, curl up and go back to sleep. But it was impossible; you can't sleep for just five minutes, so I turned off the light but stayed sitting on the bed, my eyes staring into the dark. I didn't think of anything; or rather, I thought of the colour of the dark. What colour was the dark? The colour of well-toasted coffee? Of black smoke? Of ebony? Of ink? And what consistency did it have; what was it made of? Was it a swarming of black molecules against an imperceptibly luminous background, or a swarming of luminous particles against a uniformly black background?

I remember rejecting these definitions one after the other because I wasn't satisfied with them. But to compensate I felt that the darkness was attracting me, that I was hungry for it the way one is hungry for food after a long fast. I also remember that every now and then I switched on the light, looked at my watch, saw that two minutes had passed, then three, then four, and that after each time-check I turned the light off again to enjoy, if only for a minute, for thirty seconds, that exquisite darkness.

Finally, I turned on the light knowing that this was the last time I'd turn it on and that it was now time to get up. It was right at that moment, right in the split second when I turned on the light, that I ceased to register what I was doing, because from that moment on I don't remember anything at all.

I look at the yellow-and-black rectangle of the back of the transport van. I see that it hasn't moved, but then the traffic light down there beyond the van is red. I've still got a minute – if the cars don't move when the light goes green, maybe two minutes.

A Bad Memory Block

So I return furiously to the reconstruction of when I woke up. My memory turned itself off at precisely the moment the light went on. What does this mean? How could such a thing have happened? Why did it happen to me of all people?

I tell myself that it isn't difficult to imagine what I did. I'm a person of fairly regular habits: I'll have got up, showered, shaved, etc., etc. But, I realize, I don't remember all this; I'm simply reconstructing it on the basis of my memory of other wakings in the past. And yet it is this morning's washing and dressing I must remember, this morning's and no other's. Only if I remember it, will I then be able to remember what happened later: to find, that is, the bush which hides the track.

I make a big effort. I repeat to myself: "So, I turned on the light ... so, I turned on the light ... so, I turned on the light and ..."

Too late. The traffic light is green now, and almost immediately the whole street is on the move. The cars are moving; behind, in front, and on both sides of my own; the yellow-and-black rectangle of the transport van is moving. So, I'll know soon enough if the thing has already happened or if it's still to happen. But I realize with anguish that I won't discover it myself with my memory; it will be objects and circumstances that will reveal it to me.

The Devil Comes and Goes

It is relatively easy to hide; the problem is how to pass the time while you're hidden. In this bolt-hole or bedsit, or whatever you want to call it, I haven't got any records, I haven't got a radio and I haven't got a television – just a newspaper which the woman who lives in the flat below brings me every morning along with the day's shopping. So, I've no alternative but to pass the time thinking about myself, which is exactly what I would rather not do. Unfortunately I don't know how to do anything else, or rather, there's nothing else to do. So, I reflect, calculate, meditate, speculate, analyse and so on and so forth; but, above all, I daydream. It has been raining for some days. The noise that the rain makes – drumming on the little tin roof over the french window outside on the terrace, like a person chattering in a low voice, pausing every now and then to get his breath back – encourages my daydreaming.

I daydream lying on the tattered pallet that serves as both bed and couch; I daydream with my forehead leaning against the glass of the french window, looking at the small terrace boxed in amongst the old roofs with their tiles, chimney stacks, attic windows and belltowers, small and large; and I daydream standing in the black, poky kitchen, waiting for the water to boil for tea. And so I imagine that one day I'll hear the lift stop at my floor – an unusual, even unique event this, since my bedsit is nothing other than the room that leads out to the terrace where nobody goes. And then, perhaps, I'll hear a light, slow, maybe limping step approaching my door.

Next a finger, his finger, will press the doorbell. There will be a short, elusive sound that I'll recognize, and I'll go to open the door, though not without a certain slowness and repugnance: even if invoked and expected, his is not a pleasant visit. The first surprise will be to see him appear in the likeness of a little blondish girl with watery blue eyes, a nose with wrinkled nostrils and a squeamish mouth. She'll be dressed in a puffy, little white fur or fake moufflon coat. I'll be struck by the fact that this fur won't be wet at all, even though it is teeming down outside: which adds up; the devil will make his fur coats, but he isn't such a perfectionist as to make them wet. In her tinkly, pert voice she'll say: "I've come to see you. What are you doing?" I'll answer: "You can see what I'm doing: nothing. What about you? Where have you come from?" She'll make a vague gesture: "I live round here, in the same street. Mummy went out so I took advantage of her being away to come and visit you." I won't say anything; I'll be thinking it's all lies – the mother, the street, the visit – but it fits with the metamorphosis into a little girl. Then I'll ask: "But why are you limping?" "I hurt myself. I fell down the stairs carrying a milk bottle." At this point she'll take off her fur coat, saying: "It's really hot in here. Do you always keep the heating on?" And I'll see she's wearing a tiny blouse and a very short little skirt: the rest is all legs; strong, long, muscular woman's legs. On her breast she'll have a curious pendant, a claw cased in gold. It could be a lion's claw, the kind you see everywhere in Africa. But lions have light-coloured claws, whereas this one is black.

While I'm watching her, the girl will wander round the bedsit asking lots of questions about this or that object, in the way children do. What's this? What's this for? Why've you got this? Who gave you this? And so on and so forth. They will be the most everyday objects, but I'll be on my guard because I'll be thinking that very soon she'll go from the insignificant objects to the significant ones. And indeed, suddenly she'll open a drawer in the bedside table and her little hand will reach inside to grip the butt of the gun. "And what's this for?" "For defending yourself." "What

do you mean?" "For defending yourself, by shooting." "Shooting?"
"Yes, see these holes? In every hole there's a bullet. When you press
the trigger the bullet comes out of the barrel at a terrific speed and
goes and smashes into something – the cupboard, for example –
and it makes quite a hole because it has a very high impact
velocity." "And if instead of the cupboard there's a woman, or a
man or a child, what happens then?" "Somebody will get hurt. Or
die." "But have you ever shot at anybody?" I'll be silent for a
moment, telling myself that by now the mask has been thrown
aside and the interrogation is taking the course I'd foreseen. Then
I'll say: "Yes, to defend myself. Only once, though." And jumping
immediately to the most extreme conclusion, she'll say: "So, they're
dead. Who was it, a girl like me?" "No, it was a man." "A bad
man?" "Who knows, I didn't know him." "You shot him because
you didn't know him, then?" "If you like." "And the second man,
why did you shoot him?" "No, no second man, there wasn't any
second man." "Didn't you have the courage to shoot the second
man?" "What are you talking about? I'm telling you: there wasn't
and never will be a second man."

She won't say anything: she'll skip about the room for a while
more, then go to sit at the little table in front of the typewriter and
say: "What's this?" "You can see what it is – a typewriter." "And
what do you write with it?" "My homework." "Let me write
something too." "Write away." She'll sit at the table and slowly,
painstakingly, banging the keys with just one finger, she'll write
something on the piece of paper. I'll go to look over her bowed
head; I'll see the following phrase appear: "You don't have the
courage!" She'll finish writing, then get down from the chair and
start skipping around the room repeating like a chant: "You don't
have the courage, you don't have the courage!" I'll say: "If you
don't stop it, I'll send you packing." But still skipping she'll go on:
"You don't have the courage, you don't have the courage!"

So then I'll go to the french window and lean my forehead
against the glass. I'll see the terrace boxed in between the other
terraces, some lower, some higher, and right opposite me, in the
low, grey light of the rain, an elaborate baroque belltower. Just
under the bell housing, I'll make out a broad slab of travertine
which – I don't know why – I'll never have noticed before. Then,
sculpted in large, ancient letters in the pitted, yellow stone, all shiny

with rain, I'll read: *Errare humanum est, perseverare dia-
bolicum.* Under this maxim, I'll make out some other words in
Latin, the date, the place, the name of the person who laid the
stone.

At that moment I'll hear the voice of the little girl behind me
saying: "I'm going back to Mummy now. She'll be worried about
me by this time, not finding me home." Automatically, without
turning, I'll say: "Oh, go to hell!" Immediately, I'll hear his voice,
his real voice, answer calmly: "I will, don't worry, but with
you." Still without turning, I'll exclaim: "Finally, you've revealed
yourself! A little girl, eh! And what will this hell be like, pray? Fire,
gnashing of teeth, the stench of roasted flesh?" "The repetition of
what you already know." "But who says I'll repeat it in the first
place; and then who says that in my case repeating will amount to
infernal torment?" "On the contrary, there won't be any torment.
You'll be fine, happy even, within the limits of common humanity."
"So why do you say it'll be hell then?"

"Hell isn't suffering more; it's repeating what's already been
done, and through that repetition . . ." "Remaining oneself?" "No,
not at all, becoming another." "Another? I don't understand." "It's
simple: you make a mistake, you recognize you've made it, you
are always yourself. You don't recognize it, rather, you commit
another, identical error, you are another." "Another in what
way?" "Without even the memory of the person you were before
repeating the mistake." "Ah, so that's why you were chanting,
'You don't have the courage, you don't have the courage!' a few
minutes ago."

"Finally, you've understood." "What did you mean, though?"
"I meant that you invoked me, you proposed to sell me you know
what, if in exchange I would let you start life again at the precise
point when what happened, happened. I've come and I'm telling
you: I can do what you want, but only in one way – by having you
become another through repetition." "But first you'd have to find
convincing reasons to make me repeat." "Don't worry about that.
I'm a master at finding reasons." "Repetition. A moment ago I
looked out of the window and for the first time I saw that stone
there. Which says just that; that to repeat is diabolic." "Right, no
need of something in Latin to appreciate that. A moment's reflection
would have been enough." "Imagine that I repeat. Wouldn't I be

able to recognize for the second time that I've made a mistake?"
"Oh, no. No, too easy. What would I be left with? A piece of paper?"
"I don't like this pact. Leave if you want. We'll talk about it
another time." "You invoked me, saying you couldn't cope with
being who you are any more; you said you were ready to be
someone else, anyone else. And now you tell me we'll talk about it
again!" "I want to be another, yes, but with the memory of having
been who I am." "I can't do things like that. Apart from anything
else, what would I get out of it?" "So, I'll say it again, go away."
"I'll be back. See you soon."

At this point there'll be a brief silence. Then the little girl's voice
will say: "It's late. I'm going home to Mummy. 'Bye." I'll turn and
the little girl, already bundled up in her fake moufflon coat, will
come and throw her arms round my neck and kiss me on both
cheeks. I won't return the kisses; I'll open the door for her and
watch her as she goes off down the landing. Once again I'll notice
that she has a limp.

I have this daydream every day and with repeating it, I develop
it, make it richer. Now, for example, while I'm boiling a couple of
eggs on the burner, I imagine that instead of the little girl, it is the
student on the first floor who rings my bell, a beautiful, pale, young
woman with green eyes. She'll come with any old pretext; we'll
chat; she'll say yes, and it'll end in the foreseen and foreseeable
fashion. Then right at the moment of maximum abandon, I'll see
that she has the pendant with the black claw hanging on her
breast. And as, completely naked, she goes from the bed to the
window and, looking out, exclaims: "What a lovely terrace you
have, what a lot of nice flowers, what a nice belltower!", I'll notice
that she has a slight limp. Limping, she'll wander round the room,
the way women do sometimes in a new man's house, and then
she'll open the drawer . . .

What Use Have I Got
for Carnival?

❧

Carnival! What use have I got for carnival? Carnival, at my age, in my position!

In the dark, trying to get to sleep and not managing it, I'm haunted by a memory: that of the young girl I see every morning (she's on her way to school, I, to pick up the papers), who has a dejected, repressed, fearful look about her. She's a very ordinary young girl, blonde with long straight hair, eyes a clear blue, and a pale face. Well, today, after breakfast, taking my regular constitutional along the Zattere, I found her completely transformed – not just in her physical appearance but in her behaviour too – and I realized that this transformation was entirely due to the carnival: to the fact, that is, that she was masked. She was dressed up as Harlequin, all multi-coloured diamond shapes with white tights and little black shoes.

When she saw me, she flashed me a smile of innocently provocative recognition, threw a cloud of confetti over me, then ran off with a stifled laugh into a nearby backstreet. My mind goes over and over this meeting and I ask myself what happened to turn such a sad, shy young girl into a happy, cheeky one. At last I conclude that the carnival had been at work. The dejected face she usually carried about was really only a mask, whereas the Harlequin mask was her real face.

Someone turns on the light on my bedside table. I see a Negro woman with enormous lips bend down towards me, her eyes big as two fried eggs. "What are you doing already in bed at this hour? Everybody's off out in the street; everybody's dressing up and you go to bed at ten o'clock. Come on, get up, get dressed! I've bought you a mask. Isn't it terrific? Look! Enough, I'm off, I'm going to the square. See you there. 'Bye." It's my wife, a fairly serious woman, a school headmistress, who has gone to the opposite extreme and dressed herself up as a savage; or rather, thanks to the carnival, she has discovered she is a savage. I tell her she looks good and that we'll meet in the square. The Negro woman disappears with a flounce of plastic banana leaves.

I get up and sit on the bed, take a look at the outfit my wife has bought me, and am horror-struck: it is a mask of the devil with an obscene, fiery red mouth, a goat's beard, black cheeks, a frowning forehead and horns. Automatically I take it, fit it on my face, get off the bed and go to look at myself in the mirror.

Later, I go out, one hand pressing the mask on my face while under my jacket the other fingers the handle of a knife which, just as I was leaving – I've no idea why, perhaps prompted by the mask – I couldn't help taking from the kitchen drawer. There is a bit of fog; the night echoes with the wail of a siren. I turn. Far away, taller than the houses of distant Giudecca, I see a huge, white, transatlantic liner glide quickly by with all its lights on. I'm in a bad mood. I have the impression my wife has bullied me, both in forcing me to dress up and then by buying me this of all masks. And yet, and yet . . . something tells me that, as with the shy young girl, the carnival is at work, and will go on working.

Here is the landing stage on the Grand Canal. A *vaporetto* arrives just as I do and I see that it's jam-packed with people, most of them wearing masks. The *vaporetto* comes alongside the landing stage. I'm the last one on, and I find myself crushed against the rail. Behind me is a crowd of faces of all kinds: lunatics, Chinamen, blockhead peasants, redskins, old drunkards, and so on. I grip the rail with both hands, turn my devil's face to the Grand Canal and reflect, as usual, that at night this famous waterway of ours is truly sinister, with all the buildings dead and dark and the dusky water glimmering faintly with oily reflections. Then suddenly I change my mind. We pass a tall, narrow building I don't ever remember noticing before with all its windows lit and the black irregular profiles of strange figures, clearly masked, standing out against the light. These figures wave their arms, laugh, threaten, move. The *vaporetto* glides by; the building disappears in the dark. I'm left with the disturbing impression of having made a mistake, had a hallucination.

But here comes another reason for unease. Someone, a woman, squeezes up against me, presses her breasts against my shoulders, then her belly against my buttocks. True, the boat is very crowded, but the woman – no doubt about it – is doing it on purpose. Naturally, the devil whose likeness I have on my face wakes up at this intimate contact, thinks thoughts best gloated over in silence, makes crazy plans, arouses unreal hopes. I try to cope with the situation by pressing myself as close as possible to the rail and concentrating my attention on the familiar gloom of the Grand Canal. Except that a sweet little voice whispers in my ear: "Dirty Devil, why do you tempt me?" At which, flaring up, I whirl round.

It is Death, or rather, a woman who for some reason has dressed herself up as Death. Probably it is a very young girl, as the non-disguised parts of her body suggest: slim but rounded hips; a slight outward curve of the abdomen and long, attractive legs – all encased in a pair of very tight blue jeans. From the waist up, this girl with the soft breasts and muscular stomach is masked as Death. Despite the cold she's wearing a black cotton mantle on which the upper part of a skeleton has been roughly chalked with ribs and breastbone prominent. The mantle is held at the neck, which is really beautiful, round and strong, a little flared at the base, like the necks of some peasant women in the mountains. This neck supports a small, snarling skull, which, again, is chalked on to a background of black cardboard.

Would you believe it? The devil isn't at all frightened by this funereal apparition, and rightly so, because, as everyone knows, death and the devil go arm in arm. Tough and sprightly as anything, the devil replies: "What do you want, Death?" At once the sweet little voice says: "I'm Death and I want you." "Oh, you do, do you? Then we're getting on fine, because I'm Life and I, in turn, want you." "You, Life? But aren't you the devil?" "Right, don't you know that the devil is Life?" "I imagine Life differently." "How do you imagine him?" "Differently. With the face of a handsome young boy perhaps." "Rubbish! Think about it. You'll agree I'm right." "Goodbye, Devil, see you in the square. 'Bye now." She pulls away from me, mingles with a group of masks and gets off at the landing stage at St Mark's. Without hesitating, adjusting the mask on my face and gripping the knife under my jacket tighter than ever, I rush after her.

There is an enormous crowd of people in the narrow streets, eighty per cent of them masked. While I'm following Death who, being very tall, shows her small, wobbly, snarling head above the level of the crowd, the devil suggests a whole course of action which, out of duty as his host, I'm obliged to listen to. So: "You follow Death until you're under the arcade to the left of the square. At a certain point there's a passage under a portico. Find a way to make her change course, make her cross the bridge and draw her into the building site where there's a house being renovated a bit further on. In the site, in a dark corner, get out your knife, point it against her belly and tell her you know what. The rest will follow by itself." A magnificent plan, with just one small problem: I absolutely don't want to know. I say: "Nice, very nice, but quite out of the question." "Out of the question, eh!" he says, sardonic: "For the moment though, you're already doing what I want. Otherwise why, for example, would you be slipping your hand under her arm now and telling her: 'Beautiful, isn't it?'"

He's right. With the pretext of marvelling at St Mark's Square transformed by the carnival, I've slipped my arm under Death's. But the square really is stunning. The façades of the palaces are lit as bright as day with all those rows of windows making them look like galleries in the theatre. The basilica shines with gold trimmings, its cupolas like so many tiaras of fantastic oriental queens. The belltower rises, straight and pink, like a colossal brick phallus. In the vast rectangle of the square, a boisterous, merry crowd seems to be suffering from a collective epileptic fit. Everybody is jumping, dancing, chasing each other, gathering, dispersing. Everyone is shouting, singing, calling, answering. There must be a Turkish drum somewhere, big as an enormous barrel, because at intervals you can hear its dark, regular boom. Above the crowd, like snowflakes swept away in a gale, fly musical notes of every kind. I grip Death's arm and whisper to her: "Death, what do you say? Isn't it marvellous?" "I say, let go of my arm, dirty Devil." "What about going down there, round by the Merceria? There's a little building site where we could easily be alone, away from this crowd." "Be alone, why?" "No reason, to get to know each other, to talk."

She doesn't say yes or no, she seems tempted and at the same time scared. Her hand tries to prise mine off her arm, but she doesn't put much effort into it and soon gives up. I persist: "So, let's go, come on." And I start to move off, when something unexpected happens. A group of masks suddenly surrounds us, links hands, forms a circle and begins to dance frenetically round and round. Despite their whirling speed, they sing some dirty song, and every so often come right up under my nose sticking out their tongues and making faces at me. I hug myself tightly to Death, but she pushes me away. Then, when the circle of dancers slows for a moment, she breaks the chain of linked hands, wriggles out and disappears in the crowd. Mad with anger, I hurl myself against the circle, but it is another minute before those lunatics let me through.

I start to run, progressing by shoves. Suddenly I see Death in the arcade, apparently heading right for the place I told her about. Delighted, I make a dash, then stop dead: under the black mantle I make out a pair of men's trousers, brown with a turn-up. So I turn back, and there's Death again: it's a woman, but not her; this one's got boots. Another rush through the crowd. I see my third Death at the entrance to the Merceria – a dwarf woman. What an idea, dressing up as Death when you're so small! But there's the fourth Death now on the Schiavoni bank: a drunken Death, tottering and stumbling with blue sailor's trousers sticking out under the mantle. Then the fifth Death appears as I turn the corner of the Doge's Palace – a short, stout Death, holding the hand of a little boy dressed up as a cowboy from the Wild West.

I give up, set off under the arcade and am passing the doors of the Florian when – surprise, surprise! – who should show up, but the girl dressed up as Harlequin. She is standing near the door. Beside her there is another girl dressed up as an eighteenth-century cavalier with a three-cornered hat, wig, black velvet suit, white tights and shiny shoes. A friend of hers, no doubt. I stop and with a cavernous voice say: "Harlequin, I recognize you, you know."

And she, innocently: "I recognize you, too." "And who am I?" "You're the man I see every morning going to school." I'm speechless. How did she manage to recognize me under the mask? I throw a handful of confetti over her, then cross the square, reach the passage under the portico, cross the bridge and push on in the dark inside the building site.

Here is a wooden barrel full of water. I throw in the mask and then watch for a moment. It floats on the water: the light of a street-lamp makes the mouth glow red, lights up a reflection on the lacquer of the cheeks. I throw the knife in the water too, and leave.

That Damned Gun

What to do? After two or three hours of furious insomnia, I get out
of bed in the dark, grope my way to the chest of drawers, take the
gun, then open the door and go through to the sitting room. Here
again it is pitch dark; it must be three o'clock, the darkest hour. I
turn on the lamp near the fireplace; I've got a bit of a headache
from the wine I drank, but my mind is lucid, too lucid! Mechanically,
I let myself drop, just as I am, barefoot in pyjamas, into the armchair
near the black, nocturnal mirror of the big window. I hold the gun
tight in my fist, my finger on the trigger, a gesture expressive of a
whole relationship between me and this object I half-love, half-
hate. Right, because in the end, either the gun will destroy me, or
I will destroy it . . .

But let's go back. No one, except Dirce, who at the moment is
fast asleep back in the bedroom – no one but she knows of the
existence of this gun, a nine-calibre job made by an American
company with the serial numbers filed away and a supply of twenty
bullets, five of which are in the cylinder, one in the barrel. No one
knows, but unfortunately Dirce knows that no one knows; and,
ever since the day I began to feel I'd had enough of her and to talk
about splitting up, from that very day on, she – there can be no
doubt about this – has been blackmailing me. It's a hypocritical

blackmail of course, disguised as concern. Like this for example: "You do know that for having that gun with the serial numbers filed, the one your nice-guy friend left you, they could put you away just like that?" Oh yes, because I should have told you that to justify the gun to her, I invented the story of a friend in trouble who wants me to keep the thing for him. Actually it was me and only me who got myself into this mess. God only knows why. Having a gun had become an obsession, so I bought one on the black market, and now here I am with an illegal, super-illegal, gun that will mean a minimum of three years' prison if they find it.

Dirce knows this and doesn't think twice about reminding me of it with a jokey threat in her voice: "You're in my hands with that gun. If you don't toe the line, I'll go to the police." Or, more ominously: "Did you see in the paper? They arrested a guy for keeping a simple air gun. I hate to think what they'd do to you: yours is a weapon of war, no less." Or again, magnanimous: "Don't worry, I'm silent as the grave. I don't even speak in my sleep." Until one day, after a very violent argument at the end of which we almost came to blows, she warned me openly: "If I were you, I wouldn't talk so much about splitting up. Be careful, very careful. I know a lot of things about you." "The gun, eh? Always the gun!" "The gun and more."

At this point I can hear someone exclaiming: "If this gun is so compromising, then why not dump it in a safe place, in the river, down a drain, into the sewer, wherever?" And I reply: "For one thing, I've got to like it, it's a very beautiful piece of equipment, it cost me a load of money. And then, I should have thrown it away before Dirce got to know I had it." Unfortunately, damned fool that I am, the first thing I did when she came to live with me, out of vanity and exhibitionism, was to show her it, brag about its fire power, dismantle and reassemble it under her nose. I can't even deny having boasted that I had good reasons for keeping an illegal weapon in the house. The fact is that I did everything, but really everything, to justify that threatening remark – "The gun and more." Now, after what happened at the party at Alessandro's place, I begin to understand what that dark and ominous "more" might be.

Right, Alessandro! Let's talk about Alessandro. And first of all about Alessandro's nose. Yes, because the impression of treacherous, sinister ambiguity this mystery man inspires in me, stems entirely from his nose. What is Alessandro's nose like? It's a nose that's not right; a nose that if looked at face on seems hooked, with wide nostrils and the tip pointing down, and if looked at in profile seems straight with narrow nostrils and the tip turned up. The nose, in a word, of a double, triple, or even quadruple personality. A secret-service nose, a spy's nose. In short, a nose which is all plan; but what that plan might be, God only knows. Or rather, I don't know, but Dirce, it seems to me, gives various signs of being perfectly well informed of what it is. Otherwise, why would she, during one of our usual quarrels, have casually thrown in: "You know Alessandro, the one who's always inviting us? Well, I reckon he'd give anything to know about your gun." "Why's that?" "Obvious: to tell the police, or to blackmail you into doing what he wants." "But what does he want?" "As I see it, the first thing he wants is me. But other things too." "What things?" "Other things."

But we'll let that pass. Instead, let's examine yesterday evening in some detail. I'll do it as if I were working on a film-editing machine (that's my job, film editor); I'll stop the film of my memory every so often on a frame – that is, on a particularly significant moment. Here's the first frame. Dirce and I are in the car outside Alessandro's gate. Without getting out, I say: "But come on, let's hear the truth: does Alessandro invite us because he's in love with you, or because he wants to become a close friend of ours so as to spy on me more easily?"

"The way I see it, both."

"But who *is* Alessandro in the end?"

"Who knows? A bit of a strange character, that's for sure."

"You see, even you think so. What does he live on, for starters?"

"Import-export, he says."

"Right, the usual so-called business deals. Everything about him arouses suspicion. For example, the way he dresses, so grey and bureaucratic. You feel that one day he could chuck away the grey stuff and appear in military uniform with all kinds of stripes."

"Right, I hadn't thought of that, it's true."

"So what do you advise me? For example, what should I do with the gun?"

"You want us to split up. Yesterday you even took me by the arm and literally threw me out of the flat, in my nightdress, on the

landing. So, tough luck, you're not getting any advice from me. All
I'm saying is: watch out."

"Watch out for whom?"

"First of all, watch out for me."

Nice, eh! But we won't dwell on it, our film of the evening runs
fast on the memory's editing machine. Here's another frame. There
are about twenty of us in Alessandro's sitting room. Sitting room!
Let's say, rather, permanent exhibition of oriental-style cushions –
cushions you crouch on, one against another, one on top of another,
as best you can. In parenthesis, how can you chat on the floor, eat
on the floor, in short, live on the floor? Obviously, the underlying
implication behind all these casual, super-soft cushions is the most
brazen and at the same time the most hypocritical promiscuity . . .

And now, as with one hand I hold my plate of pasta and with
the other grip my fork – all the time trying not to lose my balance
or knock over the full glass of wine I've wedged in my cushion – I
can't help looking at Dirce, directly opposite, crouched like me on
a cushion with her shoulders against the wall. Needless to say, the
master of the house, the ineffable Alessandro, is crouched next to
her, and, for all my eyes are pretty sharp, I can't make out where
he's got his hands. Naturally they have already eaten, or more
likely, they aren't going to eat, they have something better to
do. They're going to chat, laugh, communicate. How do they
communicate? Soon said: Dirce sits with her legs crossed and every
now and then pretends to totter and falls on Alessandro, who, in
turn, leans with his hand *behind* Dirce and, while talking to her,
brushes her ear with his lips . . .

Of course, as soon as I feel threatened by a rival, this girlfriend I
run down so much, who I've been planning to drop almost from
the first day of our relationship, this far from beautiful, even ugly
Dirce, as if by a miracle, starts to attract me again.

Let's press on. Here's another frame. Oh dear, very disturbing.
I've got up with difficulty from my cushion now and, glass in hand,
I head straight for Alessandro and Dirce. I stop, standing in front
of them, and raise my glass in a sarcastic toast: "Your health! What
a lovely couple you make! You look really good together." "Don't
we?" Dirce comes back bitchily: "And to think we've known each
other so long and didn't realize . . ."

Another frame. I'm drunk, or rather, I'm pretending to be. I've got a bottle in one hand and a glass in the other. Walking unsteadily, I go out in search of Dirce and Alessandro who, naturally, have disappeared. In the sitting room the little party continues. We've got to the rite of the joint now, the stub that everybody passes around with compunction having taken a drag themselves. With an exaggeratedly uncertain step I wander round the house. First of all I look in the bedroom, all in Turkish or Arabic style, in a word, oriental. A very low bed, rumpled, loaded with guests' coats, then bric-à-brac, shawls, beads, coloured prints, daggers, the inevitable cushions and – what do you know, look what's here – in a box of Turkish Delight that I open because I like sweets, a gun. A very small gun, though, a lady's kind, with a mother-of-pearl butt; in comparison with mine it's a toy, a trifle, a joke. Who does Alessandro think he's frightening with a gun like that?

From the bedroom I move to the study. Surprise: nothing oriental here; the furniture is Swedish in style, austere, bare, simple. By the way, what does Alessandro study? There aren't any books, just the telephone. I smell a rat. Here's the bathroom, very small, full of towels, dressing gowns, toiletries, with nude women from sexy mags pinned on the walls over the bath opposite the toilet.

Where else is there to go to find the two unfindables? I walk to the end of a little corridor and out through a french window into the garden. It is tiny, choked with trees, plants, climbers and weeds; damp, dark, full of uncertain glimmers, weird shadows. There they are, over there, in an unequivocal position: holding each other tight, her hands on his shoulders, his hands who knows where? They separate as if scalded. I take aim and throw my glass at Alessandro's head . . .

Penultimate frame. Back at home, Dirce and I have an extremely violent argument, at the bottom of which, rather than their embrace in the garden, is, as always, the question of the gun. I have some very hard words to say about her shameless behaviour. And she, sitting on the bed, merely repeats: "Watch how you talk!" She says it once, twice, three times, with such a threatening voice that in the end I can't help bursting out: "You mean the gun, eh!" "Yes, but not just the gun." "I haven't got anything to hide." "If you haven't got anything to hide, then why file off the serial numbers? Why not ask for a gun licence?"

I don't know what to say, so I attack her: "Spy, snoop, informer, bitch!" She's unruffled. Calmly, she says: "Alessandro has a gun too, but he went and got a regular licence for it." Overwhelmed with hate, I scream: "He has a ludicrous little-girl's gun. You're not going to compare that with mine?" "Yes, but yours is illegal and his isn't." "So?" "So, you have to legalize your position, that's all." Wearily, I say: "Enough, let's go to sleep now." She doesn't wait to hear it twice; strangely docile, she gets up, does her usual strip-show, like every evening, gets into bed without a word, turns her back to me and, so it seems, drops off to sleep immediately. I, on the other hand, after getting into bed next to her and turning off the lamp, don't go to sleep and don't even try. I lie on my back, hands behind my head, and spend three hours weighing up the pros and cons of the situation ...

Last frame, the one I'm in now: I'm sitting on the armchair in my pyjamas, the gun in my fist, in front of the window in the sitting room. While I've been thinking the room has grown less dark, the dirty pallor of the city dawn already blending with the black of night. Suddenly I make up my mind, get up from the armchair and go back to the warm, intimate darkness of the bedroom. I grope my way to the dresser, open the drawer and put the gun back in its usual place. Then I get under the bedclothes again, put my arms round Dirce and draw her towards me.

In the dark, I feel her pull back with a stifled cry, pushing her hands against my chest. At which I whisper: "Do you want to marry me?" A moment passes, to me it seems like an hour; then with characteristic lack of trust, I hear her whisper: "What's got into you?" "Nothing's got into me. I want to marry you." She's silent a moment longer, then with remarkable penetration says: "For me, I'm happy. Nothing I'd like better. Although, really, nothing will change, will it? It's different for you; obviously you've thought it over and seen that it's worth your while: nothing wrong with that, of course." Then, more tenderly: "Well, hello, hubby sweetie. But, for the moment, why don't you take that damned gun and go and chuck it in the fountain in the park over the road? Go, come back, and then we'll have a nice sleep, like a real husband and wife."

I've Stuttered All My Life

I leave the house looking right and left to see if he is there. I live in a private road, or rather, a dead end, lined by the gardens of not more than three or four villas. I see there are only a couple of cars parked along the pavement and that they are luxury cars, just as the whole area is a luxury area. He, on the other hand, uses a small economy car to tail me: although it is good camouflage in city traffic, here, in this millionaires' drive, it would be as conspicuous as a millionaire's car in a poor area.

So he's not here. I get in my car with a painful sense of frustration. What can I do now, without him, in this empty hour of the early afternoon? The fact is that I only came out for him. I wanted to confront him. Force him to give me an explanation.

But wait: as I take a left turn at random, adjusting my rearview mirror at the same time, I see his car following me. It is so anonymous that, paradoxically, I could distinguish it among thousands. I look again: through the rear windscreen I can see his face, likewise completely anonymous. But first of all we must be clear about what is and isn't anonymous. Someone might think, I don't know, of a civil servant or office worker, correctly dressed, without colour. No, these days anonymous doesn't mean the office worker; if anything it means the man without work. That's how he is anonymous. Bearded, moustached, long-haired, with a loud red-and-black-checked jacket and blue jeans for trousers, he is truly anonymous; there are thousands like him in the city. He is the new anonymous man, colourful, noisy, flashy. He could be a good man, a murderer, an intellectual, anybody. To me, he is simply *him*, someone who has been following me for a week, who tails me wherever I go at whatever time of day.

Driving slowly to let him keep up, I go back once again over his possible reasons for following me. In the end, these reasons boil down to just one: I am the only son of a very rich man and, as a result, I am probably much hated. So, that gives us just two hypotheses as to the purpose behind the tailing: there is what I shall call the realistic hypothesis, and then there is the symbolic hypothesis. The first hypothesis, obviously, would entail a kidnap with the intention of making my father pay a more or less huge ransom; the second, less obviously, would entail murder, in so far as I would be seen as a symbol of a certain situation. In other words, the idea would be to strike, through me, a blow at the society of which, despite myself, I form a part.

Now I feel, and am, completely foreign to all this. To such an extent that I chose not to go to the police because, in a certain sense, informing them would be equivalent to getting involved. So, no police. I want to confront the man tailing me and show him that he's following the wrong man and that he can't get anything out of me, money or revenge.

Meanwhile, I keep driving and every now and then I raise my eyes to the mirror to see if he's following. Yes, he is. Two problems present themselves now. The first can be solved: it's a question of the car; if I want to confront him I'll have to park it and continue on foot. But the second problem is almost insurmountable: my stutter. My stutter is severe in the extreme: I rarely manage to get beyond the first syllable of a sentence. I stammer and stutter and usually the sentence is completed by the discerning and pitying listener. Then I nod my approval enthusiastically. I haven't spoken, but I've been understood all the same.

But with him this method won't work. I can't really expect my murderer to finish my sentences for me. It's true that he did do just that this morning, but the circumstances were such as to make me fear the worst. Judge for yourselves. I went into a travel agency to book a flight to London where I'm going to continue my studies in physics. Since I couldn't do anything but repeat, "The f,f,f,f ... the f,f,f ... the f,f,f ...," he, who in the meantime had come to stand beside me at the desk, finished it for me with sinister generosity: "The gentleman means the fourth. I'd like to book a seat for the same day myself." I left the agency feeling pretty shaken. Time was running out now, not just for me, but most of all for him. I absolutely must force him to give me an explanation before my departure.

I enter the underground garage where I shall park the car. I drive slowly in the immense, shadowy space packed with cars parked herringbone fashion between the giant pillars. I see that he has come into the garage behind me and is following me at a distance. I spot two empty spaces, turn sharply and slot the car into the row. He turns too, and comes to park in the empty space next to mine. For a moment I think of getting my explanation in the garage. But the emptiness, the silence, the murkiness of the place dissuade me: it would be the ideal place to do somebody in and leave as if nothing had happened. Anyway, he doesn't seem interested in the garage. He gets out, closes the door, walks quickly ahead of me between the cars and disappears. The tailing is over perhaps? But riding the escalator that goes from the underground park to the surface, I'm forced to think again. As I lower my eyes, I see him letting himself be taken up, apparently totally absorbed in a thoughtful smoke.

Via Veneto. I start to go down the street with the air of a foreigner who, having eaten a big meal alone, sidles along Rome's most famous pavement with the intention of picking up, or rather, having himself picked up by an available tart. Obviously I don't have any such inclination. But the idea of behaving as if I were looking for a woman appeals to me because, to my eye, it confirms what I've already mentioned, my total estrangement from the system which lies at the source of my present persecution.

Suddenly I spot the woman I'm pretending to be after, there, in front of me, walking a few paces ahead. She is young, but with something tired about her face and body, something despondent and subtly impure. She is blonde and the colour of her hair seems to be picked up in her face and neck, both tanned by recent trips to the beach, and then again her dress, a kind of tunic made in a washed-out, dead-leaf yellow. She walks with more than an average swing to her hips, but even this professional invitation seems to be

performed with weariness and despondency. Then, with the kind
of move you'd expect, she stops in front of a shop window, and tries
to catch my eye. At which moment I glimpse my bearded shadow
pausing with the air of a connoisseur in front of a display of English
paperbacks in a newsagent's kiosk. And I have an idea, the idea of
a stutterer who, finding it impossible to communicate by word,
resorts to figurative, metaphorical language. I shall stop the woman
and use her as a symbol to send a message to the enemy organization
that wants to have me kidnapped or killed.

No sooner said than done. I approach her and say: "Are you
free? Can we go somewhere together?"

A miracle! Everything happened so naturally I didn't realize that
for the first time in my life I wasn't stuttering. Perhaps the tension
inevitable in such an unusual, menacing situation, has brushed
aside my stutter. I spoke! I spoke! I spoke! I experience a feeling of
deep, boundless joy and at the same time a sense of immense
gratitude towards the woman: as though I'd been looking for her
all my life and finally found her, right here, on the Via Veneto.

Beside myself, I scarcely hear the woman answer: "Let's go to
my place. It's not far." I take her arm and she squeezes it against
my hand in a gesture of complicity. We walk, with me in a daze,
for about ten minutes, until we arrive in a deserted little street lined
with modest old houses. As we go into the hall, I glance over my
shoulder and see that he has stayed outside to wait for me, leaning
against a lamp-post. We climb up two floors; the woman takes a
key from her bag, shows me into a dark porch and then takes me
through to a small sitting room full of light. I go to the window,
which is open, and see that he is still down there, in the street,
blatantly watching me.

The woman is at my side now. She says: "Let's close the window,
no?" Then, in just a couple of words, I explain what I want her to
do: "You see that young guy there, on the pavement opposite? He's
a friend of mine, terribly shy with women. So, I'd like you to arouse
him, make him lose his shyness. All I'm asking you to do is show
yourself at the window, just for a moment, naked, but completely
naked. For that moment you'll be the symbol of everything he
knows nothing about."

The woman accepts immediately: "If that's all you want." With
a magnificent gesture, as if raising the curtain on an exceptional,

unique spectacle, she bends, takes the hem of her dress in her hands and lifts it as far as her breasts. I'm surprised to see that she's got nothing on underneath; almost, you might say, as if she'd planned for this. Naked from her feet to her breasts – her small, curved belly, past its prime, pushed pertly out – she goes to the window and presses her crotch to the glass for a moment. I watch all this from the other end of the room, my eyes fixed on her thin, sun-tanned back. Then the woman carefully lowers her dress again and says: "There. Done. This time it looks as though your friend has got over his shyness. He made a sign to say he's coming up."

At these words there is a silent explosion inside my head. I see myself in front of the shop window again; I remember catching a glimpse of a strange exchange of glances between the woman and the man tailing me. I want to shout: "But you know that man; you're in it with him; you lured me into a trap."

Alas, none of this comes out of my mouth. I just stutter: "You, you, you, you ...", and point my finger at the woman. Without altering her tired, disappointed look, she agrees: "Yes, I,I,I ... But your friend's here now; there, he's knocking at the door. You stay here while I go and let him in." She pushes me towards a couch and walks out quickly. Immediately afterwards I hear the key turn in the lock.

So I go to the window and wonder if maybe the thing to do would be to jump down into the street, even at the risk of killing myself. Yet I reflect that I don't want to save myself, but to explain myself, have myself understood, communicate. The soft, indirect light from the overcast sky dazzles me. I stand still, enchanted, in a dream. I'm involved in life so deeply that in a few moments perhaps I'll be kidnapped and killed, and at the same time I'm outside it, completely alien. Will they understand that? Will I succeed in explaining it? Meanwhile, behind me, the door is opening.

In My Dream I Always Hear
a Step on the Stairs

Like many people, I'm in the habit of taking a nap after lunch. Since I eat and drink a lot, I get to sleep easily. I sleep in my study, a magnificent loft with big windows and a view of the entire city. As soon as I wake up, I jump up off the couch, make myself a really strong cup of coffee and then, without wasting a minute, sit down at my desk in front of the typewriter. I'm a screen-writer by profession. At the moment I'm writing the dialogue for a film on a difficult subject: terrorism. What connection is there between the subject of this film and a dream I've been having for some time? I don't know, but perhaps, by telling the dream, I'll come to understand.

The dream goes like this: it sounds as if someone is slowly climbing the stairs that lead to the loft, wooden stairs that echo loudly. It is a thoughtful step, hesitant, weighed down by a menacing intention. The steps stop, start, stop again, start again, and finally come to a halt outside the door. Then, after a long silence, a hand knocks. I wake up, go to the door, throw it open, and find no one there.

Even while I'm dreaming, I know for certain that this person

In My Dream I Always Hear a Step on the Stairs

climbing my staircase is the devil. At least, I know while the dream lasts. I even know, quite definitely, what the devil has come to visit me for: to propose the usual pact signed in blood – I'll give you success, but in exchange you have to sell me your soul. I decide in my heart to meet this proposal with a firm refusal. Perhaps it's precisely because of this decision that I wake up at this point.

What does the dream mean? It's obvious: the devil wants my soul and is offering me success in exchange. But I don't want success. I'm not a very ambitious person: all I want is to live out the daily routine with a certain degree of comfort, which, in any case, my screenplays amply guarantee.

I have the dream again. There is the hesitant step on the echoing stairs, the pause for breath, the hand knocking. But this time I don't wake up; instead I shout for him to come in. Then an extraordinary thing happens. I see the door-handle begin to move down with incredible slowness, millimetre by millimetre. A painful slowness that I can only explain by an intention on the part of the unknown visitor to scare me. Why not open the door straightforwardly? What does that slowness mean? On asking this last question I wake up and realize it was all a dream. All, that is, except for the fact that someone really is knocking at the door. I shout, "Come in," and then, with a sense of horror, see the handle begin to move down incredibly slowly, just like in the dream. I can't help thinking: "This is it, this time it really is him, it really is the devil." Since I'm a man who has read little and nothing out of the ordinary, it is hardly surprising that while the handle is moving I try to imagine the devil's face. But the only thing I can think of is the typical Mephistophelian mask, with arched eyebrows, a hooked nose and a little pointed beard. Finally, the door opens and in the gap the head of a young man appears, with a drooping moustache and long hair. He doesn't look diabolical, but he does have a priestly air about him, though in the way so many youngsters do these days, hiding the usual craving for life under an ascetic exterior. With a deep, bass voice, he says: "Can I?" Subdued and charmed by his confidence, I tell him to come on in. He comes in and there he is in the middle of my study with his tight blue jeans and leather jacket: the typical long-haired type you see hundreds of in some parts of the city. But immediately two things strike me as out of the ordinary: a big black leather bag with lots of compartments that he carries slung over his shoulder, and a hand crudely bandaged with bloodied gauze. I have no idea what's in the bag, but the bandage explains the slowness with which he opened the door. Looking round suspiciously, he says: "Anyone here?"

"No, just me."

He goes to the table and dumps his bag. He explains: "I've got something in here that'll have to be hidden. You can tell me where. Are you expecting anybody?"

"No, nobody. I wasn't even expecting you, actually."

I say this to have him appreciate that his presence is inexplicable to me. But he takes me seriously: "Yes, I know. But I've been to Milan, then Naples. Anyway, you're ready, aren't you?"

Embarrassed, I say: "Ready? Yes, I'm ready."

"Right, because now we really need you."

This remark intrigues me. Who is this "we"? And why do they need me? To gain time, I ask: "What have you done to your hand?"

He points to the newspaper I read this morning and left spread out on the armchair with a big, black headline on the first page. He says: "Yep, it happened yesterday evening; they wounded me in that shoot-out. But I nailed the guy who got me, oh yes!"

I don't know what to say. It occurs to me that this man I've never seen before and who might just as well be a right- as a left-wing terrorist for all I know, or even a robber caught in the act, has obviously got the wrong door: there are all kinds of people in the block, of course, the local terrorist or criminal too, most probably. But how am I supposed to convince him that he's making a mistake? That sinister remark: "I nailed the guy", prevents me from coming out in the open. If he's got the wrong door, he'd be perfectly capable of nailing me too, if only to eliminate a witness. Carefully, I ask: "How did you manage to find me? Did you tell the porter you were looking for Signor Poietti?"

He doesn't bat an eyelid on hearing my name. He says: "I came straight up. Why should I have asked? I've been before. I remembered perfectly well where you lived. Are you still asleep or something?"

I don't know why, but I say: "Yes, I was sleeping. I was having this recurrent dream. I've still got it in my head."

Unexpectedly, he asks: "What dream was that?"

I tell him the dream and he comes out with a short laugh showing

white, wolf-like teeth: "Tell me, you wouldn't be thinking of
betraying us?"

My surprise is genuine: "What are you talking about?"

"The devil could be somebody in the police you've already sold
your soul to, or you're about to sell it to. But watch out! I've got a
toy in here with three balls in it: one for him, one for you and one
for me."

It is exactly this pulp-novel banality that scares me. I protest:
"Are you crazy, or what?"

Impassive, he goes on: "In any event, the devil's making a
mistake with you because you've already sold your soul to us and
you can't sell it twice." My blood freezes. So I've already sold my
soul: in plain everyday language, sometime – I don't know when
or where – I've joined up with a terrorist or criminal organization,
one of those illegal groups it may be easy to get into but certainly
impossible to get out of. With fake nonchalance, I say: "Can I ask
a question?"

"What question?" he asks threateningly. "People don't ask me
questions."

"Don't get worked up. All I'd like to know is how you came to
know me, who introduced us?"

"Who introduced us? Casimiro, for God's sake!"

Casimiro, who's he? Never heard of him. Quite convinced now
that I'm the victim either of a mistake or a conspiracy, I say in a
conciliatory voice: "Ah, Casimiro! Of course, Casimiro, yes, who
else. When?"

"You don't trust me, eh? Well, right, we met right here, in your
study. I was on the run then, too, and Casimiro asked you to put
me up for the night. I slept here, you even gave me this key. I used
it just now to open the door." And he shows me the key.

By now I've definitely made up my mind. "Okay," I say affably,
"you hide your bag where you want. Meanwhile, I'll go downstairs
and buy something to eat for this evening."

What's come over him? He pulls a huge gun out of his jacket and
points it at my chest. "No," he says, "no way are you going to call
the police." At the same moment, thank God, someone knocks at
the door. The knocking gets louder and louder, more and more
insistent and I . . . wake up.

So it was all a dream within a dream, so to speak! But the

knocking continues. I run to the door, open it, and there is Casimiro of all people, my very good friend. I throw myself in his arms, and say: "Just think, I had a dream about you. I was saying I didn't know you at all, didn't know who you were."

"Great!" Casimiro says. "Nice friend you are."

Then I tell him my dream. He gets serious, thinks, and says: "But you know, something like that did actually happen. In '68 I came to see you one evening with a guy called Enrico. He was involved in the protest movement, on the run after some kind of clash with the police. I asked you and you let him sleep here. I even remember that we were very merry that evening; we ate and most of all drank a great deal." Surprised, I ask: "This Enrico isn't one of the ones in yesterday's shoot-out, by any chance?" And I show him the paper where, under the headline, there is a row of photographs.

He looks and shakes his head: "No, he's not one of these."

He hesitates, then adds: "But you didn't give him the key that day. You gave it to me. I had a girlfriend and I didn't know where to meet her because I lived at home at the time. So I asked you to lend me the study and you gave me the key. I even remember what you said, joking, when you gave it to me: 'the pledge of my allegiance,' you said."

Revealing Thunder

For five days I'd been on the run, zig-zagging to get them off my trail, from Paris to Amsterdam, from Amsterdam to London, from London to Hamburg, from Hamburg to Marseilles, from Marseilles to Vienna, from Vienna to Rome; sometimes by train, sometimes by plane, without sleeping, or sleeping little and uncomfortably – by now I was more interested in sleeping than in living and I think I could have fallen asleep in front of the very firing squad my fleeing was intended to avoid. Arriving in Rome, I was so sleepy that when my son came to meet me, as agreed, at the main station, the first thing I asked him was whether he'd found me a place where I could sleep safely. He replied that I would have a flat all to myself and could sleep there as much as I wanted. Nobody in the world knew of the existence of this flat apart from himself.

While we spoke, he had taken my suitcase from my hand and was walking beside me as we came out of the station. I couldn't help looking at him: I hadn't seen him for nearly two years. I had the impression, confusedly, given my extreme tiredness, that he hadn't changed at all, except in two details: the beard, which he hadn't had before; and a new, disturbing fixedness in his eyes. I thanked him for coming and for having found the flat. I told him that his mother, who'd stayed in Paris, sent him her love. I also told him, with genuine satisfaction, that he looked in great shape, better than the last time we'd seen each other two years before. He answered that this was due to the satisfaction he was getting from his job: he had got involved in an import-export business; the money was good. For the moment he was living in a hotel, but soon he'd be setting up house for himself, especially seeing as he'd got engaged to an Italian girl and was planning to marry her as soon as possible. While he was telling me all this, smiling, we had reached the car. He put my suitcase in the boot. I got in, he took the wheel and we left.

I don't know Rome very well, but I followed our route carefully, out of curiosity more than anything else, and got the impression that, traffic-light by traffic-light, we crossed the whole ancient centre of the city, before going over a bridge to the other side of the Tiber. Even while driving, my son didn't for a moment stop chatting affectionately, saying how happy he was to see me after such a long time and making plans for my and his mother's future.

We were driving along the Tiber now. From the car I could see the opposite bank, thick with trees, their full-blown, silvery leaves leaning down to skim the yellow, gleaming water. Behind the trees were rows of houses and above the houses huge, black, threatening storm-clouds climbed quickly up the sky to blot out the part that was still blue. My son told me a storm was coming, no doubt about it: the weather had been the same for some days – fine in the morning, then deteriorating, and each night without fail a violent storm would break.

For a while the car drove down the wide tarmac surface of the road that runs by the Tiber, with river parapets on one side and an uninterrupted row of apartment blocks on the other. Then it stopped at a quiet spot with no traffic, crossed by one of those red-and-white barriers put up when a road is closed. My son explained that the river bank had collapsed along this stretch; they'd been working on it for some time, which was why there was no through traffic here, and why it was a veritable oasis of peace in the middle of the crowded, hectic city. I got out of the car and looked around. He was right, the Tiber was almost deserted here: two or three kids were chasing each other on skates; a pair of lovers were walking slowly, arms round each other's waists. In a car parked by the parapet, a man and a woman were listening to the radio.

I raised my eyes to the sky: the storm was gathering all the time; the blue was reduced to a small patch with clouds pressing turbulently round it, one against another, as if for lack of space. All smiles, my son once again remarked how quiet the place was: "Isn't it just the ideal spot for someone who doesn't want to be noticed?" Without thinking, I replied: "It'd also be the ideal spot to murder someone, precisely because no one would notice." My son slapped me on the back: "Come on, enough! From now on you don't have to think of things like that any more. From now on, you must trust me; I'll see about organizing a safe, calm life for you."

He had taken a bunch of keys out now and had gone to the door of one of the smaller blocks there. There was no porter, he said, so I could go in and out as often as I wanted without being seen or spied on. We went into the entrance hall but didn't take the lift: the flat was on the ground floor. My son opened the door and led me into the entrance corridor of a small flat which gave me the impression of being decidedly squalid – that particular kind of dull, weary squalor you find in houses that have been left empty for a long time. The furniture was completely anonymous, more suitable for an office than a flat, and there was only the bare minimum: a couch and two armchairs in the sitting room; in the bedroom, just the bed, a table and a chair. There was also a little spare bedroom, near the small entrance corridor, with a rumpled pallet that seemed to have been slept on recently. In the kitchen, standing in front of the cooker, I saw a young African woman. I asked my son who she was and he said she was a Somalian maid who would do my cooking and cleaning for as long as I stayed in the flat. "She speaks our language," my son added. "You can trust her a hundred per cent."

We sat down in the bedroom, me on the bed and my son on the chair. Almost immediately, the Somalian woman came in carrying a tray with the dinner she'd just finished cooking. I watched while she bent down, gracefully laying the plates on the little table, and noticed that she was tall, supple and elegant with broad shoulders, round, strong arms and narrow hips – a real beauty of her type. Having set out the meal, she made a slight bow, looking me straight in the eyes as if she wanted to tell me something, and left the room. My son suggested that we eat. I glanced at the plates and saw that they were filled with the traditional food of our country, cooked, so it seemed, with great care. But as soon as I thought of stretching out my hand to take something, I felt a sense of repugnance that was as insurmountable as it was mysterious. I told my son I wasn't hungry, only sleepy, and to let me rest now. We'd see each other tomorrow and then I'd do all the normal things one does in life, starting with doing justice to the excellent food prepared by the Somalian maid.

My son was a little upset by my refusal. He insisted that I eat at least something; otherwise I'd be ill, he said, seeing as on my own admission I hadn't eaten all day. I replied that fear had completely taken away my appetite. I'd sleep now; through sleeping, my fear would pass, and when I woke up I'd be hungry again and then I'd think about eating. Disappointed but resigned, my son called the maid by her name. She reappeared. While she was putting the plates on the tray she again bowed towards me, looking me straight in the eyes, then went out. My son suddenly got to his feet, threw his arms round my neck, kissed me on both cheeks and said to go ahead and sleep: we'd see each other tomorrow.

I don't know why but despite the torment of my terrible urge to sleep, as soon as my son had left the room I remembered that while he was embracing me I'd felt his hand move, not around my shoulders, which would have been the normal thing, but along my sides and right down as far as the base of my spine: an unusual, improbable gesture on his part – the way you feel a suspect to see if he's armed. This recollection was followed by a sudden desire to look at my son again. I moved fast to the window, undid the shutters and looked out.

He was coming out of the building. He got into his car and once again, for no reason, I lingered at the window to watch the car as it moved off. But it didn't go very far. At the red-and-white barrier it stopped. A man sitting lazily on the parapet, legs dangling, got down and ran over to the car. My son opened the door for him and they drove off.

I thought nothing of it. My mind was filled with sleep the way a thick fog fills the landscape, blotting out whatever's there. I shut the window, threw myself on the bed without undressing and lay for a short while on my back with my eyes open. The bedroom door was ajar. I told myself I ought to lock it, but I didn't. The Somalian woman must have been in the kitchen; I could hear her quietly singing some lament or other from her own country. Lulled by this soft singing, which, like her looks of a short while ago, seemed meant exclusively for me, I fell asleep.

Sleep brought no peace. It was as if I were protesting against something, perhaps against sleep itself. All the time I sensed I was clenching my teeth hard and bunching my fists in anger. At some point in the night I heard the thunder roll, dark and booming, and then, in the intervals between the thunder, came the patter of the rain. I seemed to see the huge, tarmac surface of the road by the Tiber boiling under the pelting downpour; then lightning flashed brightly and I glimpsed a man sitting on the parapet, legs dangling: he got down and went towards a car parked under the rain, and I knew that my son was in the car. I saw this scene over and over again: the man was sitting, then he got down and ran towards the car and then there he was again sitting, getting down, running, and so on and so on.

In the end, from hearing the thunder and pelting rain, a question formed in my still-sleeping mind: where and when had I heard this thunder, this pelting rain before? And still asleep I answered my own question: in childhood. I'm nearer sixty than fifty; my memory took me back a half-century. I was at home: I would wake with a start in the dark, hear the pelting rain and the crashing thunder, and then I'd get out of bed and run to hide in the next bedroom between the warm, safe arms of my mother. And likewise now. With an instinctive, irresistible impulse, I got up, crossed the room and went out into the corridor.

The door to the room where the Somalian woman was sleeping was ajar. I looked in through pitch-black darkness alternating with the violent, fleeting brilliance of the lightning. I decided not to turn on the light. I thought it would be enough to glimpse the woman between one flash of lightning and another, as I had glimpsed my mother fifty years before. And so it was. Every so often there was a flash and I saw the Somalian woman sleeping soundly, her cheek resting on the palm of her hand, her body covered by a sheet, her bare arm folded. I watched her like this between one flash and the next for a long time. I remembered the way she had looked straight at me while she was serving and then clearing away the dinner, and I wondered what she might have wanted to tell me and whether it really was her who wanted to tell me something, or me who wanted to be told something. In the end I felt calmer and in control of my nerves. So I withdrew, closing the door behind me, and went back to my own room. The fact is that while I was watching the sleeping woman I had taken a decision: now all I had to do was to act on it.

Stretched on my back on the bed, I waited a couple of hours more. Then, with the first glimmer of light I got up, took my little suitcase and left the room on tiptoe. In the corridor I stopped for a moment outside the Somalian woman's door and listened. But there was no sound: she was sleeping. I opened the front door, crossed the hall and went out on the road along the river. It was dawn, with all the trees sodden with rain and the tarmac scattered with shining puddles of water. The sky was the colour of putty, somewhere between white and grey. As I closed the door to the block, the lamps along the pavements went out all together. I started to walk at a good pace towards the nearest bridge.

There's a Neutron Bomb
for Ants Too

❧

At seven in the morning, at the seaside, having opened the window wide, he likes to throw himself completely naked on the bed, pick up the first book, magazine or newspaper that comes to hand and for ten or fifteen minutes read anything at all, so as to wake up properly, re-establish contact with the world. He likes it to be something dramatic, catastrophic even, perhaps to counterbalance the sense of profound tranquillity which wafts in through the window, full of a still cold and empty sky tinged here and there with vague traces of a red, dawn glow.

This morning he reaches a hand to the floor and at random picks up the newspaper that he left there the night before when sleep got the better of him. He opens it. Something catastrophic, then. Ah, here's the headline he was after, and four columns of it, on the pros and cons of the neutron bomb. Excellent, what could be more catastrophic than the end of the world? He rearranges the pillow under his head, lifts the newspaper to eye level and reads.

The thing is, he tells himself as he reads, that at a certain point – difficult to say when, perhaps in the Renaissance period – man probably took a wrong turn and is now rushing towards his own extinction. It has happened before: lots of animal species have taken wrong turns and become extinct – the dinosaurs for example. Only when this premise is taken as granted, he goes on, can one consider the question of the neutron bomb. In any event, how do things stand?

This is how: 1) The neutron bomb kills men without destroying houses, works of art, monuments, etc., etc. 2) It has a selective, circumscribed effect: it kills a limited number of people and, what's more, kills exactly the ones who have to be killed. 3) In contrast with the traditional atomic bomb, it can be used without provoking the end of the world: it can aspire to become, in its turn, one of the so-called conventional weapons. 4) As a conventional weapon it will very probably be used in Europe, the predestined battleground for a war between the USSR and the USA.

Always bearing in mind the premise that man is seeking his own extinction, he asks himself what can be done to prevent the use of the neutron bomb. This time he thinks for a long while, rejecting one after another solutions that immediately strike him as superficial and partial. In the end he hits on the only possible answer: the remedy for all this is that man stop seeking his own extinction.

It is time to get up. He throws his legs off the bed and goes to the bathroom. After about twenty minutes he emerges washed and shaved, in t-shirt, shorts and sandals. He goes to take a look at the beach from the sitting-room window: it is still divided into three colours: the white, completely dry sand; the light brown sand still damp from yesterday evening's stormy waves, and finally the dark brown sand washed by the sea. The sky is already bright and blue, but the sun still hasn't appeared. For a moment he studies the perfectly calm sea, motionless save for a short-lived wave that forms and dies a couple of yards from the shore; then he goes into the kitchen to get his breakfast.

Oh no! During the night, perhaps because of the sultry heat there has been for some days, the ants have gone on the warpath. A black, swarming line of dense back-and-forths has reached the jar of honey which someone carelessly left out on the table. The jar is dotted with ants; a surprisingly large number of others have managed to get through the tiny space between the glass of the jar and the metal of the lid and are now drowning in the honey. The jar is fit to be thrown out. This morning he'll have to do without his honey.

The black line of ants comes down the table-leg, crosses the kitchen floor and goes out under the french windows. He opens them and follows the busy army of insects step by step. Their line runs along a fair stretch of the villa wall, leaves it at the corner, crosses the paving and disappears in the flower-bed, under the leaves of some shrubs. "I'll soon sort them out," he says to himself, angry with the ants that have come into his house and attacked the honey.

He hurries back to the kitchen, looks through the cupboards for the insecticide spray but can't find it. Meanwhile, the ants continue to come and go up and down the leg of *his* table, across *his* kitchen floor, along the wall of *his* villa and across the paving of *his* garden. This thought makes him angrier still. Hardly thinking what he's doing, he grabs a piece of the newspaper, rolls it up and touches a lighted match to it. The paper flares. He moves the flame close to the table-leg: the ants burn up immediately and fall one after another to the floor.

The door opens and his wife comes in, dressed like himself in t-shirt, shorts and sandles. Neatly combed, fresh, attractive. "What are you doing?" she exclaims. "You can see, can't you?" he answers. "But we've got a spray for ants. And I didn't like your expression while you were setting light to the poor things." "What expression did I have?" "I don't know: cruel. Wait, I'll get you the spray." She goes into the sitting room, comes back with the red-and-green can of insecticide spray and hands it to him: "Here, take it."

He turns it round in his hands and reads the standard instructions under the design of an enormous black ant: "Spray product holding can at a distance of 5–10 centimetres from surface to be treated ..." He takes off the lid, points the can towards the floor where the ants' line is still intact and, pressing the nozzle with his finger, directs the spray towards the insects. The effect, it occurs to him, is instantaneous, even if that instantaneousness is more an impression that he has spraying than a reality for the ants being sprayed, because it is impossible to tell what time-scale ants have. For him a moment is a moment; for an ant, though ...

Instantaneous or not, the effect is certainly lethal. The moment they are attacked by the stiff little cloud from the spray, the ants scatter, lie motionless, upside down, on their backs, in a word – dead. He doesn't have time to dwell on his observation of the ants' death, because from the table where she has sat down with her cup of tea his wife spurs him on: "It's not enough just killing the ones that've come into the house. You'll have to follow them outside, get the nest if possible."

Without a word, he follows the army of ants, routing them piecemeal with the insecticide spray. He has left the kitchen now and is spraying the villa wall. Then there is the rearguard on the paving. At the flower-bed with the shrubs he stops and thinks: "I've taught them a good lesson. That's enough for today. They won't come back, at least not for a few days."

But this thought prompts another: why, after their lesson, won't the ants return? Because they have "understood"? Or for lack of troops, because they are waiting for the nest to generate new ants to fill the gaps the insecticide has made in the army? The question is certainly important: in the first case there would be a kind of awareness; in the second, the blind, life instinct.

On the other hand, he thinks, how can one answer such a question if, in reality, it is impossible to have a direct relationship with the ants? He'll have killed a thousand, say. But this slaughter has taken place in silence; he hasn't heard anything. And yet, who knows? Perhaps the ants were moaning, shouting, screaming. And again: who has ever seen the "expression" of an ant as it dies from insecticide? To the human it looks like a black dot, nothing more.

He goes back into the kitchen now. His wife has picked up the paper that he brought in from the bedroom: she's reading and, as she reads, she lifts her cup of tea to her lips from time to time. Suddenly she asks from behind the paper: "Can someone please tell me what this neutron bomb is?"

He sits and pours himself some tea. Then he says: "It's a cliché, but, in the end, why be afraid of clichés. We are ants and our insecticide is the neutron bomb."

"But we think. You're not going to tell me that ants think. Why don't we use our power for thought to find a way of doing without the neutron bomb?"

He thinks it over, then answers with a sigh: "We don't use our power for thought because, deep down, we want to die."

"But I don't want to die. And the ants, what do they want? You're not going to tell me that the ants want to die too."

"No, on the contrary, the ants want the honey, that is, they want to live."

"So, how can we explain it? Men, according to you, want to die, while ants, on the other hand, want to live. But in the end the insecticide wipes out both of them."

He sighs again. "Haven't you read Ecclesiastes? A few thousand years ago, the man who wrote it said: 'There is no new thing under the sun.' This thought from Ecclesiastes was valid until, let's say, 1945, until the atomic bomb. Now it isn't valid any more: there are lots of new things and, at least for the moment, we haven't managed to get a clear idea of them. The latest of these new things is the neutron bomb. Could you say, talking about the neutron bomb, no new thing under the sun? Oh no, definitely not. And so, maybe, when it comes to things you can't talk about, it's better to keep quiet."

The Voyeur's Stroll

Clunk, clunk. The key turns violently in the lock the way keys will when they want to express repugnance and refusal. And in fact, immediately afterwards, to avoid any misunderstanding, his wife's voice shouts quite explicitly from the other side of the door that she doesn't want to make love with him, not today, nor tomorrow, nor ever again. She has already shouted the same thing on other occasions during this, their first year of marriage: the words fill him with greater desperation than a frank and decisive refusal would. So it's always going to be like this; these bars will form the cage they'll be trapped in for who knows how long? He goes out across the terrace of their villa, crosses the dunes, comes out on the beach and mechanically begins to walk along by the sea.

His mind blank, he walks on, looking one moment at the black, elegant ripples the waves have left on the wet sand; now at the sky with its scattering of hazy heat clouds; now at the sea, murky and motionless, with lots of litter and other rubbish drifting on the surface without managing either to come ashore, or to sink to the bottom. From out of his distraction, comes one, clear decision: he'll push on with this involuntary stroll and go as far away as possible; that way he won't be home for lunch. Who knows, maybe his absence will make his wife more affectionate tonight?

With this mean idea of not going home for lunch in mind, he walks faster now, as if he had a goal, a definite place to go. It is September and all the villas along the dunes are closed and empty, the groups of bathing huts locked and deserted. Scattered here and there along the beach a few couples are sunbathing. After the groups of bathing huts, there is a long stretch of coast without villas or huts, nothing but brushwood, beach and sea. The solitude begins to weigh on him and he decides to go just as far as a group of pine trees he can see in the distance, jutting down to the beach. Is this the goal he has walked several kilometres for? Without knowing why, he says to himself: "Perhaps. Let's see now."

He reaches the pines. First disappointment: the wood is closed off with a barbed-wire fence that goes right down into the sea. He looks into the trees, putting his hands on the wire and pushing his face as far forward as he can.

The wood is deserted: the tawny, sun-streaked pine trunks lean this way and that, towards or away from each other. In the middle of the pinewood is a large old villa with a faded Pompeii-red stucco and all the windows closed. There is a deep silence, in which he senses he hears the singing of the wind down on the sea, soft and plaintive, like a distant harp. Then, perhaps prompted by this gesture of looking through a barbed-wire fence, he remembers those photographs of concentration camps with prisoners looking out, their hands holding the wires. Only in this case, he thinks sadly, he is the prisoner, even though he seems to be free.

All at once, as if in response to his reflections, he realizes that the pinewood isn't deserted after all. He sees a car, a sparkling electric-blue car, parked the other side of the fence; and then, in a hollow, a lot of clothes, men's and women's, scattered on the ground over a carpet of pine needles. He raises his eyes, looks towards the sea and so spots the couple, a man and woman, completely naked, wet and dripping from head to toe. Obviously they've just taken a dip and are now climbing back up the gentle slope towards the hollow where they've left their clothes.

The moment he sees them, he knows that he isn't so much seeing as watching them, and as he moves from seeing to watching, he realizes that he is already snooping on them. He thinks he ought to nip this indiscreet temptation in the bud; leave without more ado. But he can't. What prevents him is the idea that he is watching something which, in the end, in a mysterious way concerns him. And then, he didn't come on purpose to watch them: it was pure chance that he looked through the fence just as they were coming out of the sea.

But these are equivocations. Otherwise why, after a first glance at both of them, would he examine, with scrupulous attention, the man before the woman? He knows that he is doing so partly to give himself an impression of disinterested objectivity and partly, and more probably, to reserve the woman for longer and more detailed contemplation, the way some gluttons will keep the best tit-bit till the end of the meal. Meanwhile, despite this lucid analysis, he goes on watching the couple with an insatiable appetite. The man is young and small but strong-limbed with powerful arms and legs. He is balding in front and his face seems thrust forward in an expression of lust. Now it's the woman's turn. She is big, with a statuesque indolence, indefinably but quite definitely beautiful. He studies her in detail and notices several interesting correspondences: between the roundness of the arms and that of the thighs; between the black of her hair and that of her crotch, between the shape of the neck and that of the waist . . .

Suddenly, he realizes that he can no longer watch, or rather snoop, without a feeling of strained and furious impatience. Yes, he isn't so much watching these two while they act as wishing them to act. It is a desire similar to that of the sports spectator who urges his favourite player to do this or that, shouting and gesticulating, and he catches himself muttering through his teeth: "Now what are you doing? Why don't you get close to her? And you, why are you looking at the pinewood instead of at him?" Yes, he *wishes* them to move towards a greater intimacy; that intimacy, he can't help thinking, that his wife denied him this morning when she slammed the door in his face.

But the couple don't oblige; they take their time, as if they had something else in mind. Then, while the woman bends to pick up a towel and, standing up, starts to rub it slowly over her body, and while the man crouches to light a cigarette, it occurs to him that he is watching a prearranged performance that could very easily not develop in the direction of the erotic intimacy his desire suggests. The truth is that he is a theatre or television spectator watching a story he knows nothing about and which he has to follow with the patience and respect due to every work of art.

This thought introduces a new element into his curiosity which alters it profoundly. No, he isn't a snooper spying on his prey like a hunter lying in ambush; he's a critic watching a performance with detached attention, and he hopes that the actors will play their parts well. But what, in this case, does "well" mean? Ah, that's it, he exclaims to himself: it means not following the script rudely interrupted by his wife this morning, but following *their* script. Does it say in this script that they have to make love after a swim in the sea? Yes? Okay, fine, let them make it. But if, on the contrary, it says that they have to open the little picnic hamper resting against a pine tree and eat their lunch and then sleep, well then, they absolutely mustn't make love, whether he wants them to or not.

Brusquely and unexpectedly, the calm, serene scene breaks up and moves along the lines he had wanted it to a short while ago. Having finished drying herself, the woman bends to pick up her t-shirt from the ground, when the man gives her a thoroughly vulgar slap on the backside and grabs her by the hips. Indignant and nauseated, just like a theatregoer who sees the players acting badly, he hopes for a moment that the woman will reject such a brutal, unseemly assault, take offence, put her partner back in his place. Not a bit of it. The woman frees herself and runs, but she does so with an indecent waving of arms and legs, breaking out into giggles of complicity and shouts of fake fear which unfortunately leave no doubt as to her intentions. Then everything happens in the worst, most banal fashion. Still chasing each other, the two run towards the sea which can just be seen down between the pine trunks. The woman goes in at a rush; the man grabs her and falls with her in the shallow water amid splashes of foam. The last thing that occurs to him, ironically, as he walks off, is that nothing more exactly resembles the agony of a big fish, pierced by a harpoon and thrashing in a net, than a couple embracing and making love in the sea.

While going home his mind is blank again, as it was coming. He just walks along, looking one moment at the beach, then at the sky, now at the dunes, now at the sea. But when he arrives at the villa, a decision emerges from this silence in his mind: to cancel out the uneasy and humiliating feeling that he has been snooping, he must go back to the pinewood with his wife and do there with her what he saw the couple doing.

Nothing easier. His wife, as expected, is in a different mood; she is once more in an affectionate state of mind and she readily agrees to take a walk the following day as far as the marvellous, mythical pinewood that he claims to have discovered.

Everything goes exactly as it did the day before, with the same sky, the same sea, the same deserted bathing huts and the same closed villas. Everything, except for one important detail: however hard he tries, he can't find the pinewood again. It came after the long, uninhabited stretch of coast and before a certain promontory. But although he goes up and down the beach several times, the pinewood, villa and fence don't materialize, remain a memory which he himself begins to doubt. In the end, with his wife laughing at him, he comes to the only conclusion that now seems possible: "Would you believe I went and dreamed it!"

Strangely, she immediately accepts this explanation. "You saw a wonderful place in a dream and right away you thought of going there with me. Don't you think that's nice?"

But that's not how it is, he thinks with some bitterness. And, in fact, he doesn't have the courage to tell her that in his dream he didn't see himself with her, but two strangers who he seemed to be snooping on with envy, with excitement, with disapproval. True love, on the contrary, would have consisted in seeing no one, and saying to himself: "Look! The perfect place to come tomorrow with her."

The Hands Around the Neck

❦

His wife said: "Squeeze my neck with your hands. Isn't it odd? A big athletic man like you, with such small hands? Squeeze me so that your fingers meet. Don't be afraid of hurting me. I want to see if you can do it."

Timoteo walked out of the sitting room and went to lean against the railing on the terrace, opposite the sea. The thatched terrace shelter was held up by two roughly trimmed pine trunks that still had pieces of bark here and there. They had more or less the same diameter as his wife's neck. Mechanically, he circled one of the trunks with his hands, tried to join his fingers and didn't manage it. Then he leaned his hands on the railing and looked at the sea.

A dark, oblique rain-cloud, like a theatre curtain raised on one side only, hung over the surface of a sea that seemed near-black, with green and violet reflections here and there and fleeting crests of white foam. The foam crests appeared, ran rapidly across the water driven by the wind, and disappeared, reabsorbed.

There'll be a storm soon, Timoteo thought; he'd have to get rid of the body before it began to rain. But how?

Going out to sea with the rubber dingy and throwing the body in deep water with a weight tied round the neck or feet was impossible now, given the imminence of the storm. Which left the grave. But he'd have to hurry, because digging a grave under the rain would be neither easy nor pleasant. The grave would fill with water; the drenched sand of the sides would cave in. And the rain would whip against his angry face.

He stayed a moment longer to look at the sea which was getting darker and darker, then tried to circle the pole with his hands again, almost hoping that this time he'd be able to make his fingers meet. But the fingers were still at least half-an-inch apart. Timoteo went back into the sitting room and through to the kitchen.

His wife was standing in front of the cooker, tall and loose-limbed with her cone-shaped neck, wider at the bottom than the top, clearly visible under the careless, compact mass of her thick hair. Timoteo looked at her neck: it was strong, thick, nervy, with just a hint of a swelling in front, like a goitre almost; and yet he found it beautiful exactly because it was expressive. Expressive of what? Of a will to live, a blind, instinctive, stubborn, arrogant will to live.

His wife's crumpled, thin-cotton nightdress was still stuck between her ample buttocks: she had come into the kitchen straight from bed, still half-asleep and she hadn't realized. Timoteo stretched out his thumb and forefinger in a pincer and freed the nightdress with a light, respectful movement, taking care not to touch her body. Then he said: "So he used to ask you to make love on the table and you did what he wanted, eh? Show me how you did it."

His wife protested: "It happened so many years ago, before I knew you. And you get this fixation now."

Timoteo insisted: "Go on, show me."

He saw her shrug her shoulders as if to say: "If you care that much!" She left the cooker, turned to the table, bent at a right angle till her stomach, breasts and left cheek were squashed down on the marble surface. Then her hands went to lift up her nightdress, showing her white, oblong, oval-shaped buttocks. In this position, the slit between her thighs appeared under her buttocks, obscured by the dark pubic hair. Her legs were long, smooth and thin, like a boy's. She stayed bent over the table with her hands open near her ears, her eyes open, as if waiting. Timoteo said: "You look like a frog. So then he used to squeeze your neck while you were bent over the table like that and he pressed down on you and you made love?"

"Yes," his wife answered. "He wanted me to put myself like this;

he had a real fixation, like you." Her voice was strained and after a moment she added: "So if you don't want to make love, I'll get up; this marble's sawing up my stomach." Angrily, Timoteo replied: "Get up!" She obeyed, first pulling her nightdress carefully over her calves and then tidying her rumpled hair with a toss of the head. Timoteo looked at her again as she stood in front of the cooker, watching the coffee pot, and once again he noticed that her neck had a conical shape with a slight swelling in front – the neck of an attractive young woman that any man would have been able to circle his hands round. But he couldn't; his hands were too small.

His wife said: "Coffee's ready. Shall we have biscuits or do you want me to make you some toast?" Timoteo answered: "Biscuits. But where on earth's the spade, the one with the green handle?" His wife replied that it was in the broom cupboard. Timoteo took the spade and went out into the garden.

Outside the kitchen there was a small concrete yard scattered with broken boxes, empty bottles and open tins. After the yard came a big flower-bed where Timoteo was planning to plant some shrubs; beyond that the slope of the dunes rose up, steep and sandy. Because of the drought, the sandy soil of the flower-bed looked grey and crumbly, almost a powder.

The body was lying where he'd put it during the night: on its back, with legs and arms apart, and head thrown back. Not having the spade, which he hadn't been able to find, he'd gathered some loose soil with his hands and scattered it over the body, as if he'd wanted not so much to cover as to clothe it with earth.

And in fact he had barely hidden it, and what's more, very unevenly: the face was covered, but that slightly swollen part of the neck his fingers wouldn't meet round was visible; the breasts likewise pushed out of the soil, as if from a strange bra; the pelvis was full of earth, but the curve of the belly protruded. Timoteo gripped the handle of the spade and traced the outline of a grave in the soil with the blade. He'd have to dig inside that outline now to a depth of at least a couple of feet. He began to dig energetically.

His wife looked out of the kitchen door and said: "Sometimes you act like a real nut. Last night, for instance, you interrogate me Gestapo-style to find out how I used to make love with Girolamo on the table. How did you put yourself? How did you bend over?

How did he lie on top of you and how did he squeeze your neck? Then, just like a nutter, you take the gun and run downstairs to shoot that poor stray dog that had started to scrabble about in the rubbish. Okay, we are in an isolated village, but think if you'd killed a man! Now stop digging – you can bury it later – and come in and drink your coffee." Timoteo answered: "I want to finish the grave before the storm comes."

It was dark in the kitchen. His wife was sitting with her eyes turned to the table, thoughtful. Irritated, Timoteo asked: "I don't suppose you can tell me what you're thinking?" "I'm thinking of what we were doing when you heard the dog and jumped out of bed and took the gun, just like a nut." "And what were we doing?" "I told you to squeeze my neck, like Girolamo used to. I'd been struck all of a sudden by how small your hands are. He could circle my neck with his hands. I wanted to see if you could. But it was all a joke. And instead you ..." "Yes?" "You pulled a really terrible face ... Look, do me a favour: get up and put your hands round my neck. But so that I can look you in the eyes. I want to see if you have the same expression as last night."

Timoteo obeyed, but saying: "You, with this fixation of yours for having your neck squeezed." He got up, came to stand next to his wife and put his hands round her neck. She threw her head back and looked him in the eyes: "No, you don't have that expression, so terrible ..." She broke off, pulled one of Timoteo's hands away from her neck and kissed it with fervour, "... and so fine!"

Timoteo grabbed the left hand and left foot and pulled the body towards him. It was very heavy, but it moved. As it shifted, the soil covering it underwent a sort of earthquake: the ampler parts of the body, already half-uncovered, emerged completely, the soil running off them in little avalanches. Timoteo pulled once: the body slipped into the grave and lay there on its side with the head resting on one ear, the face half-hidden by the hair and the arms and legs bent – as though sleeping.

Timoteo picked up the spade again and began to throw the earth back into the grave, first over the legs and then up and up as far as the head. He wanted to leave the neck – which could now be seen sideways on, from the ear right down to the breast – until last: it was the part of her body that most attracted him, because of its arrogant animal strength and vitality.

The Hands Around the Neck

His wife said: "Come on, don't stand there in a trance like that, goggle-eyed. What are you thinking about? The dog? Poor thing, we shouldn't have put the bin out at night. Everybody knows this beach is full of stray dogs; people leave them when they go back to Rome after the holidays. Come on, drink your coffee so we can take a walk by the sea before the storm comes. It's so nice walking by the sea, on the sand, in the rain."

The grave was filled with earth now, but it was a soft, dark earth and it made a mound that was visible, partly because it rose above the flat ground and partly because it was a different colour. Timoteo hesitated, then climbed on the mound and carefully trod it down till the earth was level. Then he took a spadeful of grey top-soil and spread it meticulously over the grave so as to cover the darker colour of the earth he'd turned over.

His wife said: "Let's go." Timoteo asked: "But aren't you going to change? You're still in your nightdress." He saw her shrug her shoulders: "So? A nightie is a piece of clothing like any other." Timoteo said nothing and followed her out of the house towards the steps that went down through the brushwood from the dunes to the sea.

Levelled off and dusted to perfection the grave couldn't be seen at all. An ugly stray dog, yellow and brown, came out from the dunes and went straight to the grave. He sniffed it and then, to Timoteo's relief, went to cock his leg way beyond it. So, it was safe now: not only could the grave not be seen; it couldn't be sensed either.

His wife walked ahead of him, by the sea on the still dry, grey sand. The first drops of rain began to spot the sand, thicker all the time. Then the thunder rolled like an enormous iron ball over the glassy, booming surface of the sea. Now, as if gathered by the cold, biting wind, the rain drops beat against his wife in gusts. Where they struck her, the thin cotton of her nightdress stuck to her body, letting the pale colour of her skin show through. His wife held her head leaning towards one shoulder; all one side of her neck was visible right up to the ear.

His wife said: "Squeeze my neck with your hands. Isn't it odd? A big athletic man like you, with such small hands? Squeeze me so that your fingers meet. Don't be afraid of hurting me, I want to see if you can do it."

179

The Woman in the
Customs Officer's House

❧

I'm an orderly man, not just psychologically, but professionally too: my official position is customs officer at the airport. Like all orderly men, however, I occasionally like to forget order and let the contraband of the imagination slip through. Saturdays and Sundays, in fact, I dedicate to daydreaming. I take off my uniform, lie on the bed and think about anything that has particularly struck me of late. Today, as soon as I was stretched on my bed in the silence of the empty house, it didn't take me long to find the thing that had recently prodded my imagination.

It was the suitcase of a mature woman who must have been beautiful in her youth. Her embarrassed behaviour had made me suspicious; she was too polite and accommodating to be sincere. When I put to her the usual question about whether she had anything to declare, she started as if I'd laid an accusing hand on her shoulder. She quickly repeated that she had nothing, nothing at all, only personal items of clothing. I looked at her carefully: she had one of those worn-out faces, with delicate, well-formed but plain features, where the most striking thing is the effort to hide age with artifice. Her hair was curled and puffed up over her forehead and ears; there was eyeshadow on her eyelids and under her eyes, lipstick on her lips, powder on her cheeks. And she had an expression – how can I put it? – a pathetically, heartbreakingly frivolous and seductive expression.

She was wearing all kinds of things which, on the spot, I wasn't able to identify very clearly. I noticed a little neckscarf, a velvet jacket, a wool cardigan, a pullover, a blouse – all in different styles and colours. Perhaps because of her complicated way of dressing, or perhaps because of her insecurity, I thought she might be something of an adventuress – a literary characterization, but none the less real for that – which could mean anything from drugs to espionage. Indicating her elegant suitcase, the collapsible kind, I brusquely ordered her to open up. Immediately she objected: "But I've told you I've got nothing to declare."

"Open it, please."

She sighed, took a bunch of keys from her handbag and opened the suitcase. I pulled apart the two halves with a kind of sadistic violence and plunged my hands inside. The case contained a mess of scraps of cotton, silk, and I don't know how many other soft, light, slinky materials: a typically feminine mess, I thought, because it would never occur to a man to put his things in a suitcase in such a promiscuous fashion.

My hands rummaged amongst all those soft, vaguely perfumed scraps and, meanwhile, I reflected that rather than dressing themselves as men do, women tend to decorate themselves, and the clothes they wear don't adhere to their bodies but wrap around them in a seductive, mysterious way, concealing what's there, suggesting what isn't there. Then what can one say, I went on thinking, still rummaging, about the fact that women's clothes don't stay still on their bodies like men's do, but move, flutter, puff out, crumple, flap and so on. Or, going to the opposite extreme, they adhere too tightly, and then the female body seems imprisoned in all kinds of elastics, suspenders, girdles, bras and other such harnesses. So, either the fluttering, seductive gauziness, or the tight, hermetic sheath. I finished rummaging without finding anything and pulled my hands out of the scraps, closed the suitcase and chalked a cross on the leather to show that the bag could go through. The woman thanked me, perhaps a little too warmly, with a wide, brilliant smile, then disappeared pushing her luggage trolley.

Thinking over this tiny incident now, I come back doggedly to the difference between men's and women's clothes. Why is there this difference? What is it that makes women dress so differently? Why are their clothes cut to emphasize curves, whereas men's tend to create a straight line? What does the woman's preference for light, transparent, soft, silky, fluttering fabrics mean? I hammer away at these questions and in the end, with going over and over the same things in my confused mind, I fall asleep.

I sleep perhaps for half an hour. Then the sound of the doorbell – a fearful noise – that jerks me awake. I listen, wondering who it can be, visiting me at this hour of a Sunday afternoon. I slip on my shirt and jacket, go barefoot to the porch and put my eye to the peep-hole.

Huh! A woman. A woman, forty-odd, with a worn-out, delicate face which I have the impression I've seen before. Then the velvet jacket open over a blouse, the badly tied neckscarf and all the frills around her face suddenly remind me where I've seen her: a few days ago, at the airport. She was arriving on a plane from, let's see, Madrid. I look down and a glimpse of the collapsible suitcase that I rummaged through so long and in vain confirms my memory. I attach the chain, open the door just a little and ask: "Who are you looking for, madam?"

With disconcerting familiarity, she replies: "I'm looking for you, sweetheart."

"Excuse me, but I don't know you. I've never seen you before and ..."

"Come on, come on, don't give me that. Open this door and let me in."

Intrigued by such a display of self-confidence, I slip off the chain and open the door. She comes in and immediately I'm engulfed in a cloud of perfume, a sweetish, heavy yet penetrating and somehow spicy perfume. She comes in with a lively flouncing of her generous, pleated skirt and says in a shrill voice: "I'm looking for you of course, Athos Canestrini, you."

"But I'm telling you, I don't know you."

"That's right, you don't know me, or rather, you don't want to know me. That doesn't stop me from looking for you."

"What's that supposed to mean?"

"Hmm, I'll tell you soon enough. For the moment, though, show me to the bedroom."

"Wouldn't it be better if we went into the sitting room?"

"Oh no, oh no. We've got to go to the bedroom."

"But why?"

"You'll soon see."

I show her to the bedroom. It is a big room with two windows, a double bed, a cupboard, a dressing table, a few chairs – the usual furniture. Coming in, she says: "What a cold, austere and most of all . . . deceitful room."

"Deceitful? Oh, that's nice! And why?"

"Because in reality, you would like to have a different room."

"Like?"

"A, so to speak, more feminine room. But I'll sort the place out for you now, you watch."

She puts her suitcase on a chair and begins to pull out piles of toiletries which she arranges one by one on the marble top of the dressing table: brushes, little brushes, combs, bottles, little jars, boxes, pots, make-up cases and so on. She arranges everything nice and neatly around the mirror. The suitcase seems bottomless; the more she pulls out the more there is. Finally she says: "There, finished. Now the dressing table doesn't look so sad."

I say nothing, just watch her. Out comes an embroidered, thin-cotton nightdress, a silk slip and other lingerie which she goes and hangs on the clothes hangers. Meanwhile, in the midst of everything else, she has somehow managed to throw tights, slips, blouses, skirts and I don't know how many other clothes over the chairs. And again, from the same magical suitcase, out jumps a pair of black pyjamas, a pair of green slippers, a pink dressing gown. Turning to me, satisfied, she says: "What do you say? Isn't that better?"

I watch her, amazed. Suddenly she says: "Come here."

I go towards her. And there we are, both of us, side by side, in front of the mirror above the dressing table. She says: "Look, look carefully. Don't you think we're alike?"

I look and see that she's right. We have the same features, the same eyes, the same nose, the same mouth. We would be even more alike if it weren't for that frivolous, pathetic expression on her face, which, thank heaven, I don't have at all. She says calmly: "Understand now? I'm you and you're me. That is, I'm the female version and you're the male version of the same person, the same Athos Canestrini. Well, I'll undress now. I'll lie down on the bed and take a little rest. And you, what are you going to do?"

Bewildered, I stammer: "But this is my house, I'm going to do what I've always done up until yesterday. Rest, read, think, daydream maybe."

"Daydream about what? That I take your place. You don't have to anymore: it's happened. From now on, there'll be the male version of Athos Canestrini at the airport and the female version at home. So, 'bye now. You've got to go to the airport. See you this evening."

"But what'll you do here, in my house?"

"That's my business. Why should I tell you? In any event, I'll make it brighter, cosier, more frivolous."

Meanwhile, without making a fuss about it, she undresses. She isn't embarrassed about showing me a body in which, as with her face, artifice emphasizes rather than hides the signs of age. I feel there's nothing more I can do. I leave the room, followed by her voice warning me: "Shut the door properly." Here I am in the passage. As I open the front door I narrowly avoid bumping into the most ordinary of beefy-looking men: dark, with ruffled hair, a face with thick, sensual features, an athletic body. In a voice with a strong local accent, he says: "Mrs Canestrini?"

"There are no women here." And . . . I wake up.

So, it was all a dream: that woman with the suitcase at the airport must really have made a big impression on me! I look at my cold, sad, bachelor's bedroom and say to myself that perhaps there was some truth in my dream: the unconscious aspiration to have a more lived-in and livable house. I start to think of the improvements I was intending to make: flowers, paintings, knick-knacks, rugs, cushions, drapes and so on. Amid these pleasant fancies, I once more fall asleep.

Printed in the USA
CPSIA information can be obtained
at www.ICGtesting.com
LVHW091134150724
785511LV00001B/131